She dre̶ eyes. "Oh, but you are, Your Grace." In a mirror image of what he had done earlier, she raised her hand to his cheek, but held it suspended there as though waiting for his permission.

He closed his eye and braced himself for it.

"I don't know what you want from me," she said, her voice soft and questioning, her hand poised in the air, still not touching him.

He looked at her then and felt the fury melt into something else, something that made him walk a step forward and take her hand in his, his other hand on her arm, to draw her close to him, to lower his mouth to hers and to kiss her.

To taste her, to capture some of her essence, her sparkle, to feel what it must be like to be so—so her.

She didn't push him away. Didn't slap him, or demand he marry her, or mock him for daring to touch her with his imperfect self.

Instead she placed her arms around his neck and held him to her, her soft mouth moving on his, her fingers caressing his neck.

Not as though he were a monster. Or even a duke.

Just as though he were a man.

By Megan Frampton

Dukes Behaving Badly

ONE-EYED DUKES ARE WILD
NO GROOM AT THE INN (A NOVELLA)
PUT UP YOUR DUKE
WHEN GOOD EARLS GO BAD (A NOVELLA)
THE DUKE'S GUIDE TO CORRECT BEHAVIOR

ONE-EYED DUKES ARE WILD

MEGAN FRAMPTON

AVON BOOKS

An Imprint of HarperCollinsPublishers

AVON BOOKS
An Imprint of HarperCollins*Publishers*
195 Broadway
New York, New York 10007

Copyright © 2016 by Megan Frampton
ISBN 978-0-06-241278-2
www.avonromance.com

First Avon Books mass market printing: January 2016

Avon Trademark Reg. U.S. Pat. Off. and in Other Countries, Marca Registrada, Hecho en U.S.A.
Avon, Avon Books, and the Avon logo are trademarks of HarperCollins Publishers.
HarperCollins® is a registered trademark of HarperCollins Publishers.

Printed in the U.S.A.

10 9 8 7 6 5 4 3 2 1

Acknowledgments

Thanks to my editor, Lucia Macro, for her encouragement, enthusiasm, and something else beginning with "e." Thanks to my agent, Louise Fury, for her support and continued guidance. Thanks, as always, to my critique partner, Myretta Robens, who tells me to keep going every time I doubt what I've written (spoiler: that happens a lot).

And finally, thanks to my husband, Scott. I love you, and I know you've got my back.

GEORGIANA AND THE DRAGON

By A Lady of Mystery

Georgiana stopped as she walked toward the well. What was that smell? It was as though someone had set the woods on fire, or something, only there was no smoke, or burning trees, or anything but the odor itself.

She shifted the bucket in her hand to the other hand, pushing her hair out of her face. It was windy, and perhaps there was a distant fire somewhere, someone burning brush, and that was the cause of it.

Shaking her head, she continued walking, counting her steps, as she always did, on the way to the well. It was her task to fetch the water every day, sometimes twice a day, for her father's smithy.

It was hard work, but Georgiana never begrudged it; her father worked hard to keep her and her sisters fed and clothed. Her mother had died when her youngest sister, Mary, was born, and Georgiana had only the slightest recollection of her. Nor did she have time to wonder about distant fires. She had water to collect, and soon—the King had honored her father by giving him the task of shoeing his horses, but the job had to be completed before the King went hunting in the spring. That gave her father just a month to complete it all, in addition to his usual work.

Chapter 1

Lasham took too big a swallow of his wine, knowing his headache would only be exacerbated by the alcohol, but unwilling to forgo the possibility that perhaps, for just a few minutes, his perception would be muffled, blurred a little around the edges.

So that he wouldn't be in a state of constant keen awareness that he was the Duke of Lasham, that he was likely the most important person wherever he happened to be—according to everyone but him—and that he was under almost continuous surveillance.

The ballroom was filled with the best people of Society, all of whom seemed to be far more at ease than he had ever been. Could ever be, in fact. He stood to the side of the dance floor, the whirling fabric of the ladies' gowns like a child's top.

Not that he'd been allowed anything as playful or fun as a top when he was growing up. But he could identify the toy, at least.

"Enjoying yourself, Your Grace?" His hostess, along with two of her daughters, had crept up along his blind side, making him start and slosh his wine onto his gloved hand. Occurrences like this weren't the worst part of having lost an eye— that obviously would be the fact that he only had one eye left—but it was definitely annoying.

"Yes," he said, bowing in their general direction, "thank you, I am."

The three ladies gawked at him as though waiting for him to continue to speak, to display more of his wondrous dukeliness for their delight. As though he were more of an object than a person.

But he couldn't just perform on command, and his hand was damp, and now he would have to go air out his glove before bestowing another dance on some lady he would be obliged to dance with, being the duke, and all. Because if his glove was damp, it might be perceived as, God forbid, *sweaty*, and sweaty-handed dukes might mean that the duke had gotten said sweat because he was enthralled with the person with whom he was dancing, which would lead to expectations, which would lead to expect a question, and Lasham knew he did not want to ever have to ask that question of anybody.

It was bad enough being the object of scrutiny when he was out in public. At home, at least, he

was by himself, blissfully so, and taking a duchess would require that he be at home by himself
with somebody else, and that somebody would
doubtless have ducal expectations of him as well.

"Excuse me," he said to the silent, gawking
ladies. He sketched a quick bow and strode off,
trying to look as though he had a destination
rather than merely wishing to depart.

"It is my trick, I believe." Margaret leaned forward to gather the cards and swept them to her
side of the table, along with the notes and coins
that had been tossed in. She glanced to either side
of her, noticing the telltale signs of disgruntle-
ment on her companions' faces. She would have
to start losing for a bit, then, in order to win more
in the end.

Not that she cheated, of course; she was just
very, very good at cards, and the people she
played with were usually quite bad. Plus she was
able to recall just which cards had been played,
and that no doubt helped her as she weighed what
cards might be coming up next.

It got to be boring, after a while, constantly winning. Though the winnings at the table helped to
keep her suitably decked out in the gowns she required in order to keep her place in Society, and
also would help some of her other less superficial
interests, so she didn't really wish to be losing.
Who would wish to lose, anyway?

But sometimes, after she'd won yet another
considerable sum, she wished she could be sur-

prised into a loss. To find an opponent who would be worthy of her skill and her attention.

That, it seemed, was not to be. Might never be.

Not that she wasn't grateful to be here at all; she certainly was. The cold truth of it was that she was invited to these events not because she was a good cardplayer, but because she was a scandal, but not too scandalous. So any hostess who invited her would be seen as daring, and she would add color to the festivities, simply because of who she was.

That she was able to support herself and the causes to which she'd dedicated her money was a welcome side effect of her scandalous wake.

"It is your deal, Lady Sophia," Margaret murmured as she passed the cards to her left. The lady took the cards, nodding, and Margaret leaned back in her chair, glancing around the room.

She'd been back in London for only a few months, as soon as she'd found out her parents had departed, and it already seemed as though she hadn't ever left. She'd missed it, even though she'd liked living out in the country, just walking alone for hours at a time and thinking. Just thinking.

Thinking was at more of a premium here, what with all the other things she had to be doing as well: attending social gatherings such as this one, visiting with her sister, the Duchess of Gage, and her new niece, plotting out how to get her heroine even more in danger with the dangerous hero in her ongoing serialized story, which had just been increased to a weekly publication—another delicious bit to add to her scandalous reputation.

Avoiding her parents.

She felt her jaw clench as she thought about them, how they steadfastly refused to acknowledge her in public since she'd rebelled against their plans for her. As though she would marry someone as loathsome as Lord Collingwood, not that he had any desire to marry her, either. He had just wanted the funds her parents had promised along with her body, and had been dumbfounded when their second—in so many ways—daughter had refused to go along with their plans.

It hurt, even though she should have been accustomed to it by now. And it must bother them, as well, to know that she had returned to Society and had continued to be accepted at parties, and that she was perfectly able to survive on her own. If they thought about it at all, of course.

"Lady Margaret?" Oh, she'd been too engrossed in thinking to realize it was her turn to play. She took a quick survey of her cards, sorted them into their respective suits, and glanced at what had been played. Jack of hearts, two of hearts, and the ten. She had four additional hearts in her hand as well, which left six other cards. She figured out which ones were missing, then tossed her queen into the pile and took the hand, before laying down a six of diamonds.

It wouldn't do to play too many hearts, she thought to herself ruefully. Not that she had ever given her actual heart. That organ remained intact, not even dented by her close encounter with Lord Collingwood. Her pride, now that stung, but pride would heal; a heart would not.

The play lagged as a footman bearing wine approached the table. Everyone but Margaret took a glass, and then out of the corner of her eye she spotted a large black shape reaching for a glass as well.

It was a man, of course, a gentleman, since if it were a bear or a mobile rock or something there would have been more screaming and less allowing of the bear/rock to take a refreshment. And as she turned her head to look at him, she felt something inside her stutter to a stop, her breath caught in her throat as she looked.

He looked as though he could have walked right out of the pages of one of her more outrageous serials. He was tall, very tall, taller than all the other gentlemen in the room. And broad, as well, with shoulders that would have strained at the seams of his jacket if the garment in question had been less impeccably cut and less exquisitely molded to his form. His very excellent form.

And that was without even mentioning his face, which was just as excellent. He was clean-shaven, a rarity among the gentlemen in the room, and that meant the sharp planes of his face were clearly displayed. Of course what most people likely noticed was the black patch that covered his left eye, the ribbon tying it on also black, which happened—fortunately—to match the black of his hair and his eyebrows.

As she regarded him, he caught her eye and stiffened, as though he'd recognized her and didn't want to associate with her, or he hadn't recognized her but hadn't appreciated her gawking at him.

Either way, she thought with a mental shrug as she returned to the play, he clearly didn't want to have anything to do with her. Pity, since he looked as dangerous as she felt.

"My trick, I believe." Lady Sophia scooped up the coins from the table and Margaret leaned against the back of her chair, only about the seventh most shocking thing she'd done this evening.

The first, of course, had been having the audacity to win at cards despite being a female with a slightly tarnished reputation. The second and third likely had to do with the hat and gown she was wearing—she refused to continue to wear the pale colors of an unmarried woman. The colors didn't suit her, for one thing, and for another, she had no desire to indicate her unmarried status. So instead of insipid ivory, she was wearing blue, and not the wan blue of an early morning sky. This was the fierce, triumphant blue of a cloudless summer sky at midday.

The numbers leading up to seven likely had to do with declining to dance when asked by gentlemen who thought that because her reputation was tarnished, her behavior would be equally suspect, and taking a second glass of wine. Although she wasn't entirely sure, she imagined that she had likely done things to tick up the number of shocking events that she wasn't even aware of.

And that was why she'd been invited anyway, wasn't it?

It didn't miss her notice that leaning against the back of the chair was just as shocking as refusing a blackguard or a dance. Now if she were a man, she could get away with such behavior. She could lean against chairs, drink as many glasses of wine as she chose, and never have to dance with anyone she didn't wish to. She sighed as the possibility floated above her, like a tantalizing balloon she just couldn't catch.

And then, out of the corner of her eye, she saw another black shape, only this one didn't intrigue her as the pirate had. She knew this man, and she wanted nothing to do with him. Hadn't seen him, in fact, since before her parents had announced she was to be married to him. He hadn't even had the courtesy to come proposing himself; he'd allowed them to tell her what was to be done. Even thinking of it, thinking how close she had come to surrendering her freedom, made her grit her teeth and raise her head as though in challenge.

Although that was incredibly stupid, wasn't it, because then it increased the chances he'd spot her.

"Excuse me," Margaret said, nodding to one of the people watching the card game, "would you mind taking my seat? I find I am in need of some air," and she left without waiting for a reply, walking through the crowd quickly in the opposite direction from Lord Collingwood.

Lasham took a sip of his wine with the nondamp hand, squelching the desire to find out just who the lady was who'd met his gaze so—so directly. He wasn't accustomed to that, not at all; ladies didn't look at him either because they were awed by his title or because they were frightened by his eye patch. But her—she'd looked at him, and looked at him some more, so he had to avert his own gaze from hers.

He had noticed, however, that while she wasn't as young as most of the debutantes currently giggling in the ballroom, she wasn't old, either. Nor was she beautiful, not in the way of most beauties, but there was something—something *sparkling* about her, as though she'd been dusted in starlight or something like that. A ridiculous thought, and he didn't know where it had come from.

Her hair was a rich, lustrous brown, pulled back from her face with one curl resting coquettishly on her shoulder, which was bare. Her eyes were brown as well, huge, with thick lashes surrounding them. Her mouth was wide and sensuous, if a mouth could be sensuous, and as he regarded her, he'd seen a tiny smile creating a dimple on one cheek. Unlike the usual beauties, she looked utterly, deliciously approachable, which was why he absolutely must not find who she was or plot to meet her. She looked dangerous, if not in reality, then to his peace of mind.

Lasham continued threading his way through the crowd, nodding to people here and there, keeping his focus away from anyone's eyes so as to avoid conversation. He just wanted, *needed* a moment away from the party, from the constant scrutiny, from people who kept regarding him as though waiting for him to do something remarkable. Or unremarkable.

He arrived at a door near where the servants were bustling in and out, turned the handle, and stepped inside, shutting the door softly behind him. He stood in what appeared to be a small library, the streetlamps outside lighting the room enough so he could navigate, even with only one good eye.

He went and leaned against the windowsill, looking out at the street below, the carriages and their patient horses and coachmen waiting for the partygoers to finally decide they were done for the night. At the yellow glow of the streetlamps making the night seem as though it were faintly tinted, at the dark streets with the day's detritus still scattered on the ground.

And he was at last, finally, blissfully alone.

He heard the door open just as he was beginning to gather his resolve to return to the ballroom, to do his duty to the debutantes currently on display, to dance for the next few hours until he could return home and collapse into bed, only to get up and be the responsible duke all over again the next day.

A woman stepped into the room, darting a glance behind her as she shut the door. It was she, of course. The sparkling woman from the card table. That was why she'd been looking at him. He felt the sour taste of it in his throat, the certain feeling that she'd marked him as someone she could manipulate.

"You should go," he found himself saying, even though it was entirely rude and entirely unlike him.

She started, as though she hadn't noticed him, and Lasham felt a twinge of uncertainty.

"I should go?" Her voice held a note of amusement. "I've just arrived; it seems to me that you should be the one to go, since you've been in residence longer. Do allow someone else to have a turn, my lord."

My lord. So she didn't know who he was. Did that please him or annoy him?

"No," he said, and the word, the word he wished he could say to all those people who wanted things from him, wanted him to appear at their events just because he was a duke, slid from his lips as easily as if he'd been saying it his entire life.

"No?" She repeated him, imbuing the word with humor, again, as though that was what she always did. She walked farther into the room, her skirts rustling with a soft *sh-sh-sh.* "Then we are here together. Perhaps we should be introduced, although there is no one here to accommodate us." She stepped closer, stopping to rest her hand on the back of one of the sofas. "I am Lady Margaret Sawford." A pause. She tilted her head at him. "And this is where you should offer who you are."

"Oh, yes." Had he ever encountered such an odd woman? But not odd in an unpleasant way. In fact, the way she was looking at him, so directly, so appraisingly, was entirely refreshing. Of course once she knew who he was, that would all change. *Yes, Your Grace, I will leave immediately.* Or, worse yet, maybe not—*No, Your Grace, what will people say if they knew we were alone together? You have compromised me, and now you must do the right thing.*

"I am the Duke of Lasham. I am pleased to make your acquaintance, Lady Margaret."

She nodded her head, and he saw her smile. "Excellent, Your Grace. Now we are improperly introduced." She gestured to the sofa. "Would you mind if I sat? I promise not to speak, I just want to sit in here a moment."

Lasham couldn't speak himself, he was so taken aback. She—she wasn't here to entrap him, or engage his interest, or anything beyond, apparently, wishing for a moment alone.

He watched as she looked at him for a few more seconds, shrugged, then sat down and leaned her head back, closing her eyes.

"You can sit as well, if you want." She spoke with her eyes still closed. "If you're not going to leave, which you said you weren't."

"But—" And here Lasham finally found his words. "But if we are discovered, that will put you in a very awkward situation. That is, we being together, it isn't—well, it isn't proper," and didn't he sound like the most stuffy prig in the world, lecturing her on propriety when he'd himself told her no.

She chuckled. "And then what? You will no doubt make all sorts of proper offers, and then I will very improperly say no, and my reputation will be blackened a bit more." She opened her eyes and turned her head to regard him. "It is not the end of the world."

He gaped at her. Not the end of the world? Who was she? Where was the usual response of *Oh,*

Your Grace, of course, yes, I will leave, or yes, I will marry you, or yes, it will be just as you wish.

And this woman, this person who'd dared to stare so boldly at him, who'd refused his request, even knowing it came from a duke, had just informed him it would not be the end of the world if they were discovered. That she would not insist on marrying him, or otherwise forcing his hand in any way.

And, contradictorily, that just made him want to know her more.

Georgiana and the Dragon

By A Lady of Mystery

⧜⧜⧜

"Hello?" Georgiana called as she made her way to the woods. The bucket swung against her legs, a few drops of water splashing her gown. She should just dump the water and carry the empty bucket, but what if something actually was on fire? Then she would feel foolish for having done so.

Another roar sounded. Was it an animal? A wounded hunter? Whatever it was, it sounded as though it needed help.

Georgiana quickened her pace and more water sloshed out, some of it spilling on her soft shoes, making her curse. Not too loudly, of course; her father and sister would both be horrified if it got about that the eldest Smith sister did anything so indelicate as curse.

She ducked her head into the trees, the bare branches brushing her hair. It was a good thing she was as short as she was, even though she normally hated it. At least she wouldn't get poked in the eye with a branch. The worst that would happen was that her hair would get more mussed, and it was already very mussed, thanks to the wind.

"Hello?" she called again, only more softly. Now that she was in the woods chasing down a mysterious roar, her decision didn't seem as intelligent. What could be in here? Who was in here? What was whatever or whoever it was doing in here?

She didn't think any of the answers would be good ones.

Chapter 2

Damn. He wasn't nearly as dangerous as he appeared to be, Margaret thought. Instead, he was lecturing her on propriety, and standing over there by the window as though she might launch herself at him and he needed a quick escape. Not that she wouldn't mind launching herself at him—closer scrutiny proved that he was, indeed, quite as remarkably good-looking as she'd first assessed, but he would have to keep his staid opinions to himself for him to be quite launch-worthy.

"Why are you here, anyway?" Now he sounded piqued, as though he'd assumed she'd *followed* him here, of all things.

"Escape, mostly," Margaret replied quickly. She heard him move, and then he sat down next to her on the sofa. The sofa was quite large, so they were still a good distance away from each other—definitely too far for launching, for example—but that wouldn't matter if anyone caught them. Now she almost wished for someone to catch them, just to see how pokered up he'd get.

"Why did you feel a need for escape?" His voice was low, and had a richness to it that made her body prickle in reaction. Every part of him but the best part—his brain—seemed designed to entrance her. Pity about the brain, then. She opened her eyes again and glanced over at him. Yes. Still quite handsome. If only he wouldn't speak.

"People." He made a gesture as though she should continue. So she did. "People who chatter about you, and ask questions, or don't ask questions, or expect you to do something just because it's what you're supposed to do."

His voice rumbled with a low hint of humor. "I wouldn't know anything about being talked about and people who expect you to do something just because you're supposed to."

She couldn't help herself, she started to laugh. Because of all the ludicrous things she'd ever said, or even thought, that one had to be the most ludicrous. Of course he knew just what she was talking about; he was a duke who looked like that and also had an eye patch. People must always be leaping out of his way like they were wee tugboats and he was a mighty yacht, and then they all likely gaped at him whenever he was in the room.

She had just basically told a lion it was a hardship for her to have to walk to the buffet table when the lion had to chase down its prey and kill it.

"I am glad I amuse you," he said in a stiff voice. Oh goodness, he really was entirely proper. So disappointing.

But she couldn't say that to him, not without making it sound as though she wished him to be improper, with her, and she did not, despite his good looks and that raffish eye patch. "No, I apologize, it is just that I was thinking about how I was complaining about people being around and commenting on everything I do, but to you, a duke with, no doubt, all sorts of people trying to get your attention or who stare at you, or talk about you when you're not there, my complaints must seem frivolous."

He chuckled in reply. "Yes, I can see that. I shouldn't have taken offense."

Margaret shook her head. "But if you did take offense, then you should have. That is, if that is how you feel, you should be free to express it. Just as if you really wish me to leave the room, you can tell me that, and I will hear you out and make my own decision. That is what humanity is all about, is it not? The ability to decide for oneself?"

She felt him exhale beside her, a sound that seemed as though it came from his very soul. "You have obviously never been a duke, my lady," he said at last, sounding weary.

She couldn't help but laugh in response. "No, that is fair to say. I have not." Perhaps that was the trouble. Perhaps he'd never been able to get beyond his title, beyond who he was supposed to be. She'd seen her sister have the same problem— well, not the being-the-duke problem, although her sister was now a duchess—but the same problem of feeling as though she could only do what was expected of her. What would he do if he could do what was unexpected? And what was preventing her from asking?

"What would you do first if you weren't a duke?"

A very long pause this time, accompanied by a few huffs, as though he were thinking and not being pleased by his thoughts.

"I would—well, I have no idea, honestly."

"Perhaps you should discover it. And then do it."

He snorted. "That is easy to say, my lady, especially for someone who isn't a duke. But being me is being so much more than me, if that makes sense. It is being someone who is in charge of hundreds of lives, and livelihoods, and future generations as well. I cannot just give it all up because I am tired of having people expect me to make their decisions for them."

"Why not make a few decisions for yourself?" Margaret said in what she thought was a reasonable tone.

He snorted again, only this time more derisively. Apparently not such a reasonable tone after all. "I wish it were that easy."

"If you want to be stuck in your existence, always doing things that are expected of you, then go ahead, and do what you think you should be doing." She turned and looked at him, a challenge in her stare. "Or if you want to do something that pleases you, just you, and you make that decision, on your own, you can see how it feels." She shrugged. "If it doesn't feel right, you can stop. But you should at least have tried."

He rose quickly, smoothing his already perfectly smooth jacket on his body. "Thank you, Lady Margaret. It has been a pleasure to meet you." Even though it didn't sound as though it were a pleasure, and the way he moved swiftly out of the room reinforced that intimation.

Margaret shrugged again, relaxing against the sofa cushions. A few moments alone without a very proper duke would be quite welcome, she assured herself. Very welcome indeed.

If it doesn't feel right, you can stop. Long after Lasham had left the darkened room, long after he'd danced all the dances with the white-gowned debutantes, long after his carriage had trundled through the dark London streets to his town house in Mayfair, long after he'd gotten into his enormous bed, surrounded by pillows and draperies and all sorts of things deemed necessary for his sleeping dukeliness, long after he should have been asleep, her words haunted him. *She* haunted him.

It wasn't as easy as she'd said, was it? Was it? The possibility felt as though it were dancing in his head, just beyond reach, just beyond comprehension.

What would he do if he could do anything he wished? He didn't know the answer to that question, especially since it could not be answered with either a yes—the answer he heard and gave most often—or even a no, which he'd rarely ever said.

It had been drummed into his head since the

day he'd been born that he had to do what was right. Not what he wished to do. And he couldn't even say what he would wish to do when she'd asked.

He had told her no, though, hadn't he? He'd told her he didn't wish to leave the room when she'd asked. He'd shared a moment with her before he left the room, leaving his potential for recklessness there as well, returning to the world where he knew what was expected of him, and what he expected of himself.

But for a moment, just for that moment of shared humor, of warmth, he'd felt what it could be like to do what he wanted to, even if he wasn't certain at all what that was.

"This one is lovely." Margaret sighed aloud. She stood in front of the painting and just stared, feeling as though the colors in front of her had leaped off the canvas and were saturating her soul. She found herself in the National Gallery at least once a week, scandalously on her own since she didn't see the point of forcing her maid to accompany her, the one who told her mistress tartly she'd seen all the art she wanted to see, thank you very much; she'd wait in the carriage.

Margaret felt a small smile curl at her mouth as she recalled Annie's words. When she'd left London after refusing the Collingwood—she wouldn't call it jilting him, since she'd never said yes in the first place—Annie had insisted on accompanying her, even though she'd never left

London before. But wherever Margaret went, so did Annie.

Except for the National Gallery.

She started as she heard someone clear his throat behind her. And turned to see him, the Pirate Duke who was not at all piratical, standing as though he were posing for his own statue—head high, shoulders pulled back, his hands clasped behind him. If only he were nude, the look would be perfect.

"Pardon me, Lady Margaret." He sounded entirely uncomfortable. Perhaps he was imagining himself nude as well? Margaret stifled a giggle and schooled her features into a look of calm repose.

Or as calm as she could get, given that she was imagining him as a statue in the altogether.

"Good afternoon, Your Grace." She dipped a curtsey and then turned her gaze to his face. Not speaking; he had addressed her, after all, he could have just left her alone as it seemed he'd wished to last night.

But the silence just . . . lay there, and she nearly opened her mouth to say something, anything, just something, so he wouldn't just be looking at her, or not, since his gaze kept shifting away from her face to other spots in the room, then returned back to her.

Finally, after what felt like an hour, he opened his mouth.

"Do you like paintings, my lady?"

His voice sounded as though he hadn't ever spoken before, each word shiny and new when it emerged from his lips.

"I do, Your Grace." She gestured to the painting behind her. "I love the colors in this one. And how, for once, the lady is the focal point of the picture." She paused, then spoke again. "Even if the lady in question is running away."

"It would be foolish to stand your ground against a dragon, wouldn't you say?" the duke replied, gesturing to the painting. "George there seems to have it well in hand."

Margaret chuckled, at least as much at how unexpected it was to hear him converse nearly normally as at what he'd actually said. Not that she knew how he conversed; perhaps he was normal, and not all standoffish with everyone else in his acquaintance, and she was just a special case.

Although that would imply he knew anything about her, and from their conversation the previous evening, he did not. So he must be this rigid all the time.

"What do you suppose happened after this?" She tapped her finger on her chin. "Maybe they went down to the pub and shared a pint of ale or something to celebrate the dragon slaying." She turned back to look at him. "And who do you suppose had to clean it all up? The dead dragon and everything?" She made a hmphing sound. "I would imagine it was the lady, since she didn't do anything but run away. Although she was probably terrified. That hardly seems fair."

The duke's expression turned rueful. "People's situations seldom are."

Now she was curious, again, about this man

whom she'd written off as being the stodgiest duke in the world. Intriguing.

"Not that I have anything to complain about myself," he added, the low rumble of his voice doing something interesting to her insides. "I haven't encountered any dragons, nor any ladies in need of rescuing, thank goodness, and I don't know that I would wish to change my situation even if I could."

"Why not?"

He frowned, as though perplexed by her question. "How could I know that the person who would inevitably replace me would be as conscientious as I? Would do the right thing, all the time?"

Ah. So that was it. "You do the right thing all the time?" Margaret repeated, stressing the "all."

He was apparently so absolutely proper he didn't even hesitate, or blush when he answered. "Yes. I do, my lady."

"Pity," Margaret murmured, turning her gaze back to St. George and the very unlucky fire-breathing creature who'd happened to encounter him.

She didn't speak again, just stood there, unmoving, looking at the painting even as her mind raced with questions and possible conversation. Eventually, after a few moments, she heard him clear his throat again, saying, "Good afternoon, my lady," and moving away before she could reply, much less turn around.

What was he thinking, going up to speak to her like that? What must she think of him?

It wasn't as though there was anything to be gained from conversation. It was just that . . . that when he'd seen her, standing in front of the Tintoretto, it had seemed as though he'd conjured her out of his own imagination, and he hadn't actually realized he had very much of an imagination. At least not as far as ladies in art galleries went.

So that was surprising, and then that she was here where hardly anyone in their world visited, except to see and be seen, and she was definitely not doing either one of those things. Of course he wasn't, either; he felt as though the gallery was a refuge. A place he could go where he didn't have to feel as though he were as much on display as the paintings were.

He liked the way she spoke so confidently about the painting, about the colors and the lady and even what would happen to the dragon remains. It was all so different from the conversations he usually had with—well, anybody.

"Your Grace!" He turned as he heard the words, knowing it was hardly likely that there was another duke hanging about the National Gallery.

"Good afternoon," he said, nodding to the group of ladies, all of whom he recognized from various functions, although he wasn't quite certain of their names.

The tallest one, a Lady Dearwood, he thought he recalled, stepped out from the crowd and smiled at him. "Are you a fan of the visual arts, Your Grace?" She gestured to the group. "We are here for our monthly visit, we come once a month"—as the phrase "monthly visit" would imply, Lasham thought—"to gaze upon the majestic beauty of the pictures and become inspired in our own artistic efforts." She leaned forward, as though confiding in him. He resisted the urge to draw back. "We are all amateur daubists, you see, Your Grace."

"I see," Lasham replied, wishing he hadn't given in to his desire to visit the gallery today himself. Not if it meant encountering a young lady who made him want to do something wrong—not that he knew what that would be—and another group of women who couldn't just call themselves painters, they had to be "amateur daubists."

But if he hadn't come, he wouldn't have heard her talk about the Tintoretto so intriguingly. He wished it were possible to ask a lady to walk with him through a museum without immediately causing comment—if not from the lady herself, then from anyone who happened to see them—so he could see what she thought of the other works on display. The Titian, the Rubens, the Claudes.

"Are you a painter yourself, Your Grace?" Lady Dearwood's voice interrupted his thoughts. Just as well, it wasn't as though he could actually have any of the things he'd been imagining.

"No, I just—" How to say it without sounding as though he were as insufferably pompous as Lady Margaret no doubt thought he was, although these ladies might be pleased at how ducal his approbation—or lack thereof—was. "I appreciate art." And left his words sitting there, hanging awkwardly in the air between them.

Wonderful, Lasham, he thought. No wonder he

usually kept silent in company beyond the minimum of polite conversation. He was clearly terrible at saying anything without sounding like a prig, a snob, or a . . . or a duke.

Although he had managed to utter a few sentences to her without having any of that happen.

"As do we!" Lady Dearwood exclaimed. She patted him on the arm with one gloved hand, her enormous skirts brushing his legs. He resisted the temptation to step farther away. "Please say you will join our artish excursion, Your Grace? It would be an honor."

And a chore, Lasham thought as he nodded, holding his arm out for Lady Dearwood to take. Those damn skirts making him nearly stumble.

Margaret hadn't meant to keep track of where he was; it was just that he was so—so present, and large, and very definitely male, and he seemed to loom in the corner of her eye, even though that sounded entirely odd, and she kept feeling this prickling awareness of him. Only every time she happened to very casually and surreptitiously glance his way he was most definitely not looking at her, but at something else. Anyone else, in fact.

But it was hard not to notice him, especially since he was the large black center of some sort of lady bouquet, with women arranged on either side of him, in back, and one in front who seemed to be clearing the way of interlopers.

"This one, Your Grace," the one on his left arm declaimed as they drew up to a bland landscape scene, "this one makes one's heart yearn. Don't you think?" The lady—Margaret thought it might be Miss Edwards, she always bet too much on long shots and got conservative when she had a winning hand—did some sort of eyelash-batting in his general direction, only of course he couldn't see it, since she was on his blind side.

Margaret didn't think Miss Edwards would appreciate that if she pointed it out. But the thought of doing so did make her chuckle.

"Yearn, yes, Miss Edwards," the duke replied, still using his I-have-barely-ever-spoken-to-another-human-being tone he used with her. Had he ever had a normal conversation? Or, worse yet, was this his normal conversation?

Lady Dearwood—it was hard not to notice her, the lady was so tall, and wearing some sort of cascading ruffly dress that doubtless looked good at some point, just not on a woman who more resembled an Amazon—had hold of his other arm and drew him away from the painting, a pointed sniff indicating what she thought of Miss Edwards and her yearning.

And then he did meet her gaze.

"Your Grace!"

He'd known where she was the minute he stepped into the large room. Not that she drew attention to herself, or was dressed outrageously, or was talking loudly, or anything.

She just—what had he thought the night before? Of course. She sparkled. It almost seemed there

was a nimbus around her head, which was ridiculous and definitely put paid to the idea that he
had no imagination. Here he was, imagining her
as some sort of astral body, or heavenly creature,
when all she was was a plainspoken lady who
was most definitely not impressed with him. And
yet—and yet she had said "Your Grace" with such
authority, as though she wanted to speak to him.

And since the entire room was silent, no doubt
waiting for his reply, it seemed that everyone
wanted him to speak to her. If only to answer.

"Yes, Lady Margaret?"

She moved closer, her eyes locked on his face,
looking right at him, a sly smile on her lips. Very
few people ever just looked directly at him as she
was; normally they focused intently on his one
eye, or darted glances back and forth between his
patch and his eye, the movements getting more
frantic the more uncomfortable they became. But
she—she just kept her gaze on him, looking at
him as though he were a normal man.

Albeit a man who had a title, an eye patch, and
the company of no fewer than seven "amateur
daubists."

"I am ready to be escorted to my carriage." She
addressed the ladies surrounding him. "The duke
was kind enough to offer to do so when my maid
was taken ill," and here she looked down and
made some sort of gesture that implied she was a
helpless creature, when Lasham already knew she
was nothing of the sort, "and he said I should find
him when I was finished."

She paused and returned to looking at him,

and he could have sworn she winked. As though they were two regular people sharing a joke, not a very confused duke and a sprightly, sparkling woman who appeared intent on removing him from where he was.

Rescuing him. That was what she was doing, wasn't it? She had seen his discomfort and was responding to it with a clever subterfuge that would extricate him from the situation without his having to be rude, which he definitely would never be, or having to endure hours more of the yearning and the daubing and whatever else the Monthly Ladies' Meeting Every Month Group decided to discuss.

"Of course, Lady Margaret. I am so pleased to be of service." He removed the lady from his left arm, then Lady Dearwood on his right, making a small bow to each of them in turn.

And then he looked at her, his rescuer, and wanted to kiss her, he was so grateful. Although that was not all of why he wanted to kiss her, although he hadn't quite realized just how much he wished he could until this very moment.

But instead of doing anything so shocking he just waited as she slid her gloved hand into the crook of his arm, which he'd presented to her as though it were a present, instead of her offering him the gift of escape.

Escape. He wished he actually could.

They walked slowly to the exit; he felt the weight of all the other ladies' stares as they moved, unable to see her face because of the enormous bonnet she was wearing. Thank goodness men didn't wear bonnets, or he wouldn't be able to see anything at all.

Wouldn't be able to see the sycophants bowing in front of him, the gossips talking about him behind his back, see the way everyone changed their attitude simply because he was a duke.

Perhaps he should start wearing a bonnet after all.

His arm, and it seemed his entire body, was rigid as they walked to the exit of the gallery. What had seemed like a lark to Margaret now held much more weight, as though this meant something, which of course it didn't. She'd seen his distress, she'd figured out the reason—she hoped—and she'd done something about it.

"You did wish to leave, didn't you?" she asked in a low voice as they kept walking. Please let him say yes, or otherwise she would feel like the most managing kind of female.

Not that she wasn't, but she'd already managed a few things today, namely to do with her next deadline and a contribution to the women she was trying to help, and she didn't know if there was a quota and she'd have to be less managing tomorrow.

She didn't think that would be possible.

"Yes, thank you. You came to my rescue, just as St. George did," he said, his voice sounding relieved.

She exhaled. "Whew, thank goodness. Because I know I don't know you, and perhaps you like being the object of all that attention. Only . . ." And she paused and tightened her grip on his arm—his very hard, muscled arm she couldn't help but notice. "From what you said the night before, it seems as though that is the last thing you want. To be the object of attention."

The duke tipped his hat to a lady entering the gallery, then held the door open for Margaret to step outside. He held his arm out for her again. "I don't know if I would say that is the last thing I would want, Lady Margaret," he replied, his low, resonant voice sounding so intensely male it made her insides flutter, just a bit, "but it would have to be in the top five."

"What would be the other four?" she asked, allowing a flirtatious tone to creep into her voice. Because of course she still found him immensely attractive, and there was nothing wrong with flirting, even though the object of flirtation might be the dullest duke she'd ever met.

But since she'd only ever met two, and the other one was married to her sister, she couldn't really say she had much basis for comparison.

And he might be the dullest duke but he was also—no offense to her brother-in-law—the most attractive duke she'd ever encountered.

"To sing in public, to be forced to drink inferior wine, to tell a joke and have no one laugh, and," he said, glancing her way quickly, then returning to looking straight ahead, "to wear one of your bonnets." He paused, and then the amused tone was gone entirely. "That is to say, not that your bonnet is unattractive, on the contrary, it is quite lovely, as bonnets go, only I wouldn't—that is, I couldn't—"

She took pity on him, even though she couldn't help laughing. "I understand precisely, Your Grace. My bonnet is fine for me, but not for you. I will bear that in mind before I ask you to don any of my clothing."

And then she felt herself start to blush, because if he was wearing her clothing then what was she wearing? And then she thought about how he'd have to remove some of his clothing to put hers on, and then he'd be naked, as she'd thought about him before, and goodness knew that she didn't doubt he'd rival all the statues she'd ever seen, but it would be he, and that would be entirely awkward.

She really wished she didn't have such a vivid imagination.

"Thank you." His voice was as luscious as the rest of him, Margaret thought—low, and rich, and resonant, and its timbre sent a little shiver through her. "You did rescue me, and I am very grateful."

"You are welcome." They stood at the bottom of the stairs, and Margaret glanced down the line of waiting carriages until she spotted hers. "Ah, there is my carriage." She spotted Annie's head popping out of the window, no doubt growing more and more impatient for her mistress to stop "gawking at them pictures," and go do something useful. Like take a nap or have a cup of tea or any of the myriad things Annie thought were more useful than viewing art.

"Allow me to escort you the rest of the way," he said, not waiting for a reply, but drawing her arm through his again and starting to walk. What did it say about her that while she did not like being told what to do, she did like it when he took such masterful command?

She probably did not want to examine that too closely.

"Thank you. You know," she said in a thought-ful tone, "you should probably visit the gallery earlier in the day so as to avoid such situations as you just encountered. Ladies such as those seldom rise before noon, and then it takes them at least an hour or two to dress, and more time to gather themselves sufficiently to venture outdoors."

"Do you generally visit earlier?"

Oh. She hadn't thought he'd think—well, at least she *hoped* he didn't think she was one of those types of ladies, the kind who was angling for attention. Although he had asked.

"I am not nearly as regular as that, Your Grace." She shrugged. "I arrive when I do," which made it sound as though she were flighty. Which she was not. Managing, yes, but flighty, no.

"Ah." Did he sound disappointed? Could it be that he actually wanted to be in her company again? She forced herself not to ask just that, because she didn't want to embarrass the poor gentleman again, and she already knew he was entirely proper and would likely think she was being shockingly forward.

"Would you like to meet again at the gallery?"

And then there was the fact that she *was* shockingly forward, and she just didn't care. And if he did want to meet her here at some point in the future, why shouldn't they do just that? She'd already shocked Society once, it wasn't as though she could ruin herself again. Or, she thought as she glanced over at the duke, perhaps she could. He was so very attractive.

"Uh, well, that would be pleasant." He sounded as rigid and proper as he had the night before, but Margaret could already tell it wasn't so much that he was an absolute stick-in-the-mud as that he was just uncomfortable. Maybe there was something to the Piratical Duke and his Very Proper Demeanor after all.

Damn it, and now she was intrigued, and she couldn't afford more distraction from her deadlines and her work among the unfortunate women she'd been helping. She almost wanted to reprimand him for being so attractive and layered, only then he would be utterly confused and no doubt shy away from any contact with her. And, damnation, she didn't want that.

She wanted the opposite, in fact.

"Excellent, Your Grace," she said, using a tone that she would employ if she were, for example, trying to persuade a bear or some other enormous solitary beast to keep her company.

Not that she was in the habit of such things, of course. But she couldn't help but think of her first impression of him, as a solid, and solidly handsome, force that might be able to move mountains, if it were so inclined, or make things happen that seemed impossible.

It remained to be seen if the reality of the duke could live up to Margaret's now very active imagination.

And luckily she was very interested in being the one to see it.

GEORGIANA AND THE DRAGON

By A Lady of Mystery

⁓⁓⁕⟳⟲⁕⁓⁓

The moan of pain—and Georgiana could tell whatever it was was in pain, that much was clear, even if she couldn't ascertain who, or maybe even what, was making the noise—was closer now, and she walked with more confident steps, knowing that whatever it was wouldn't be able to hurt her.

At least she hoped not.

She walked for at least ten minutes, stopping every so often to listen for the moans, which were growing fainter.

"Hold on, help is on the way," she called, feeling incredibly foolish but not able to stop herself. She didn't think the moans were made by a human, which meant it couldn't understand her, so why was she trying to reassure some sort of beast? Also, she couldn't ignore the prickling feeling that although whatever it was might be in pain now, it might also be hungry, and she might be dinner.

There were a lot of bad "mights" in there.

But she kept walking, knowing that if she were in pain in the woods she would want someone—or something—to hear her and try to help.

Chapter 3

Lasham felt himself wince as he recalled what he'd said to her, the lady of sparkles. "Wear your bonnet," or some such nonsense, something that managed to make him seem bizarre and insulting all at the same time.

Perhaps for his next trick he could tell her she was stupid and not worth his time. Or would that be too subtle?

"Lash!" He jerked his head up, forgetting bonnets—thank goodness—for just a moment as he heard his friend Jamie's voice. The man himself soon appeared in Lasham's line of vision, a wide grin on his face.

"What are you doing in London?" Lasham asked, shaking his friend's hand. Unlike Lasham, Jamie thought London wasn't busy enough, and was usually traveling in some distant land, only returning home when his mother demanded she be able to see her only son.

Jamie shrugged, his movements precise and elegant. "I got bored of not speaking the language."

He made a show of looking Lasham up and down, one eyebrow raised. "You are looking as forbidding as usual." He reached out and tapped his finger on Lasham's eye patch—the only person from whom Lasham would even come close to tolerating such behavior. "It's a pity you won't travel with me, Lash. Your appearance would scare even the most recalcitrant individual into handing over their treasures."

Jamie didn't just see the sights when he traveled; he had developed a robust trade in art, tracking down items in the most remote places and selling them to fellow British folk who weren't as brave as he in venturing beyond their own world. He didn't need the money but it seemed that he did need the danger. Something Lasham envied—he wished he could join his friend on one of his adventures, but then he'd be neglecting his responsibilities.

If it doesn't feel right, you can stop.

Jamie and Lady Margaret were very similar. Perhaps too similar—he didn't think he'd be in too much of a hurry to introduce them to each other.

And he didn't want to think too much about why their meeting would irk him so much.

"Thank you, I think," Lasham replied, his tone dry as dust. Jamie enjoyed trying to rile Lasham up, even though he never succumbed to Jamie's frequent prodding, whether it was about his appearance, his stodgy habits, or his discomfort with appearing in public.

But Jamie was one of the few—perhaps the only

person Lasham trusted absolutely. So he put up with his ridicule because he did wonder if he was, perhaps, a little dull. Even though Jamie seemed to find him amusing enough.

"God, I'm thirsty." Jamie grabbed hold of Lasham's arm and tugged him across the street. "There's a pub there, let's just go down a pint."

"Wha—? I can't go in there, I'm—" And then he stopped speaking, because what he had been about to say was likely the most pompous thing he'd uttered that day, and that included when he'd said, "I appreciate art."

"You're a duke, I know," Jamie replied, and Lasham didn't have to see his friend's face to know he'd rolled his eyes. "Can't you forget that for just a few minutes? We all know how damn responsible you are, Lash, you don't need to prove it to all of us all the time."

Lasham shook his head, wondering who the "all" were that Jamie was referring to, but also knowing that his friend was right. That she was right, also.

He only did the right things. Until this very day, he hadn't even considered doing anything but the right things. But what would happen if he did do some of the wrong things? Would the world end? Would his dukedom be taken away from him?

"Fine, just a few minutes. And try not to pick a fight with anyone." That was how he and Jamie had met; Jamie's sharp tongue had made some of the older boys at school furious, and they'd tried to take it out of Jamie's hide. Lasham, never one to abide injustice, saw the inequity of three boys beating on one, and had joined in on Jamie's side.

And since Lash had always been tall and broad, the two of them had beaten the three boys, and had forged a friendship that had lasted for nearly twenty years in the process.

He felt a rueful smile curl his lips as he thought about that first time. If it weren't for his sense of responsibility, the one Jamie was currently decrying, they wouldn't be such good friends. Wouldn't be friends at all.

"Over here," Jamie said, leading the way to a table set to the side of the bar. The barmaid's face registered surprise—perhaps at the toffs who'd come into what otherwise seemed to be a rather dingy establishment—and she walked over to them quickly, giving Jamie more of a once-over than Lasham got.

"Ale?" she asked, since apparently that was all that was on offer. Although judging by how Jamie was regarding her, and how she was looking at him, that might change.

"Yes, thanks love," Jamie said, giving her a wink before she walked away.

"It's good to see you," Lasham said, aware of just how true that was.

Lasham had never had the knack for making friends—or enemies, for that matter—and Jamie traveled frequently and Lasham's duties kept him from socializing much, never mind that he usually loathed it.

What would you do if you could do anything you wanted?

Why did her words keep echoing in his brain? He shook his head at his own idiocy. Why wouldn't they? When was the last time he'd done anything he truly wished to?

And why had the thought just occurred to him?

"Here, have a drink, for God's sake, you look as though someone died," Jamie said, pushing the pint of beer toward him. Lasham blinked, not having realized the barmaid had returned so quickly.

He hoisted the pint and tilted it to Jamie. "Glad to see you, my friend. How long are you in town for?"

Jamie took a long draught and wiped his mouth with the back of his hand. "A few weeks. I was going to stay with my mother, but now that I've run into you . . ." His words trailed off and he gave Lasham a significant look.

Lasham was shaking his head even before he realized it. "Absolutely not. The last time you stayed with me you damaged three chairs, made the cook and the downstairs maid come to blows, and I still haven't figured out how you managed to completely disarrange my files in less than five minutes, but it took my secretary the better part of a week to return them to their rightful order."

Jamie shrugged, drank the rest of his glass in one long swallow, and gestured to the barmaid for another. "It was worth a try. One of these days, Lash, you're going to find yourself doing something that won't be what you're supposed to do."

Apparently this was the day when anyone he spoke to—all two of them, at least, ignoring the Monthly Daubists—would comment on what a boring existence he led, and urge him to do something wild. He should remind Jamie that if it weren't for Lash being responsible, being the kind of duke his title deserved, it would result in a bigger problem than just a few files being misfiled.

But if he challenged Jamie, he knew his friend would actually see it as a challenge.

"Someone might have said something similar to me earlier today." Lasham drummed his fingers on the table as he thought. "The odd thing is it has never occurred to me to do something I shouldn't be doing."

Jamie nodded in understanding. "Your father definitely wouldn't have countenanced any kind of freethinking in his son, the duke's heir, would he?"

Lasham recalled his father, just how stern the man had always been, and how a young Lasham had wished his father had been able to play once in a while.

Damn it, had he become his father?

He took another sip of the ale and realized he could do something just a bit different. That he had engaged to do so, in fact, earlier that day.

He would meet Lady Margaret at the gallery. He would attempt to respond to her flirting as though he had not just learned how to speak the English language, and he would perhaps even go so far as to engage her for a dance at the next social event they would both be attending.

That those events counted as "different" in his world was a fairly strong indicator of just how boring he—or maybe just his life—was.

"What do you know of the Duke of Lasham?" Margaret took a sip of tea as she regarded her sister, beautiful as always. As was her daughter, sleeping in a crib to the side of the sofa.

Margaret used to envy her sister her marvelous beauty, until she realized that her parents viewed Isabella as a commodity because of it, and had bartered her to a duke, nearly sight unseen. Thankfully it had worked out; Isabella was as happy as Margaret had ever seen her, but it wouldn't have mattered to their parents if it hadn't. Just as it hadn't mattered to them that Margaret had no desire to marry the Collingwood, which was why they no longer recognized her as their daughter.

A fact that hurt, even though it was not as though she particularly loved her parents. But Isabella had stood up to them when they told her she likewise had to cut her sister out of her life, and for that, Margaret was grateful. She'd also made sure Margaret was able to live on her own, adding the force of her title whenever it was necessary. Margaret hated to rely on that, but she did acknowledge it came in handy when dealing with landlords and merchants and such.

"The Duke of Lasham is the one with the—" and Isabella gestured up to her eye.

"Yes, the duke with the eye patch. How did he lose his eye, anyway?" And why was she so curious about him? She wouldn't answer that to herself right now, except to recall broad shoulders, dark hair, and a self-deprecating air that belied his appearance and title.

Isabella shook her head. "Nobody knows. He won't say, and of course no one is rude enough to ask."

Until I do, Margaret thought. Because she knew she couldn't bear not knowing something; it was one of the most delightful and most aggravating things about her, she well knew.

"Did you meet him?" Isabella said, then rolled her eyes at herself. "Of course you did, otherwise you wouldn't know about the eye patch. What did you think of him? We don't know him very well; he doesn't attend many Society functions."

"I found him"—*handsome, disappointing, curious, intriguing, more handsome, and somewhat charming*—"interesting. I met him last night, and then saw him at the National Gallery this morning. We've arranged to meet there again."

Isabella's eyes widened. "Is he courting you?"

Margaret shook her head. "No, of course not. I am so far below what he would require of a wife, and I would hate being on display as his duchess—no offense to you, Isabella, but if I had to do what you do, and if people were constantly assessing me, I think I would explode."

Isabella laughed. "No offense taken. It can be unpleasant at times, but the benefits outweigh the difficulty," she said with a knowing smile and a quick glance at her baby that made Margaret's heart ache.

Would she ever find someone to love, and who loved her, as Nicholas did Isabella? Thus far, the only men who'd seemed remotely interested in her had assumed she was mistress, not wife, material, and the men in question hadn't tempted her into either position.

"And since you won't ever tell me about the benefits," Margaret said, stressing the last word, "I won't even consider becoming a duchess." She waved her hand in the air. "Because of course all the available dukes are pining to marry me."

"Just you wait," Isabella said in a chiding tone. "You'll be going along and boom, all of a sudden, you'll fall in love." She nodded. "And when you fall, Margaret, you are going to fall hard."

"Falling hard sounds as though I'll end up hurt, or at least bruised."

Isabella smiled that knowing smile again. The one that made Margaret practically itch with curiosity. "It will be wonderful."

Georgiana and the Dragon

By A Lady of Mystery

❧〜⊙つC⌢〜❧

Georgiana walked for at least fifteen minutes, calling out every few minutes to the thing, the entity, that was in pain, holding her breath until she heard the return call. At least it wasn't dead yet.

The call sounded closer and closer, and finally, as she pushed through a thick cluster of trees, she spotted something in the distance that wasn't the same-verdant green as her surroundings.

It was orange and yellow and red, all varieties of each color swirling into one another like they were all in a mixing bowl and someone was stirring them vigorously.

She swallowed as she approached it—it wasn't like anything she had ever seen before, and yet it was noticeably breathing, and obviously it had cried out, and so it was alive.

She slowed her steps as she walked up to stand not five feet from it, hearing how loud her breathing was in the quiet of the forest.

"Hello?" she said in a low voice. "I came to help you."

The thing lifted its head and looked at her, giant eyes with bloodred pupils just staring. It opened its mouth and wisps of smoke emerged, along with another one of those plaintive cries.

It was a dragon, Georgiana realized without nearly as much shock as she should have had. What's more, it was an injured dragon. She could see one of its wings bent back at an odd angle.

She stepped forward and placed her palm on its back. "It is all right. I am here to help."

Chapter 4

Margaret strode up the stairs to the National Gallery at just past ten o'clock, hoping and also not hoping to find the duke there. It wasn't as though there could be anything—not even friendship—between them. She was a notorious author of dramatic serials, who'd caused a scandal by refusing to marry someone and revealing herself as the notorious author in question at the same time. He—he was a duke. A proper duke, one who did what he was supposed to, and never did anything wrong.

He was invited to things because of his title, not because there was even the slightest chance he would do something shocking.

She wondered what it would take to tempt him into doing something wrong, and then cursed herself for even thinking of it. Because she'd found, to her own chagrin, that her thinking about something was mere steps away from actually doing it.

It was unfortunate the same didn't apply when it came to, for example, making her writing deadlines or being able to sleep.

She walked briskly through the corridors to where she had first seen the duke the day before. She saw him before he could see her—she was approaching him on his eye patch side—and she slowed her steps, taking in his magnificence. He was so tall and broad and yet he wasn't remotely fat; he looked as much like a Greek statue as he could, given that he wasn't made of marble and naked.

She really had to stop thinking about him naked.

Because if she thought about it—well, that would be a bad thing for certain if she ended up doing something about it. Especially given how stuffy he seemed. He'd likely faint from the shock of it, and then she'd have to catch him before he fell, and how could she possibly keep that from happening, when he was so tall and broad and— drat. There she was doing it again.

At this rate, perhaps she should just save time and ask him to undress right now.

"Good morning, my lady." He must have seen her ogling him. Or maybe felt it, she had no idea, having never ogled anyone as thoroughly as she just had him.

"Good morning, Your Grace." She nodded to the painting. "You know, I was recalling my memory of the story of George and the dragon there." She shook her head and walked to stand beside him. "I find it horrible that the lady was able to tame the dragon by tossing some item of her clothing around his neck"—*Don't think about that again, for goodness' sake, Margaret!*—"and then when he was all docile, George went and killed him. That seems rather unsporting, wouldn't you say?"

Her words must have caught him by surprise, since he seemed to stifle a snort. "To be fair, the dragon was, after all, a dragon. And perhaps the lady's item of clothing had only a limited time during which it would be effective."

Margaret considered that. "Hm, well, it would have made for a better story if there was a certain time period for the effectiveness of the clothing. If I were to write it, I would definitely include that."

They both gazed at the painting again, Margaret irrationally pleased that he'd responded with an answer that showed he had actually thought about her point.

"You're an author yourself, aren't you?" His voice sounded strangled again, as though he weren't accustomed to making conversation.

"Yes, I am A Lady of Mystery," Margaret replied.

"Not so mysterious if you are telling me," he said in an almost teasing tone.

His mood—and therefore his tone of voice—seemed to vary with his breaths, first proper and somber, then light and humorous. Quite unexpected, and not nearly as dull as she'd first thought. As he'd first presented himself.

She nudged him with her shoulder, snickering as she did so. "And here you told me you did everything properly, Your Grace. But you have just made a sly joke, and I don't think sly jokes are entirely proper."

He made a startled sound, probably because she'd made him move to the side, and then turned his head to regard her.

His gaze was so intense she wanted to leap back, only of course she didn't, because part of her wanted to leap forward and find out what he'd do if she kissed him, right here in the National Gallery.

That is, she wanted to kiss him on the mouth in the National Gallery. Because "National Gallery" was not a common euphemism for anything, at least that she knew of. And if it was, then she was certainly in a lot more scandalous trouble than even she had been aware of.

"You make me do and say things I would never dream of otherwise," he said in a low voice that made her shiver. Did he know what he seemed to be saying?

Did she?

He blinked and shook his head as though to clear it. "A friend of mine just said I always do what is right, and proper, but if people don't do what is right and proper, then the right and proper things don't get done." He sounded as though he were working it out for himself as well as presenting it to her. "And the opposite of right and proper is wrong and improper, and that won't serve anybody."

She took a deep breath. "Not everything is black and white, Your Grace. There are shades of gray. There are ways to have fun without being improper." Even though her thoughts were definitely improper at the moment, but they were only thoughts, not actions.

She had to keep them that way.

He kept his gaze locked on her, the depth in his look making it seem as though he could see to her very soul. She felt a shiver of something course through her, a rippling thrill that started in her chest and traveled—well, to places she didn't think she should be contemplating out in public.

He lifted his hand, as though he were going to touch her. She caught her breath.

And then dropped his hand, quite firmly, his face setting into hard lines. "I cannot entertain the possibility of impropriety," he said, his voice as cold, properly cold, as she'd yet heard it. He bowed, then turned on his heel and strode out of the room, the heels of his boots striking the floor the only sound in the room.

It felt as though he'd slapped her.

She stared after where he'd gone, her heart racing, feeling a variety of emotions course through her—embarrassment, shame, anger, pride, and of course that desire she'd felt for him still bubbling underneath it all. The desire that had caused all this in the first place.

If she hadn't found his looks so intriguing, she wouldn't have wanted to know more about him. If his appearance matched his personality, she wouldn't currently be standing on her own, mid-morning, looking at art she had seen just the day before.

She wouldn't still be wondering what else was there to discover inside the duke who'd just behaved so, yes, *improperly* toward her.

And thinking about all that made her realize

just how shallow she was being. She resolved to forget about the Piratical Duke altogether, since he clearly was not interested in anything to do with her.

Lasham strode out of the National Gallery at a furious pace. Furious in terms of how quickly he was walking, and also furious with—with her, and himself, and anything and anyone who could make him question just who he was and the rightness of what he was doing.

Doing what wasn't right had simply never occurred to him. And he could blame that on his parents, both in raising him as they did and then having the misfortune of dying when he was too young to balance the responsibility.

But it wasn't just that. It was he, as well. Who he was, and who he'd become.

He nodded at a few people who were attempting to greet him, but didn't slow his steps, just walked out to his carriage—which was waiting for him, of course, since a duke's carriage was given precedence as the duke himself was, and he never had to wait for any conveyance.

He leaped in and slammed the door behind him, not waiting for his footman. He sat stiffly on the carriage seat, clenching his jaw and feeling as though someone were encasing him in a vicious embrace.

But nobody was, were they? He was alone. He had just rejected someone so thoroughly it was likely she would never speak to him again, and all because he hadn't wanted the temptation of what she offered. The chance that he could do things differently.

The carriage began to move, back to his house—it wasn't a home—and he felt the rage and frustration curl through him. He lifted his hand, made it into a fist, and punched the door of the carriage until his knuckles bled.

"If I may, Your Grace." His valet brushed something off of Lasham's shoulder and then stepped back, a satisfied expression on his face. "If I might be allowed to say so, Your Grace, you look unexceptional. Perfect for the evening." Unexceptional. Perfect. *Boring.*

He'd spent the hours since rushing out of the National Gallery reviewing the latest contracts he'd received for his holdings, consulting with his cook for a dinner he was to give for members of the House of Lords also in favor of passing a certain bill, and then he'd had tea, by himself, in his study with his books.

Boring. Necessary as well—he wasn't foolishly falling on his ducal sword of propriety—but boring.

Would it be possible to engage in more interesting pursuits and not neglect his duties, as she'd seemed to suggest?

Not that she would be available for anything of the sort, not now, not when he'd made his discomfort with her viewpoint so thoroughly known.

He wished he knew how he could apologize

without necessarily telling her he was wrong—
not that he wasn't, he was, but—and here he
nearly smiled at the irony of it—there were shades
of gray in his wrongness, and he didn't think he
would be able to properly explain himself, not
without somehow making it worse.

Especially since she was adept at words herself.
An author, one whose serials were hugely popular. He'd read a few of them himself, before he'd
met her, and he'd been drawn into her stories,
been able to escape his own concerns for the moments he'd read her work.

How could he possibly say anything that would
make any sense to someone who handled words
and stories and grand moments as she did?

He couldn't. He wouldn't.

"Good evening, Your Grace."

"Good evening, my lord. A delightful party,
isn't it?"

"It is. Excuse me, I am going to sample some of
Lady Marcham's cook's cakes."

"Of course, enjoy yourself."

Lasham stood at the side of the ballroom, as he
usually did, studiously looking over everyone's
heads so he wouldn't have to make eye contact.
Although that hadn't stopped anyone from addressing him. Thankfully, they seemed to find
him as dull as he found them, and generally
moved along once his polite disinterest was fully
engaged.

Going out was a recent necessity, since it

seemed—much to his horror—that his fellow lords only supported bills when they had an acquaintance with the individual behind the bill. He wouldn't be so selfish as to stay at home when there were good works to be done.

He'd arrived punctually half an hour past the stated time, he'd exchanged pleasantries with his host and hostess, he'd sipped weak punch and nodded at all his acquaintances.

And that had taken all of fifteen minutes, but he couldn't leave for at least another twenty minutes or he would be seen as rude.

"Lash!"

He turned abruptly at the sound of Jamie's voice. Of course his friend would have found a way to finagle an invitation, even though he'd just arrived in town and, as far as Lasham knew, had never met the Marchams.

Jamie stood next to him, on his good side, of course, since his friend was always conscious of just what and how well Lasham could see.

"I knew you'd be here. That's actually the only reason I wanted to come."

"To see me? You could have called at my house, I was there all afternoon." *Doing boring things while being boring and wishing I weren't so boring.*

"Yes, I could have, but I was otherwise engaged," Jamie said with a wink.

Jamie had clearly not spent the afternoon being boring. At least, for the lady's sake, Lasham hoped not.

"And now that you've found me, what did you want?" Lasham shook his head in frustration.

"Not that I am not delighted to see you, that is. I didn't mean it to sound so. That is—"

Jamie held his hand up, a grin on his face. "I know what you mean. You are pleased to see me, you cannot wait until you can leave this event, and you want to know what I am about. Isn't that right?"

Lasham exhaled. "Yes. Precisely."

"Well, it's just that I was hoping you could drop me at my lodgings this evening. I haven't yet secured a carriage, since Mother's is being repainted or something. You'd think the woman would be certain to keep all of the things I might possibly require at the ready in case I visit." Jamie spoke in a mock-outraged tone that showed just how much he cared for his mother.

"Since you told her you were coming, of course," Lasham replied dryly.

"I barely ever know when I am arriving, so of course not." Jamie paused and folded his arms over his chest. "Still and all, unless I wish to hail a hansom, which I don't, I have no way of returning home tonight."

"If it means we can leave soon, I would drive you to Scotland," Lasham said.

"Ha! I knew I could depend on you. And your misanthropy."

Lasham drew himself up to his full height. Which meant, since Jamie was nearly as tall as he, that he was eye-to-nose with his friend. "I am not misanthropic, merely . . ." What was he? Why did he have only one good friend in life? And a good friend who frequently left town? What did that say about him?

And why couldn't he seem to just . . . get over it, the way Jamie would, if he were in the same situation.

Although Jamie would never be accused of being boring or stiff or proper, that was for certain.

"I know, I know, don't get all stiff about it," Jamie replied. "Let's go, I don't think I can stand to look at your solemn party face any longer."

They said goodbye to their hosts, then asked a footman to bring them their cloaks. They stood just outside the entryway to the ballroom, Jamie eyeing all the ladies who walked in and out, and Lasham watching his friend, wondering why things seemed so easy for Jamie.

And then feeling like an idiot because life was not hard for him, not at all. He was a duke, he had more money than he knew what to do with, he was healthy, he did the right thing at all the right times, and—

And he was miserable in company, had just insulted one of the only women who had ever intrigued him, and even his best friend had implied he was dull.

"Who is that creature?" Jamie's words snapped him out of his introspection.

And then made him wish he could crawl back into it.

"That's Lady Margaret Sawford," Lasham heard himself reply. "She is the sister of the Duchess of Gage, and is A Lady of Mystery."

Lady Margaret spoke to a footman, no doubt also calling for her outer garment, then thankfully turned to speak to someone at the other end of the room. She wore a gown similar to those of all the other young ladies in the room, but on her, the wide skirts, the narrow waist, and even the puffy sleeves looked special. Sparkling. He'd never had cause to notice a lady's clothing before, but when she was wearing it, he somehow couldn't take his eyes off it. And her.

"It's no mystery how lovely she is," Jamie said, making Lasham wish he could simultaneously roll his eyes at his friend and punch him in the face.

"A Lady of Mystery. The author of those newspaper serials."

"Oh! Not that I've read the serials—been out of town, you know—but that makes much more sense than you suddenly developing a penchant for florid prose."

At least Jamie didn't *explicitly* say that Lasham had no imagination. Oh right, he'd already basically told him that earlier that day. No doubt Jamie would think repeating his opinion would be as dull as Lasham was.

"Introduce me."

"No," Lasham said in nearly a snarl.

Jamie arched his eyebrows and gave Lasham a knowing look. "Ah, so that is it, is it?"

Lasham closed his eye and exhaled, concentrating on breathing deeply so he wouldn't act on what he most wanted to do. Which was deny everything, punch the wall—again—and also ask Jamie for advice on how to grovel well enough so that a certain young lady would forgive him and remain his friendly acquaintance.

The footman arrived with their cloaks before Lasham could do any of the things on his list. He strode out of the Marchams' house without glancing in her direction—at least not that she would be able to tell—and got into his carriage, only exhaling when the footman had shut the door behind Jamie.

"What are you going to do about her?"

Lasham didn't even bother trying to say he had no idea who his friend was talking about.

"Nothing. There is nothing I can do."

Jamie uttered a snort. "I can think of plenty of things," he began, only to stop speaking as Lasham's hand clamped over his mouth.

"Shut. Up."

"Fine," it sounded like he replied, only of course his word was muffled through Lasham's palm.

He withdrew his hand and folded his arms over his chest. He didn't look over, but he could tell Jamie was staring at him.

"I can't," he began. "I don't even know what I'd want if I could."

Thankfully, Jamie did not pipe up with a helpful list of suggestions.

"I met her a few evenings ago, and she was—she was refreshingly honest." He shrugged, not able to even put the words together. "I wish I had the facility of making friends easily. She seemed as though she would be a good friend to have. Only I—"

"You did something to turn her against you."

Lasham felt the burn of frustration coil through his chest. "Not exactly, but it's that—well, I can't make it right."

There was a long pause. Surprising, given Jamie's usual habit of saying all the things that were on his mind. "You can make anything right if you want to." Jamie's tone was nothing that Lasham had ever heard him use before—pensive, almost, even though prior to this moment he would have sworn Jamie didn't have a pensive bone in his body.

And prior to a few days ago, Lasham would have said he was relatively satisfied with his life. Certainly he didn't always like the attention that being a duke brought, but it was balanced against the good he was doing for his extended family, his tenants, the citizens whose laws he enacted.

But now he knew—or at least he thought he knew—it wasn't enough.

It was almost as though he had punched himself in the gut; he felt it roil in his belly, the whatever emotion it was coursing through him like a strong liquor.

The only question was, did he want to stay drunk or get sober?

GEORGIANA AND THE DRAGON

By A Lady of Mystery

⇛⇛⇛⟳◯⟲⇚⇚⇚

"Why are you here? Why aren't you frightened?" The dragon spoke in a low rumble, wisps of steam escaping from his mouth and his nostrils.

It should have been surprising that the dragon could speak, but then again, it was even more surprising that there was a dragon in the first place, so Georgiana didn't fuss about the details of the apparently living dragon.

Now if he weren't able to fly, well, then she might quibble.

"You need help," she said in a matter-of-fact tone. "And I am actually quite frightened, only I cannot deny help to anyone just because I might be a bit fearful."

The dragon exhaled, closing his eyes and seeming to sink farther into the earth. "It's no use anyway. I don't have the energy to survive, much less to devour you."

Georgiana knew enough not to ask if he would devour her if he had the energy. Instead, she ran her palm along the ridges of the dragon's back, feeling for the injuries.

And then the dragon roared.

Chapter 5

"Thank you, Lady Marcham, it was a lovely party." Margaret nodded at her hostess, then smiled at the footman who'd arrived with her cloak.

She hadn't meant to leave so early, but she'd gotten an urgent message from one of the women she was trying to help—she'd been waylaid by a grumpy footman who'd seemed irked that he had to ferry messages to guests when he could be standing in the room looking important.

Apparently the woman's sister's husband had been drinking again, and was making threats to both of the sisters. They were barricaded in their lodgings, but the police wouldn't come because it was a domestic matter, and the women were too poor to pay anyone else to help them.

Margaret wished, sometimes, she wasn't so softhearted and observant. If she had been less of the former, she wouldn't have done anything when she'd been the latter. But since it was practically her job to notice people, and relationships, and how humanity interacted, it would be disingenuous and morally reprehensible of her to ignore the things she observed.

Which was why she was heading to Soho, if not the worst neighborhood in London, definitely among the top five. Escorted by her sharp-tongued maid Annie, her coachman who was another one of her rescues, and that was all.

She was grateful she had gotten her brother-in-law to show her a few boxing moves—not that she could knock anyone out, but she knew where to hit a man, and also knew how to best get out of the way if someone was intent on hitting her.

Thus far, she had not had to use the knowledge, but she was armed with it—or fisted with it, she thought with a smirk—and while she hoped she wouldn't ever have to put it in practice, there was something quite appealing about hitting someone who was intent on hurting you.

"Where we off to now, then?" Annie said as Margaret got into the carriage.

"How did you know we're not just going home?" Honestly, she should teach Annie how to play cards; the woman was downright frightening with how she was able to predict things.

"Because it's early, you've got that set look on your face, and I saw some sort of grimy fellow come up not fifteen minutes ago with a note, and then a footman darted inside with it. You should write me as one of them detectives in your serials, you should."

"I do not write mystery stories, Annie; my nom de plume is A Lady of Mystery. Not the same thing."

"Fine, just ignore me then," Annie said with a wave of her hand, nearly as regal as the Queen herself.

"Yes, we're going to help the Banner sisters. You remember, the ones who do that nice lacework? The younger sister's husband is a brute, and apparently he's been drinking again."

"So we're going in there to stop him, a grown, drunk man." To call Annie's tone of voice dubious was to be optimistic in the description.

Margaret pulled the edges of her cloak more tightly around herself. "Well, yes."

"And you're probably going to take the women out of their lodgings and bring them to that house, and then to the Agency." A sniff. Margaret had already had an earful about the Quality Employment Agency, and how "fings were never gonna be right, no matter how hard people try" many times before. It couldn't make her stop trying, not if it meant one woman was saved from a terrible fate. And she knew Annie secretly felt that way, too—she just couldn't admit to being quite as charitable as she actually was. It was only luck that Annie hadn't had to rely on the Agency for employment—her aunt had served in Margaret's parents' household, and recommended her niece for employment when Margaret needed a lady's maid. Her parents hadn't cared who had been hired, just that Isabella did not have to lend out her own servant to dress Margaret. "And we'll be getting them out if that man doesn't end up killing one or more of us."

"Uh—yes?" Margaret said, wondering if her

idea was actually as ludicrous as it sounded when told through Annie's view.

"Well, we'd better make sure we're well fortified, then," Annie said, withdrawing a small bottle from her own cloak. She unstoppered it, took a drink, then handed it to Margaret.

"Goodness, Annie, I didn't know you had this," Margaret said, taking the flask in her hand. She took a sniff and coughed.

"It's a good thing I do," Annie said. "We're both going to need as much help as we can get, and when all else fails, we can always muster up some Dutch courage."

Margaret chuckled and took a swig from the bottle. It burned going down, a fiery path that immediately helped fire up her resolve.

Annie tucked the flask back into her cloak and nodded at her mistress. "Now we're ready."

"As ready as we'll ever be," Margaret murmured.

"This is the house, my lady," John Coachman said in his broad London accent. He'd been with Margaret for nearly all of the two years since she'd left her parents' home—she'd found him wandering the road after getting let go from a glue factory. She figured he had some experience with horses, given where glue came from, and so she hired him on as her coachman. The Agency didn't, at the moment, offer employment for men, so she was grateful she'd actually needed someone when she found him.

He'd taken to the position with aplomb, and with the exception of his less than posh accent, it'd be hard to distinguish him and his work from any man who'd been born and raised in the stables.

That said, he was slight and wracked with a persistent cough, so he probably would be less help than Annie in what they were about to do.

Not that it would matter if he were the most correct coachman ever—the simple truth was that no matter how she did it, it was scandalous for her to live on her own. But she needed her independence, and her reputation was already lost, so she didn't see the point of suffering in less than ideal living circumstances. Even though her brother-in-law had offered her a place to live—she just couldn't. Besides, how much more scandalous could she get?

"Thank you," Margaret said as she descended the coach. She felt in her pocket for the embroidery needles she kept in the coach just for this type of situation—she'd never embroidered in her life, but the needles, she'd discovered, were quite sharp.

Annie followed after her, muttering under her breath as she usually did. But, as she also usually did, she followed close behind Margaret; she'd never leave her mistress alone, never mind that she thought (and frequently said) that her mistress was often foolhardy.

"I believe their rooms are on the top floor," Margaret said, gazing up. Just as though she'd conjured it, they saw two figures clearly in the midst of a struggle pass by the window. "No time to waste, we have to get up there."

By the time they'd reached the fourth floor, they had a plan.

"So you'll distract the man while I get the women out?"

Margaret didn't have to see Annie's face to know her expression was skeptical—she could hear it in her tone.

Fine. So it wasn't much of a plan.

"Yes," Margaret replied. "And John knows to summon the watchmen if he hears a scream." One thing the two women had discovered in their time together was that Annie's scream was piercing, known to momentarily deafen a few dogs, on rare occasions.

"Excellent." If Annie's tone were any dryer, they'd be in the desert, Margaret thought. Which would make a good piece of writing for her next serial, provided she survived this encounter.

Margaret didn't bother knocking on the door, she just turned the knob and entered, taking a deep breath as she surveyed the scene.

The older sister, Miss Banner, was currently atop her brother-in-law's back, her arms clutched about his neck as though she was his new neckwear. He had a grip on her arm with one hand, while the other was holding on to the other sister—his wife—so tightly Margaret could see the bright red marks of his fingers.

"Let go of—of them!" she called, only all three of the room's inhabitants were yelling or screaming or crying, so her voice was drowned out.

She shook her head, withdrew the embroidery needle, and marched over to the man, poking him in the fleshy part of his upper arm. He yelped, dropping his grip from the one sister and allowing the other to get a better position on his back, moving her hand to his eyes.

He fell immediately to the ground, his sister-in-law still perched on top of him, his wife clutching her arm and staring at the scene with wide, frightened eyes.

He didn't stay down for long, however; he wriggled out from under his sister-in-law and lurched to his feet, staggering as though he were about to fall again.

"And who the hell are you, then?" he said, addressing Margaret. He did not look at all in the mood for a discussion, so perhaps his opening conversational gambit was merely time for him to figure out how to murder her.

Or so it seemed.

"That doesn't matter," Margaret said, trying to keep her voice steady. "The point is, you are not fit to be in company with these ladies, and I will be removing them from your vicinity. Come along, then," she said, turning to speak to the still supine sister-in-law and her terrified sister.

"Like hell you—" Only then he stopped, and uttered what Margaret could only describe as a squeak.

"Precisely," Margaret replied, entirely unsure why his expression had undergone such a dramatic change, but that she should capitalize on it before he realized what he'd done.

But then she saw the ladies had equally frightened expressions, as though she had suddenly started belching fire, dragonlike, or had a squadron of armed soldiers in back of her.

She turned her head just enough to see.

Drat. It wasn't her formidable presence that had terrified them.

It was he. The Piratical Duke. The one who'd appeared to have been disgusted with her behavior only this morning.

Who stood regarding her with his arms folded across his impressive chest, his wide-legged stance and cool gaze showing he was battle-ready.

And not even armed with an embroidery needle.

He glanced at her, then moved his gaze to the other inhabitants of the room. All of them—save Annie—seemed to almost deflate as he looked at them in turn.

"I could have handled this on my own, you know," she said in a cross tone.

"Yes, you certainly seemed to have it well in hand," he said in the same desertlike tone Annie had employed earlier.

She made a harrumphing noise. "Since you're here, perhaps you can help me escort these ladies to my carriage."

She turned to look at the women. "I promise you, he is not nearly as terrifying as he looks," she began, only then realized the husband might seize on that idea to cause more of a fuss, "but he is here, and he is quite powerful, and I would do as he says." She tilted her head back to him. "So what do you say, Your Grace?"

An audible gasp emerged from all three of the

mouths engaged in the fracas as they realized that the Piratical Duke was, in fact, a *duke*.

"I say the ladies should go wherever you want them to, and the gentleman here should rue the day he crossed your path, my lady," he replied.

Margaret nodded. "Yes. Thank you. And you may escort us to my carriage, if you please, Your Grace."

The women had stopped crying and screaming enough to gather a few things they deemed necessary to take with them, and it wasn't long before the five of them were descending the stairs, the duke and Margaret in the back of the group.

"Why are you here, anyway?" she said in a low voice as they made their way down. Margaret was grateful there wasn't very much light—she'd already stepped on something sticky, and she didn't even want to imagine the dirt and grime that would be on her evening gown.

Worse was imagining what Annie would say. If only she'd had the forethought to dress appropriately both for an evening party and a perilous rescue in one of London's lesser neighborhoods.

What would such a garment look like, anyway? The mind boggled.

And he hadn't answered her question, either. She had the feeling he was ignoring her. Something she most definitely did not like. "You haven't said. Why are you here?"

GEORGIANA AND THE DRAGON

By A Lady of Mystery

"Hush, do hush, or someone will come," Georgiana said, knowing that trying to soothe a dragon was likely an impossible task.

"Someone has come," the dragon said, in between bellows, "and it is you, and I still feel terrible, and I am hoping that the person who was meant to come is out there still so I can be rescued."

Georgiana frowned. "Rescued? What do you mean? That is, you're a dragon; dragons don't get rescued."

The dragon glared at her from his yellowy red eyes. "Look, I don't know what stories you've been told, but all the stories I know mention that dragons are rescued by beautiful princesses." He seemed to look her over and let out a sniff, releasing a belch of smoke as he did so. "And I don't think you're a princess, either."

It took her a moment, and then when she understood, she knew she turned as red as the flames that emitted from him. "You're saying I'm not beautiful?"

He rolled his eyes. "And you also seem to be quite slow. Leave me, I'll wait for the princess."

Georgiana planted her hands on her hips and stomped her foot, which would have been impressive if she weren't standing in damp leaves. "Fine. You can stay here and wait, for all I care."

The dragon nodded as though in satisfaction, but Georgiana could see him grimace as he did, as though he were in pain all over.

She couldn't care about that. He'd told her to leave so

he could wait for his beautiful, intelligent princess. So she would.

She picked up her bucket, turned on her heel, and tromped out of the woods as quickly as she could.

Chapter 6

Why *was* he here? Telling her the truth—that he'd dropped Jamie off, then spotted her carriage where he knew she didn't live, so he'd instructed his coachman to follow, perhaps to be able to apologize, no doubt terribly—made it seem, well, *awkward*. Strange. Almost impertinent, which he never was.

Until now, of course. Because he had followed her, and what's more, he'd even—obviously— followed her into the building, entering the room when he heard the fracas.

"Uh, well," he said, wishing he had use of her imagination so he could come up with some reason that didn't make it sound as though he was unduly interested in her. Or even duly interested.

What the hell are you doing, then?

And why did the voice in his head sound so much like Jamie?

More questions he couldn't answer. Lovely.

"Your Grace?" Now she sounded even more annoyed. "Were you coming to apologize for earlier? Or demand satisfaction from me, or something?"

"Never mind why I was there," he said, his words clipped and forceful. It usually worked on most people.

"That is just avoiding the question, which seems awfully suspicious, wouldn't you agree?"

Lady Margaret was not most people.

Thankfully, they had finally descended the final flight of stairs, and had emerged onto the street, so Lasham was saved, for the moment, from answering.

"Don't think I won't ask again," Lady Margaret said, punctuating her words with a poke to his side. "I'm quite curious as to the answer."

Lasham was not the type of person one poked. At least he didn't think he was.

"But for now, Your Grace," she said in a louder voice, "if you would excuse us," she began, but he started speaking almost before he himself realized it.

"I insist on accompanying these ladies"—he nodded to the two women—"to wherever it is they are going. They could be in some danger still, could they not?"

Lady Margaret began to sputter some sort of aggrieved reply, but her servant answered before her mistress could speak coherently. "That'd be lovely, Yer Grace. How's about you take Lady Margaret and them in your carriage, and then if you don't mind, I can foller along in Lady Margaret's carriage. There ain't room for five in Lady Margaret's."

There was a moment of silence. Lasham knew he couldn't utter a word, not at the moment; he had never had a servant issue any kind of directive, much less what sounded as though it was an order, in his presence. Even his various footmen would just meekly inquire if he wanted more coffee when he was holding up his empty cup and looking pointedly at them. If he held a sign up that read "I want more coffee" he couldn't have been more obvious.

But this. He turned his gaze to Lady Margaret, whose expression was not the scornful, condemning one any other lady might wear, but instead was much more—well, she wasn't sparkling now as much as blazing.

"No."

"No."

They blinked at each other as they each spoke, then he saw a slight smile cross her lips, as though she was amused but didn't want to reveal it.

Perhaps she would accept his apology, no matter how terrible. Dear God, he hoped so.

She arched her brow and regarded her servant. "You see, Annie, the duke and I are in perfect agreement. He will return to his home, and I will make sure the ladies are safe, and then return home to mine." She looked at him, that brow still raised as though in challenge. "We will be perfectly safe, Your Grace, thank you for your concern." She nodded to the ladies. "Go ahead and get inside the carriage, it is too cold out here."

Lasham clamped his jaw tight so as not to explode in front of all four of the women. Even rarer for a servant to issue orders to a mistress was anyone daring to refuse to do what he'd said.

That hadn't happened since before he had become duke. And even before then it had been rare, since he'd been a duke's heir.

He strode forward and clasped her arm just as she was preparing to enter the coach herself. "You should not put yourself in such danger, Lady Margaret." Never mind not doing what he'd commanded. "These neighborhoods are not appropriate for a young lady such as yourself."

"Such as myself?" she replied, her tone practically dripping with disdain. "Believe me, Your Grace, if there was a choice in the matter I would not concern myself, but there is none. And so I am here. But now, as you have said, it is time for all of us to go home. Please do excuse me," she said in a sharp tone as she swept up into the carriage, not even looking at him as she shut the door.

Lasham refrained from punching anything on his way home. Thankfully. One outburst a day seemed like it was entirely sufficient.

He did, however, walk immediately into his study and pour himself a very large brandy.

"That bad, hm?" a voice said from Lasham's blind side, making him nearly spill the alcohol on his clothing.

Of course it was Jamie. Nobody else would dare enter his home without a proper invitation. He couldn't remember the last time he'd asked anyone to his home, in fact. And definitely people did not arrive when their host was off scaring angry men in substandard housing.

"What are you doing here?" Lasham said, turning to regard his friend. "Didn't I just drop you at your house?" He narrowed his gaze. "Your mother hasn't kicked you out already, has she?"

Jamie, who'd been reclining on the sofa, sat up, a grin on his face. "Not yet." He stood and walked over to where Lasham stood, an empty glass in his hand. He reached for the brandy bottle and poured himself nearly as hefty a glass as Lasham had. "I went home, and everyone was sleeping, only I was wide awake, and I thought I'd just turn up here."

"Like a bad penny," Lasham muttered.

Jamie ignored him. "Here's to you," he said, raising his glass.

Lasham shook his head, knowing there was no use trying to get Jamie to leave, much less not drink him out of brandy. He lifted his glass as well, but stopped when there was a knock on the door.

Both men stopped still, immediately looking at the large clock that stood in the corner. One o'clock.

"You didn't invite anyone, did you?" Jamie asked, downing his drink in one swallow.

"I didn't even invite you," Lasham replied. He strode over to the door, flinging it wide.

"What is—?" he began, only to feel his words fall away—again—as he saw her.

"Your Grace," his butler said in an anxious tone, "I tried to tell the lady that you were not at home, but she—"

Lady Margaret walked into the room, pulling

her cloak off as she did so. "But I told him you clearly were, since here you are," she said, laying her cloak on the sofa Jamie had been sitting on.

"If you'll excuse me, Lasham," Jamie said in a low, amused voice. "Good evening, my lady," he said with a nod at Lady Margaret, then smirked at Lasham, and walked quickly out of the room, pulling the door shut behind him.

"Coward," Lasham muttered, before turning to her.

She lifted her chin and looked at him, seeming as though she was really seeing him, not looking at him as though he were a piece at a museum. For an amateur daubist to admire, no doubt, he thought sourly.

But she wasn't doing that. Unlike everyone else he met, everyone with the exception of Jamie. Even his servants would stare occasionally when he'd been away from the house for a few days.

"What can I help you with, Lady Margaret?"

She lifted her chin higher, setting her jaw. That would make it difficult to speak, a fact that was borne out by how her words emerged through clenched teeth.

He couldn't help but notice, however, that she was still lovely. If also very, very angry.

"Your Grace, I am here to demand that you explain what you were doing in that neighborhood earlier this evening." She drew a deep breath and continued before Lasham could even open his mouth.

"Because if I was not mistaken—and I was not—you made it absolutely clear that you did not wish to associate with me just earlier today. Even though you are the one who suggested we meet at the museum." She crossed her arms over her chest. He tried not to notice how that made the bodice of her gown move. "And since the first words we exchanged were you telling me to leave a room, and me saying no, let me make it clear myself: I have no interest in you as anything. Not as an acquaintance, a friend, or Lord help me, a husband. Which is what you seemed to think."

Lasham drew himself up straighter, if only so he didn't have to meet her gaze so intently. He opened his mouth to reply, but she gave her head a vigorous shake and kept speaking.

"The thing is, you seemed as though you might be different. That you might be someone who would be interesting to know. Not to marry, of course," she said in a scornful tone, "although that is what everyone would think, but someone with whom I could exchange ideas and opinions. Instead you tease me with the promise of that, and then shut me down. And then," she added, her voice gaining strength and outrage simultaneously, "you follow me to a place you would not otherwise be and have the audacity to come in and rescue me. Or attempt to, at least."

Finally she closed her mouth, but continued to glare at him.

And then he felt all her words tumbling around him like a collapsing heap of bricks, pelting him so sharply they nearly hurt. The fury and frustration he'd felt earlier that day came roaring back, and he spoke without thinking. "Do you know what it is like, Lady Margaret, to be gawked at and appraised every single moment you are within sight of anyone?" He swept his gaze down her body. "You do not." He expelled the breath from his lungs. "To be judged constantly by what you could do for someone, not who you could be to someone." He turned his back to her, the height of rudeness, but he didn't care. Couldn't care, not at that moment.

Besides, she had already flouted propriety by arriving at his house at so late an hour, likely only accompanied by the order-giving maid.

"That doesn't explain why you followed me," she said in a somewhat milder, but still angry tone. "And why you were so dismissive earlier."

How could he explain to her when he couldn't explain it to himself?

He turned back around, spreading his arms out. "I don't know, Lady Margaret. Believe me, I wanted not to have done it as soon as I did." He shook his head in frustration. "Look at me." And then realized what he'd said. "No, don't look at me. Too many people do." Now the fury was back, crashing harder against his pent-up resentment. Resentment against himself, mostly, but at her for daring to make him question his choices thus far. And finding the answers lacking. "But if I hadn't been there tonight, what would have happened? You would have subdued that drunkard who was already fighting with two women? With what, your beauty?"

Her eyes went wide at that last sentence, and he could swear he'd surprised her. Hadn't she looked at herself?

"Whereas you were able to defeat him with your appearance, you're saying?" She rolled her eyes. "I don't know who's been looking at you, Your Grace, but you're beautiful also." She laughed at his expression, which must have looked as though he'd been punched in the head. Or blindsided.

Which was absolutely not funny, given that he was partially blind, but then it did make him want to laugh.

That was it. She made him want to laugh, to talk about things, to feel other than how he felt most of the time. He had no idea what to make of that. Or of her. Or of anything, for that matter.

"I am not beautiful," he replied stiffly. And awkwardly. As though nobody had ever paid him a compliment before. Which they hadn't, at least never in terms of his appearance.

She drew nearer, an appraising gleam in her eyes. "Oh, but you are, Your Grace." In a mirror image of what he had done earlier, she raised her hand to his cheek, but held it suspended there as though waiting for his permission.

He closed his eye and braced himself for it.

"I don't know what you want from me," she said, her voice soft and questioning, her hand poised in the air, still not touching him.

He looked at her then and felt the fury melt into something else, something that made him walk a step forward and take her hand in his, his other hand on her arm, to draw her close to him, to lower his mouth to hers and to kiss her.

To taste her, to capture some of her essence, her

sparkle, to feel what it must be like to be so—so her.

She didn't push him away. Didn't slap him, or demand he marry her, or mock him for daring to touch her with his imperfect self.

Instead she placed her arms around his neck and held him to her, her soft mouth moving on his, her fingers caressing his neck.

Not as though he were a monster. Or even a duke.

Just as though he were a man.

GEORGIANA AND THE DRAGON

By A Lady of Mystery

❧

"Fine," Georgiana grumbled as she trudged her way back out through the woods. "See if I come help the next time a dragon is roaring."

She chuckled at that, of course, because the most exciting thing that had happened to her—until today—was the annual fair that took place in their village, and that was only exciting because her father insisted on buying her a new hair ribbon.

A new hair ribbon did not come close to equaling finding a living dragon.

But even a hair ribbon—new or otherwise—would never make her a beautiful princess. She had to admit to being hurt by the dragon's comment, even though he was definitely not even close to beautiful himself.

Except there was something awe-inspiring about such a creature.

And he was not even close to being awed by her.

She had just resolved to wipe the whole matter from her mind when she heard another sickening roar.

Chapter 7

At first, Margaret was so startled she didn't know what to do. If she were one of her heroines, prepared for any kind of situation, she certainly would—unfortunately, in Margaret's books he would be the villain, and her heroine would be screaming for help from the trustworthy hero. Who would not be nearly as intriguing as he.

But then, as his mouth, his firm, gorgeous, masculine mouth descended on hers, she knew exactly what to do.

Which was wrap her arms around his neck and hold him closer. After all, if he was kissing her, he wasn't talking, and thus far, she'd found his conversation to be lacking in comparison to his appearance.

But his kissing. Goodness, it was wonderful. He used just the right amount of pressure and held her as though she were both precious and a strong woman—how did he do that?—and the contrast of his smooth, tender mouth with the stubble above his lip and how strong he felt when he was holding her and, oh my, she was surprised she hadn't swooned yet.

There was time for swooning, of course, but right now she'd rather be kissing him.

She wove her fingers through his hair, feeling the silky strands caress her skin. Another contrast to the huge, strong body that was right there, although not absolutely right there, not where things were starting to respond in an interesting way.

That would bear thinking about as well, but again, not while he was kissing her.

And then he leaped back, as though she'd breathed fire on him or something, his eyes—no, his eye—wide and startled, his entire attitude that of someone who'd just done something he couldn't believe he'd done.

That would make two of them, then. Although she was guessing she was the only one who wished they could do it again, and very soon.

"My lady, I must apologize, I don't know what . . ." He paused, and ran his hand over his face and down his chest.

Rather as Margaret would like to do as well, although this was likely not the time to bring it up.

"I provoked you," Margaret said with a shrug. She stepped away from him and went and sat on the sofa. "It happens."

His expression tightened. "So this kind of thing has happened to you before? Happens often, in fact?"

She wanted to say, *Yes, it happens all the time, men just leap on me and start kissing my mouth,* just to see what he'd do. Hm. Maybe she would, if only it would persuade him to kiss her again. She put her hand up to her mouth to cover her smile.

"Because you are so irresistible, gentlemen cannot help themselves when they are around you?" He stepped closer, and now she could see how his jaw was set and the pulse at his neck was beating a furious rhythm.

Or it would just make him talk more, and that was perhaps the last thing she wanted to happen.

"No, of course it doesn't happen all the time," she said, waving her hand in the air. "At least, not this specific reaction." She frowned in thought. "I do tend to aggravate people, but they generally don't kiss me in response."

A muscle ticked at his jaw. At some point, she would likely inform him he certainly appeared to have quite a temper. But not now. She wasn't that brazen. At least she didn't think so.

"I didn't mean to kiss you, my lady," he said stiffly. He wasn't looking at her any longer; instead, he appeared to be studying the door. Perhaps hoping she would soon make use of it?

"So it just . . . happened?" she said, stressing the last word in imitation of him.

Then he did look at her, and finally, finally it seemed he was calming down a bit. At least he didn't appear as though he were about to go on a murderous rampage. Maybe a nonmurderous one, but definitely there was no killing involved.

"I deserved that," he said in a much lower tone. "I don't—" and then he shook his head. "There's nothing I can say that will fix this." He looked at her again, his mouth curling up just a bit, enough to hint at a smile. "I believe we've established you don't wish to marry me, which is the only proper response I could have to having done what I did." He paused. "You—you don't wish to marry me, do you?"

He sounded so concerned Margaret couldn't keep herself from laughing. "No, of course not. Thank you for the offer, though." The thought crossed her mind that her parents would disown her again if they knew she'd turned down a duke, no less. It was a good thing she could be disowned only once.

"Well. That's settled then." He crossed his arms over his chest, only not in the predatory way he'd done when he'd appeared so unexpectedly, but this time as though he were protecting himself. From her?

She placed her palms on her legs and rose, smoothing the skirts of her gown as she did so. "Well, I should be on my way. Except that you never did answer why you happened to be there to save me," and at that she couldn't help but roll her eyes, "but I suppose that is one of the mysteries of life. Rather like A Lady of Mystery," she added, unable to keep herself from making the reference.

Only perhaps she shouldn't have. His gaze narrowed, and now those folded arms had altered so they did look rather threatening. How did he do that? Was he tightening his muscles?

And what was wrong with her that she wished she could go over there and feel them for herself?

"You shouldn't be going to those neighborhoods, Lady Margaret. It's not safe, even if you do have a bossy lady's maid to accompany you," and now she thought he had rolled his eyes—eye—but she was too outraged that he would dare to bring it up again, after all this, to notice.

"I shouldn't be involving myself in other people's hardships, you're saying?" and she took a few steps to get closer to him, feeling herself fairly bristling. "And what have you done—oh!" she said, bringing her fingers up to her mouth. "But that's it!"

"What's it?" he asked, understandably confused. She hadn't finished her thought, after all. It would be as if she stopped writing mid-sentence.

"You can do something for me," she said in a triumphant tone of voice. "Since you are so concerned for my safety." He did owe her, and he did look as he did. *And you do want to spend time in his company.* "You can escort me to those neighborhoods, as you call them, when I am needed." She looked him up and down. It was definitely an enjoyable view. "You can come along and look frightening, I will do what needs to be done, and you won't have to worry about my safety. And it will relieve your guilt about having accosted me just now," although she really did wish he were in the mood for more accosting.

He didn't reply, just stared back at her, his mouth hanging open just enough to let her know he was entirely speechless.

Although this way of getting him to be quiet was far less fun than the other way. But less potentially damaging to her reputation.

"Well?" she prompted. She hadn't counted on him being slow to comprehend; he'd seemed to understand enough when they were at the museum.

"It wouldn't be proper," he said, returning to that stiff tone of voice she was coming to loathe.

"No, of course it wouldn't," she said with a sigh of exasperation. "That's precisely the point of why I want you to come. It's not proper to do, I am going to do it, and you can make it less dangerous for me. It isn't as though I need escorting to safe neighborhoods, after all. Those I can manage on my own." She inhaled as she thought about what she could say to convince him. "You always do what is proper." *Except now, when you just kissed me*, she wanted to add, only she didn't because she thought he might insist on marrying her after all, and neither of them wanted that. "Your escorting me makes it more proper than if I were to go alone."

He appeared to be considering it. Now for the closing paragraph. It was crucial she do this well, as when she wrote the final part of each serial. "And," she said, spreading her hands out, "it is not as though you can labor under any kind of misapprehension for my motivation in wanting to keep company with you. It is not as though I wish to marry you, after all. Far from it," she added under her breath.

Even though part of her was asking if it would be so bad to be married to someone who was so attractive to look at and who could startle people with his very presence.

But that was a dangerous thought.

Not least of which was that he would speak every so often, and likely as not, he would find some way to irritate her.

"Oh. I see." He sounded—disappointed? Had she somehow hurt his feelings by letting him know she didn't want to marry him as much as he didn't wish to marry her?

Men. She'd be better off just making the fictional men in her life do what she wanted, since she had thus far had very little luck with the real ones.

"Well, then," he said, still stiffly, but less so, "then yes. If I can be of help in your foolhardy venture, I will assist you."

Margaret smiled, feeling a warm sense of relief flood over her. "See? That wasn't so bad. And to think you are in this situation because of something that just . . . happened," she said with a smirk.

He gave a tight smile in response.

"And if you would like, I did enjoy looking at art with you—that would be a perfect place to meet as well. We can rendezvous at the National Gallery or the Royal Academy or somewhere public and entirely respectable, and then we can take ourselves off to my foolhardy pursuit."

"Venture," he corrected.

"'Pursuit' sounds so much more exciting," Margaret replied. 'Venture' sounds like something people embark on, like a great ship traveling for a long time with nothing to do. 'Pursuit' is something you can actively do."

His mouth twisted in a rueful grin. "Why do I have the feeling, Lady Margaret, that you will be writing the lines of my life from now on?"

Margaret's heart thudded in her chest. If she were writing his life, she wouldn't be giving him any dialogue. She'd find something else for him to do.

The question she couldn't—wouldn't—answer was what, precisely, that thing would be.

He had kissed her. He had really gone ahead, pulled her into his arms, and kissed her.

What was more remarkable was that she had kissed him back.

He had apologized, but he couldn't feel sorry for it—he felt alive, and on edge, and curious, but not sorry. And he hadn't apologized for the earlier thing, the time when he really did regret what he'd done.

And now he'd gotten roped into accompanying her to places no young lady and no proper duke would go, just because he had kissed her.

He could have said no; there wouldn't have been any consequences. He knew she didn't want to marry him. He didn't want to marry her. She had no hold over him.

So why did he say yes?

He exhaled as he pondered it. Just two nights ago, the night they'd met, he'd been dissatisfied with his life and what he was doing with it. And he'd had no idea how to change that.

And then he'd met her, and now he had some

idea, although it wasn't necessarily the most proper one, the one most suited to his position.

But that was the point, wasn't it?

This—this *task*, odd and improper though it was, made him feel as though he had more of a purpose. As though he was wanted for who he was, not what he was.

Just in the same way that she had kissed him. As a man.

Not as a duke, not as an oddity, not as anything but who he was. Or who he might be.

And he wished he could kiss her again. What would he be doing if he had gone ahead and done more?

He allowed his mind to wander, just for a moment, to consider what it would be like to have her as a bed partner; she would doubtless continue to make fun of him, and ask questions, and laugh, and he wouldn't mind, not if it meant he could share the joke and get the chance to run his hands all over her warm, naked body.

He had a healthy sexual appetite but it was seldom practical or the right thing to indulge it whenever he felt like it, so it had been some time since he had been with a woman. And now, though it felt as though she'd awakened some sexual beast inside, it wouldn't be right to go find another woman upon whom to slake his urges.

Perhaps he had finally discovered his imagination, because his mind was certainly full of what he'd like to do to her.

Although now, alone with her in a room well

after midnight, was likely not the best time to discover he did, indeed, have an imagination.

Especially since she'd said something, and he hadn't heard her. "What did you say?"

A knowing smile was on her lips, as though she was well aware of what was distracting him. Hopefully she wasn't; hopefully that was just his guilty conscience and surprisingly vigorous imagination. "We will meet tomorrow at the Royal Academy, then."

Lasham pushed all thoughts of bed and Lady Margaret aside—or most of the thoughts, at least—and nodded in agreement.

"Three o'clock?"

He frowned. "I should check with my secretary, let me send a message tomorrow."

"Certainly, Your Grace." She smiled mischievously. "Although if you cannot make our appointment, I will still continue on my way back to Soho. Or wherever I am needed."

Aggravating woman. He wished he could just lock her in one of the bedrooms upstairs and—no, no, of course he didn't wish to do that. Where had that thought come from?

Maybe having an imagination was not all he had hoped for. Or imagined, if he were being remarkably devoid of imagination.

Now he was making his own head hurt. "Then I will see you at three o'clock, regardless of what else was in my schedule. I will have to be back home in time to dress for dinner."

He really did sound like a dullard. Perhaps he

should enlist her to write his words so he could appear to be less incredibly boring.

Though that wouldn't alter who he was inside. He had the feeling that that, too, was going to change because of her.

And he didn't know whether to be intrigued or terrified at the prospect.

GEORGIANA AND THE DRAGON

By A Lady of Mystery

Georgiana dropped the bucket and sprinted back into the wood, her heart pounding furiously, her mind listing the possibilities of what had happened.

Had someone else come upon the dragon and hurt him? Did he regret what he'd said to her? Was the dragon afraid of the dark?

She didn't know anything, of course, just that someone was in pain and needed her help. At least, she thought he might be able to use her help, even though he might not see it the same way.

She burst into the clearing where he was, startled to find another person—a young woman—standing at the dragon's side, a bow in her hand and an arrow sticking out of the dragon's hide. This was a new injury, much worse than a damaged wing, she had to imagine.

The dragon lifted his head and regarded her with those eerie eyes. "The princess came," he said in the saddest tone she'd ever heard.

Chapter 8

"And His Grace, him that had told you he couldn't be bothered with you, arrived to that house and made that drunkard stop beating on those ladies and then agreed to accompany you to more of those places?" Annie squinted at Margaret. "Tell me again how he doesn't like you?"

And he kissed me. Not that she was going to tell Annie that—the woman was already jumping to conclusions, she wasn't going to stoke the fire of her curiosity even more.

It was just after breakfast, and Margaret had yet to sit down at her desk to begin the day's writing. She was apprehensive about her work, where normally she wasn't—what if she accidentally wrote in an unexpected kiss or something?

"He is an honorable man who doesn't wish to see me run into trouble. He would do this for anyone."

Margaret picked up her teacup and took a sip—lukewarm, but that was her fault, since she'd spent most of breakfast gazing off into the distance when she should have been eating. And now she didn't quite recall what she'd eaten and her tea was too cold.

"That's why he's been going with all those old dowagers when they visit the sick." Annie put her finger up to her nose. "Oh, wait, he hasn't been doing that. It's just you he's offered to do it for, so what do you think that means?"

You should have heard his voice when he was worried I might actually want to accept his proposal, Margaret thought.

"We are meeting at the Royal Academy later this afternoon." Margaret stood up from the table, looking down at her plate. Apparently she'd had toast. "The elder Banner sister told me about some other women whose men were mistreating them in that same neighborhood, I want to see if I can find them and at least make sure they know they can come to me for help if needed."

"And you don't think that duke will scare the women half to death?"

Margaret blinked. "I hope not." *Do you know what it is like, Lady Margaret, to be gawked at and appraised every single moment you are within sight of anyone?* "Although maybe, now you mention it, I will ask him to wait just outside while I am speaking with them."

"That would make sense." *Of course it would to you,* Margaret thought fondly, *because you thought of it.*

"And after that, I will be going to the Purseleys' party. Lord Purseley believes himself a good cardplayer, and who am I to argue?"

"Just hope you can keep fleecing them lords or you won't be able to afford me," Annie said.

"I don't fleece them, Annie," Margaret said in a tone of mock outrage. "They do not play as skillfully as I; is it my fault that I am so very good?"

"Just be careful, is all," Annie chided.

Of course she would be. She had to be. Winning at cards and writing a newspaper serial were all that stood between her and having to throw herself on her sister's charity—never mind being able to spare funds to help women in less fortunate situations.

"Oh, my lady, thank you!" The elder of the Banner sisters greeted her at the parlor door. Margaret had found the lodgings for the impecunious women when she'd first gotten involved with sending potential employees to the Quality Employment Agency—the Agency could find positions for them, but not immediately, and there was an immediate need for housing, especially in cases like that of the Banner sisters.

The house was only a few doors down from the Agency, which made it convenient for everyone. That Lady Margaret was the ostensible renter for the house made it even more convenient; while her sister was a duchess, it was true that it was harder for Isabella to do things more average ladies could. If it got out that a duchess was renting a house that was not her husband's—well, there would be talk. Isabella's husband had offered to take care of it, but Margaret refused, as usual, to have a man do what she could do perfectly well.

Which did raise the question of why she wanted the duke's help, but then again, she wasn't over six feet tall with an eye patch. If he had been a woman and looked the same—well, he would have been hideous, but that wasn't the point. It would have been the same result. Although she probably wouldn't have been quite as intrigued to spend time with the intimidator.

Thus justified, at least to herself, she entered the parlor, where she saw both sisters with their lacework in their laps.

The need to make a living never stopped, did it? That was why Margaret helped—some of the first ladies she'd assisted had lost valuable hours of working time because of sick children, or violent husbands, or poor living conditions.

She'd sworn to help them whenever she could, because she was grateful her sister had done so much for her. Not all of these ladies—she could confidently say none of them, in fact—had a duchess for a sister.

That her parents had so quickly given her up made it even more real to Margaret—if she didn't have Isabella, and something happened, she would be lost. And she didn't want that either for herself or for anybody she could help.

That was why, when she'd heard about the Quality Employment Agency and how it helped women find work, she'd leaped into helping as best she could. At first it had just been sending old clothing and the occasional pound to assist, but it had grown to being more actively involved, even when she wasn't living in London.

It made her feel as though she had a purpose, which she sorely needed, given that she doubted she would ever have a husband and children.

"You are all right? You slept well?" Margaret looked from one sister to the other, noting that while both were pale, neither of them had a large, drunken man assaulting her, so she knew they were at least better.

The younger sister, the one who was married to the drunkard, put her lacework aside and stepped forward, her large brown eyes filled with tears.

"We are, and we did, my lady." She clasped both of Margaret's hands in hers and raised them up to kiss them. "We cannot thank you enough for helping, you and the gentleman."

She could admit now that the sisters' rescue had been eased by the duke's presence. Without him, even her stabbing the husband in the arm with her embroidery needle wouldn't have helped.

"You are most welcome. Are you in need of anything?" Margaret said, loosening the grip the woman had on her hands and starting to reach for her pocketbook.

"No, we couldn't," the elder sister said, moving to stand beside her sister. "You have done enough, and the lady from the Agency, the one you told us to go to this morning, she said there was likely to be work for us in a few days."

"Excellent," Margaret said, relief evident in her tone. Carolyn, one of the Agency's proprietors, was always completely and entirely honest in her dealings with prospective employees, so if she said there was work, then there must be work.

"Once we're back on our feet, we're going to work on a point lace piece for one of your fanciest dresses," the older sister said. "It isn't enough payment for helping us out—maybe saving our lives—but at least we can do something."

Margaret smiled back at them, biting her lip as she tried not to cry. *At least we can do something.*

That was all she could do, too, wasn't it? Do something. Do *anything*. Be someone who would help, not hinder. Be the person who would stand up for people who couldn't do so for themselves.

That was what privilege was. Not to mention the benefit of not caring so much about your reputation, since it was already in tatters.

The sisters' gratitude was still warming her a few hours later when she arrived at the Royal Academy. He wasn't there yet, but she didn't even bother to ponder if he wasn't going to arrive at all—he'd said he would, so he would. She knew him hardly at all, but she knew that much about him.

Meanwhile, she'd spent at least fifteen minutes in this one room, shifting on her feet as she gazed at yet another landscape painting.

Would it be too much to ask for just one person off in the distance or something? There were only so many clouds a person could endure.

She'd gotten through the day's writing, thankfully without writing anything about a one-eyed man who'd kissed his heroine. Mostly because she was writing about a dragon with both his eyes, and kissing didn't usually enter into that type of story.

"Lady Margaret." His low voice startled her so much she jumped, and she felt a wash of heat come over her face. She should not be so easily embarrassed, she seldom was, but her thoughts could not stop returning to the previous night when he'd been so—unexpected. Not to mention the way his mouth had felt on hers, how his grip on his arms had been thrillingly, entirely strong, as though she could lean into him and he would support her.

She didn't need support, she'd proven that in the past few years, but there was something entirely seductive about being able to let go, to allow someone else to be the strong one.

And here she was not replying to him while he stood there, the expression on his handsome face flickering from concerned to puzzled.

She knew how he felt. Or didn't feel, given how puzzled he looked.

"Good afternoon, Your Grace," she said, dipping a brief curtsey. She tilted her head in the direction of the paintings. "I much prefer paintings with people in them, don't you?"

He narrowed his gaze in thought. "I don't know I agree, my lady." He put his hands behind his back and moved forward, closer to the painting. "I think there is something very peaceful about a landscape. Imagine what it must be like to be the one person who can see all of that. To be alone with one's thoughts among such beauty."

"Hm," Margaret replied, hoping she wouldn't say anything to bring back that stiff-toned duke, "I hadn't thought of it that way. Of course, I am no stranger to being alone—until a few months ago, I was living in the country, quite isolated."

"Why did you come back?" It wasn't the question most people asked—usually they wondered why she'd gone away at all, and how she could have borne being away from London for so long.

But she was coming to realize that far from being a usual sort of person, he was quite unusual.

She moved to another painting, this one where it appeared to be raining. That would explain why there were no people in it—they were likely all indoors not getting wet. He stood next to her, his hands still clasped behind his back, his feet set wide apart as though he were on parade. On display.

Did he know he did that, or was it just unconscious? Had he been viewed so many times he just presented himself?

"I don't know if you know why I left, but there was some scandal, and I thought it'd be best for me to leave London for a bit."

He didn't say anything. Just waited. Not as though he didn't want to know more, however; he kept his gaze on her face, his expression showing his interest, but not as though he were impatient to hear her words.

"You see," she said, "my parents and I had a disagreement about who I should be marrying."

She shrugged. "Annie and I lived in a small town by the sea. I was able to keep up my work, and it was more inexpensive to live there."

He nodded.

"But I still haven't answered, have I?" She gave a self-conscious laugh. "I suppose I came back for a few reasons." Not all of which she'd examined, not even to herself. "My sister is here, she is the Duchess of Gage." Margaret felt that tight fierceness in her chest, the one that surfaced anytime she thought of Isabella. Even though Isabella didn't need her protection anymore, she had a perfectly capable duke to take care of her. "And my publisher is here, and he said that with the serials gaining in popularity, perhaps it would behoove me to be in town regularly." She took a deep breath. "And my parents are not here, so that worked out well." But it wasn't just about her, was it? "And then there is the work of helping people. Women, in particular." She turned and looked at him. "And that is where you matter. I am so glad to have the help of someone so ferocious. Positively dragonlike." She smiled as she spoke, letting him know she was teasing.

For a moment, it appeared that perhaps he did not know; his expression darkened, and she saw his jaw clench. *Damn it, Margaret! Have you just brought about the return of the Proper Duke?*

And then he closed his eye for longer than a blink, turning that intense gaze onto her. "I am delighted to be of assistance, Lady Margaret, even if it is just for my appearance." He spoke in that wry tone again, only this time she could tell he wasn't chiding her or anything.

She wasn't sure how, precisely, she could tell—maybe it was because there was a slight hint that his lips might smile at some point? Or that he wasn't seeming to pin her to the wall with his gaze?

"Yes, thank goodness you have that, because otherwise, what would you be?" She held her hand out and spread her fingers. "One, you would be a member of the aristocracy, the highest member, in fact. Two," she said, moving on to the next finger, "you would have wealth, power, and position." She frowned at the second finger. "Although that is inherent with being a duke, isn't it?" She glanced up at him. "I'm being redundant, aren't I?"

The duke's lips curved into a—wait, was that a smile?—and he spoke. "Far be it from me to correct the writer here on her language, but yes, being a duke does imply wealth, power, and position." His mouth twisted, and it was clear there was some past memory that disturbed him.

She hoped today was not the day she blurted out the question of what happened to his eye, although why else would he look so perturbed?

It couldn't be the fact of who he was, could it? In which case people who were not dukes were likely miserable all the time, and she could safely say she was not miserable all the time. Only when Annie got to the last biscuit before she did, and if she had to dance with Lord Tremayne, who was pleasant enough but smelled like a large mound of earth.

Thankfully he spoke before she could say anything. About biscuits, earth, or the distress of being a duke.

"Being a duke does have its . . . benefits," although it didn't sound, the way he said the word, as though he believed them to have had a beneficial effect on his life. "But there is also much responsibility." An exhale. "Something my father drilled into my head since I was small." Ah, perhaps that was the memory. His tone got strong again. "It isn't fair to people who aren't dukes to be forced to do something detrimental simply because a duke is careless, or negligent—" He shot an amused look at Margaret. "And now who's being redundant?—and I take my responsibilities seriously. I would never do anything to jeopardize my position, because that would jeopardize the position of all the people, not just of this generation, but of future generations." He shook his head. "I could not live with myself." He cleared his throat and reached into his pocket, drawing out a piece of paper. "Speaking of jeopardy, I have a few things I deem essential to discuss before we venture on this . . . pursuit," he said, quirking his mouth. He unfolded the paper, the noise of it echoing in the empty gallery.

"I have drawn up some requirements to my participating."

Margaret felt her eyes narrow. "You mean rules, don't you?" *And I have never been good at following the rules, have I?*

He looked uncomfortable. "I suppose, if you wish to call them rules. I believe they are essential to our safety, both in maintaining our actual safety, in terms of visiting the places you wish to go, and our reputation's safety, since we are both clear that we do not wish to be," and here he closed his eye and took a deep breath, "encumbered with one another."

"Well, it's a good thing I refused you then, isn't it?" Damn it. She couldn't stop herself from saying it, could she? Hopefully one of his rules wouldn't be that she would keep quiet at all times. Because she simply could not do that.

"Yes, well," he said, shifting as though not sure what to say. And how would he? She doubted very much that he had ever had to be polite about the fact that someone didn't want to marry him. Eye patch or not, he was a duke.

"Onto the requirements," he continued. "One: You will not go to any unsavory place without my company."

"I was doing just fine," she muttered.

He met her gaze. "Yes, I could see that the other evening," he replied in that cool tone.

She felt herself flinch. He was right, only she hated to admit it. Even to herself.

"Two: You will secure my participation at least a day prior." He looked up at her again. "I do have appointments I cannot break, regardless of how appealing the prospect of spending time with you might be."

Was he joking with her? Or did he really find her appealing?

And why did she care, anyway? She didn't. Not at all.

Only she did, she was very afraid she did.

"Three," he began.

"How many rules are there?" she blurted out.

He glanced down at the paper. "Five. Is that a problem, Lady Margaret? And they are requirements, not rules."

She snatched the paper from his hands and stuffed it into the pocket of her cloak, crumpling it up in her fist. "I will review your rules at a later time, Your Grace."

"I can see that rules, as you call them, are even more essential than I'd imagined," he said, smiling as though he found something amusing in what he'd said.

Goodness knows Margaret did not.

"Yes, well, fine," she said grumpily, if not very coherently. And then felt rueful, since he was just trying to keep things under control, as it seemed he required. "I apologize for my attitude, I have not always been very good at following rules." She laughed. "Not good at all, in fact." Another reason to be grateful she wasn't ever going to have to be a duchess.

"You did mention something along those lines," he said in that desert-dry voice, but that now she understood held some humor within. Albeit buried very far below. "What happened? Is it part of why you are so . . . so . . ."

"Adamant about not marrying you? Yes." She took a deep breath and stared firmly at the landscape. "I told you there is scandal to my name, and there is, and your duchess could never be seen to be scandalous. And then there's the fact that being under constant scrutiny like that"—she shivered—

"would make me want to go and do all the scandalous things, just to thumb my nose at everyone. That would definitely jeopardize your position."

"All the more important to have rules, then."

Aggravating—and correct—man. And here she was the one who was supposed to be the writer who could envision any type of scenario. She glanced around the room, noting that it appeared only aspiring artists (indicated by their mournful poses and general youth) were there, and breathed a sigh of relief.

But meanwhile, she wouldn't feel right if she didn't at least offer to release him. "I—I would not wish to do anything to damage your reputation," and she couldn't believe she was saying this to a man, a gentleman, who could likely destroy anybody with a long-enough session in the House of Lords, "so if you do not wish to accompany me—"

"Did I say that?" he cut in, in as sharp a tone as she'd ever heard him use. "I spoke of my responsibility to people, my people in this case who depend on me, but I feel responsible to more than just them. If you are doing something that can help people, and you might come to danger without me—and," he said, holding his hand up to her, "you can say you will be fine, and I will disagree, then I have a responsibility to help there, as well."

Well. There was that, then. "Um," she said, wishing she had words adequate to say in response, "then thank you." She felt in her pocket for the crumpled piece of paper. "And I will abide by your requirements, once I've had a chance to look them over."

He nodded, as though that were the end of it. And, she supposed, it was. He was stiff, and proper, but he was both of those things with an honorable purpose. Somehow she couldn't begrudge him being so correct, not when it meant he was not—incorrect, at least in terms of how he was living his life.

"Well," she said, glancing around the room with a bright smile on her face, "I've had enough of seeing misty scenes with no people and lots and lots of boats and clouds. Let's go dive into the seething populace and see who we can find today."

He—he smirked, and Margaret wanted to laugh aloud at the sight of it, but just for the joy of seeing that on his face, not because he looked odd or anything.

Oh, it was a good thing he didn't smile more often, or he would never find himself alone. She, for one, wanted to spend much more time with him, if only to see that look again. And again.

GEORGIANA AND THE DRAGON

By A Lady of Mystery

Georgiana didn't hesitate; she walked right up to the dragon and clamped her hand on the arrow that was sticking into his thick hide, her eyes already filling with tears.

"How could you do this to him?" she asked the woman—presumably the princess, who stood with her bow in her hand. The princess was remarkably pretty—beautiful, the dragon would no doubt say—with flaxen-white hair flowing down her back in tiny braids, her blue eyes wide-set in her face, so huge it looked as though she were constantly widening them.

"He needs to be rescued," the princess replied in an oddly flat tone. "He is so hideous, and he could be so much more."

"He is a dragon!" Georgiana exclaimed. "He is more already."

The princess looked at Georgiana as though she were sorry for her.

"Don't pull it out," the dragon said as Georgiana frowned and began to wiggle the arrow. "It is in deep, it will only cause me to lose more blood."

And indeed, as Georgiana looked, she saw there were rivulets of dark purplish blood oozing out of the wound, flowing onto the ground and dampening the leaves.

"What can I do?" Georgiana asked, kneeling down by the dragon's head.

"Just leave me," the dragon said, sounding so forlorn Georgiana felt the tears well up again.

"Never," she replied, kissing the dragon on his cheek.

Chapter 9

"Just stand in back of me and don't say anything," Lady Margaret said as they exited the carriage. They'd taken hers, since his was far grander, emblazoned with his family crest and all. She'd given it a sour look, muttering something about being murdered for the upholstery, and then had beckoned him over to hers, which was plain black, with a skinny scarecrow of a coachman and, of course, that bossy lady's maid.

"What if there is trouble?" he asked in a low murmur, glancing around at their surroundings.

As the worst parts of London went, it wasn't the absolute worst. That would be East London, and he would have had to insist neither of them go there, no matter how much good she thought she could do.

They were in Southwark, which was admittedly bad, but it didn't make him want to gag, nor did it make him doubt how a population could survive. There were children playing, and some ladies selling meat pies or something, and the general hubbub of commerce. But he wouldn't have wanted her to come here by herself, that was for certain.

Not looking as lovely as she did, today wearing a maroon cloak with lighter ribbons on it, the gown underneath an even darker red color that seemed to make her brown hair appear reddish in the sun. He didn't pay attention to clothing, in general, beyond ensuring everything was properly buttoned, but it was impossible not to notice her, just as if she'd stepped out of a painting and was waiting for him with a bright smile.

Which turned serious as she appraised him. "If there is trouble, just stand up straighter and try to look frightening."

"That's not much of a defense, my lady," Lasham said, still in that low murmur. Perhaps he should have included more about what might occur here rather than focus on how to set about it.

But his mind had whirled because of what had happened the night before—not just the kiss, although that was paramount in his brain—but because she'd arrived at his house at a time no decent woman (and few indecent women) would have, she'd refused to back down from her questions, and yet she'd seemed to understand when he told her what he was feeling. How he felt, most of the time.

Although right now he had to admit he felt like going home and finally getting to have that drink.

Preferably also getting to have her accompany him.

And then they would sit on the sofa and . . .

talk. Just talk, he commanded himself. Nothing else.

"Mrs. Beecham, how nice to see you again." Lady Margaret was ahead of him by a few feet, and he realized he'd been imagining again—of all things—instead of watching out for her.

A fine intimidator he was ending up being.

"My lady, thank you for the bread you brought last week." Mrs. Beecham beckoned behind her to a few smaller Beechams. It was nearly impossible to tell their sex, they were clothed in an indiscriminate mass of fabric. "And my girls"—*aha!* Lasham thought—"they are able to work, and I was hoping you might have an idea for where they could go?" Mrs. Beecham's expression darkened. "I don't want them going over to the pub or them type of places, I know what happens to girls like that."

Lady Margaret glanced back at Lasham, as if to say, *See?* and nodded at Mrs. Beecham. "I can ask some people I know whether there can be a place found for them. Do they have any skills?"

Lasham wondered that as well. What skills could they have gotten, out here in one of London's poorer neighborhoods? And how had he missed all of this, given how he was one of the most responsible nobles in the House of Lords? What else was there to find?

And what could he do about it?

He hadn't been posturing when he told Lady Margaret that he felt responsible, even though it might have sounded like that to her. He knew what it was like to have responsibility thrust upon him, thanks to his parents' death, and he did not take it lightly. He took it the opposite, in fact—he took it heavily, carrying his burden even as he attended parties, or made idle chitchat, which of course he loathed, or spent time writing out speeches that most of his peers would sleep through.

So seeing this, seeing these people, just a fragment of their lives, set something burning inside him to do something.

He stepped forward, ignoring her look of admonition. "I can help your girls, Mrs. Beecham," he said. He dug in his pocket and drew out a few coins, placing them in the woman's palm. "Take this, and then have your girls go to Lasham House in Mayfair. They're in need of kitchen maids," or they would be once he returned home and explained the situation to his housekeeper, "but have them purchase new clothing first, since what they have on won't be suitable, and they won't get wages for the first month."

He was responsible, but he wasn't stupid or softhearted. It wouldn't do for anyone to hear that his household was staffed by improperly clothed girls from the streets; if people started to gossip—*when* they started to gossip—they would wonder just what else his household, and by extension he, had overlooked.

His responsibilities were piled one on top of the other like a gigantic house of cards that just one tiny flick of the finger could overset, leaving him and everyone who depended on him to flutter helplessly to the ground.

"Thank you, my lord," Mrs. Beecham said, her

eyes wide. "My girls will be there first thing in the morning, you can be sure of that."

"Good," Lasham said, daring to look at Lady Margaret.

Her mouth was set in a thin line, and her sparkle seemed more like banked coals right now, as though the blaze was merely waiting until something flammable came to set them afire again.

He was guessing the "something flammable" would be when they were safely in her carriage, away from everyone but the bossy lady's maid.

"What were you thinking?" Margaret sat next to him, so she couldn't just stare across the seat of the carriage at him. They'd finished with the Beechams, then she had gone to check on a few families she had met before, to ensure they were still doing all right. She hadn't found the women the Banner sisters had mentioned, which had been distressing, but meanwhile, she had distributed some coins, encouraging words, and hope for the future.

That was a solid afternoon's work, and had kept her mind off what he had done and, more importantly, said.

Annie, seated opposite, was keeping herself entirely out of the conversation—she'd closed her eyes immediately upon entering, although Margaret could have sworn she'd seen her eyes open quickly a few times.

Hmph.

"I was thinking," the duke replied in that low,

shiver-inducing voice of his, "that those girls might have a chance if they had work. Do you begrudge them that?"

Oh no, he was not trying to make her feel guilty about it—was he? Well, there was only one way to find out. "Are you trying to make me feel guilty for wishing you hadn't said anything?" She let out an exasperated breath. "The thing is, I am very pleased you helped those girls out today. That is not the point."

"What is the point, then?" He sounded surprised.

"The point is that if anyone sees that you are really a fine gentleman you will be of no use to me as protection there."

She darted a glance at him—thankfully, she was sitting on his sighted side, so she didn't have to guess what he might be thinking. His brows were drawn together in thought, and he looked as though he was really thinking about what she'd said.

That was yet another thing that made him unusual—that he listened to her. That he actually seemed to consider what she'd said.

Her father never had. He'd listened to her mother, yes, but he hadn't ever listened to either of his daughters. Nor did any of the young men she met out in Society now; they thought she was an anomaly, a scandalous young lady who they hoped would act scandalously with them.

Not listening when she said no.

But he did. He would. He was now.

"I am of no use to you if I am a gentleman?"

Oh dear. He bit his words out, as though each syllable was accented with the rap of a drum. Tap, tap, tap.

"I didn't mean that, precisely," Margaret said. She could have sworn she heard a muffled laugh from Annie's side of the coach. "What I meant was, I want those people to be afraid of you. And they won't be because they will know you're too honorable to actually hurt them."

"You deem me too honorable?" Now his words were less accented and more . . . *fierce*. She really had awoken the dragon, hadn't she?

"Well," she said, drawing her words out slowly, "I do. That is why you do what you do, isn't it? Isn't that why you offered those girls the position in the first place? Because you're so honorable?"

He exhaled, and Margaret felt his shoulder brush against her. Such a terribly handsome man shouldn't also be so large—not that she had any reason for thinking that, but she did—but he was. It felt as though she were tucked into her side of the carriage seat, his whole presence commanding all the space in the carriage.

It was unnerving, and wonderful, and terrifying. All at the same time.

Rather like discovering a dragon in the forest, actually. She had to smother the beginnings of a snort, which she quickly changed into a cough.

Annie's eyes flew open. "Are you getting sick? I told you to cover your mouth when we were out in those places."

"I'm fine, Annie," Margaret said in an exasperated tone. It was bad enough that she was now beginning to think of the Piratical Duke as her own Private Dragon, now her actual dragon of a maid was starting to fuss—well, she might just be tempted to tell everyone to leave her alone.

Only she did not want that. She wanted Annie, of course, who wouldn't leave her even if she did command her to go, and she also found she rather liked having the duke around. She shouldn't admit—likely not even to herself—how much she liked having him around, even though he'd been around for only a few days.

Oh no. What would happen in a few weeks? A few months? Would she accidentally fall in love with this man who absolutely could not marry her, and to whom she'd said she'd never wished to be married?

And was she suddenly writing one of her serials instead of living her own life?

She shook her head. She was *not* going to marry the dragon.

"Lady Margaret, I will promise to be less . . . gentlemanly in the future," the duke said in a very low voice, so low she wasn't sure even Annie could hear it.

The woman had gone and closed her eyes again anyway, no doubt thinking the danger of illness was past, and not wanting to interfere with whatever scenario she'd concocted in her head.

Less gentlemanly. Of course that conjured up the memory of the last time—last night—when he'd been less gentlemanly.

And look what had happened there. No wonder his words sent a shiver up her spine and down several other parts of her.

"In fact," he said, still in that low, thrilling tone, "I was thinking that if you were amenable, we could enter into a reciprocal arrangement."

A what? And why did that sound both scandalous and wonderful?

He couldn't mean what Margaret immediately thought it meant.

"What kind of arrangement?" she asked, acutely aware of Annie snoozing in the corner. Just as she'd had the thought, however, Annie emitted a soft snore that was either an actual snore, or the kind of snore she might emit if she wanted her mistress to continue an inappropriate conversation.

He glanced over at her, a spark of—mischief?—in his eye. "I have come to realize that I am not perhaps the most adventurous of souls." He turned away to gaze out of the window on the other side of the carriage. "In fact, some have accused me of being a stick-in-the-mud. If you would, I would like you to accompany me on some . . . adventures."

Well, that didn't sound at all like the Proper Duke. And damned if he wasn't intriguing her more by the minute.

"What kinds of adventures were you interested in, Your Grace?" She leaned in closer to him, keeping her voice low in the perhaps vain hope that Annie wouldn't overhear.

She felt his shoulders shrug. "The thing is, I am not even certain what kinds of adventures would be enjoyable. That is where I would like your assistance."

She smiled to herself. "So perhaps one day

we would go eat as many ices as we could, then another day perhaps we would see what type of wine we prefer best, or another day we could visit a bookstore and see if you enjoy poetry? I am certain you have never read poetry," she added.

"No, I have not," he admitted. "And yes, that sounds—enjoyable," he said, as though he'd never uttered anything close to that sentence before.

"Then I accept. And I will have my own rules to guide us as we go along."

That startled him, since he whipped his head around to look at her. She burst out laughing at his expression. "It is not as though I have the rules with me now. But I will have them, do not mistake me." She narrowed her gaze at him. "I'll make up the rules as we go along. But you'll have to abide by them, once they're set," she said in a warning tone. It was already enjoyable to speak with him like this, to think about introducing him to things no Proper Duke would ever condescend to do.

And she shouldn't think about it too much, or else she would realize just how much trouble she could possibly be getting into.

"I don't see why you're fussing. Stop fussing," Margaret said, swatting Annie's hand away from her hair.

Annie stepped back, her hands on her hips. "My lady, it is my duty to ensure you are dressed appropriately for every occasion. The Purseleys' party is bound to be a grand event, and I don't want anyone to say you are less than perfect."

"They already say that, Annie," Margaret said in a wry tone. "Haven't you heard how I jilted Lord Collingwood and then brought scandal down on my family by being A Lady of Mystery? I think the damage is done."

Annie didn't even bother responding.

"That's why I get these invitations in the first place, isn't it? And it is not as though he will notice one way or the other how I am dressed," Margaret said. It was silly to pretend she didn't know why Annie was putting so much effort into her appearance tonight. Annie was usually most concerned with whether Margaret had a purse large enough to carry her winnings from the table, not whether she actually looked attractive. "Plus I plan on spending most of the time at the tables. I don't attend these events for pleasure," Margaret said in a dry voice.

"You can play cards and look beautiful at the same time," Annie said, not pausing from her ministrations.

Margaret sighed. It wasn't as though she would win this—well, it wasn't an argument, more like a discussion—so she should just endure whatever Annie thought should be done to her to make her beautiful.

Isabella was beautiful. Margaret had never thought she herself was; her hair was too brown, as were her eyes, and she didn't have her sister's height and presence. But as she gazed at herself in the mirror, she could partially admit that she was not unattractive.

Annie had chosen the blue gown Isabella had bought for her before she'd left London, but had done something to it, added some lace or something, to make it look like an entirely new gown. The color made her eyes and hair look rich, not plain, and the cut clung to her upper body, enhancing her bustline and making her waist look tiny.

The gown flared out into the wide skirts that were fashionable now, and the sleeves were barely a suggestion, leaving most of her upper arm bare.

Meanwhile, Annie had pulled all of Margaret's hair to the back in a low, heavy chignon, and was placing tiny diamond stars into her coiffure.

Finally, after darting in and out to smooth a piece of fabric here or adjust a star there, Annie stepped back and nodded. "You'll do," she said, satisfaction in her tone.

Margaret looked at herself for a moment. She would do. She was, if not beautiful, at least striking.

"Thank you, Annie," she said, standing and pulling her maid in for a hug. Annie made a grumpy noise, but allowed the affection.

"I'll be home late, I have to make enough tonight so the Agency can have food on hand for the women with children."

Annie rolled her eyes, but didn't say anything. Margaret knew that Annie believed in what she was doing, but she also knew that her devoted servant thought she did too much sometimes, and worried about her.

"You be careful," Annie said, giving Margaret's shoulder one last pat.

"Your turn, my lady."

Margaret smiled, thumbing through her cards. She wasn't normally this preoccupied when playing, but she also wasn't normally thinking about being kissed. And exceedingly large, often formidable gentlemen. Or one exceedingly large, formidable gentleman, to be precise. And his oddly sweet wish to be less gentlemanly.

He wasn't here, and Margaret was annoyed at herself for continuing to scan the crowd—if he did arrive, he'd be announced, and she and the entire rest of the room would know he was here. So why did she keep looking around?

She shook her head and chose which card to discard, realizing too late that her discard meant that Lord Gantrey would be able to make his play.

"Aha, my lady! Your luck isn't in attendance tonight?" She could excuse Lord Gantrey's crowing; he had always been remarkably good-natured about the many times she had beaten him. She supposed he deserved some good luck.

Although his good luck seemed directly tied to her lack of attention to the game. She would have to rectify that, handsome man in an eye patch or not. The Agency could do only so much without additional funds. Not to mention she was dependent on her winnings to maintain her small household.

She narrowed her gaze at her cards, resolving to put the duke out of her mind.

"Lady Margaret?"

Drat. She'd forgotten about him, at least as much as she could, for at least twenty minutes, during which he must have arrived and been announced. She'd won back her original stake, plus a bit more, but not enough for the evening. There was never enough.

"Good evening, Your Grace." She looked up at him and her breath caught. Goodness, he looked remarkable in evening wear. Everything he wore was severe—from the crisp black dress coat to the matching black trousers, the startling white shirt underneath the black waistcoat. And of course the black eye patch, tied with a black velvet ribbon.

He was glorious.

"Lady Margaret," he said, keeping his gaze locked on her, "I am hoping you would do me the honor of a dance later. After you've finished your game." He looked—nervous, as though she might actually decline.

She usually didn't dance, except when her brother-in-law asked her. Too often the gentlemen who wanted to dance with her were no gentlemen, and besides, time spent dancing meant time away from the tables. But she couldn't resist this, could she? The chance to be held in his arms, to clasp his broad shoulders, to embark on something adventure-worthy, after all.

"Yes, thank you, Your Grace," she said. "I should be free in about ten minutes."

He bowed, not saying another word, and headed to the corner of the room. Margaret only knew where he was because, damn her, she couldn't keep her eyes off him.

He was joined by his friend from the other night, the one whose mouth was curved up into a rakish smile, whose appraising glance seemed to take in all that was female in the room. It was intriguing, she had to admit, that the Properly Piratical Duke had an acquaintance who appeared to be less than proper. Maybe there was hope for him after all.

"Good evening, Lash." Jamie had a smirk in his voice, so Lasham knew his friend had seen whom he'd just been speaking to.

"I asked Lady Margaret for a dance." Better to just tell Jamie what he wanted to know rather than wait for the man to badger him into it.

"And did she say yes?" Jamie replied.

Lasham gave his friend an annoyed look. "Of course she did, it seems that you don't realize it, but I am a duke. For her to refuse to dance with me would be scandalous." Not that that would stop her; she'd already told him about the scandal in her past, refusing to marry someone her parents had chosen for her. Would her contrariness go so far as to refuse to dance with someone as well?

Although he shouldn't have to ask himself that, should he? He could tell, from the way her eyes lit up, that she was pleased to be asked. Plus he hadn't had to mention it, but this was part of their pact of adventuring, wasn't it?

At least he thought it was. He wasn't sure if he should ask her—what if dancing wasn't at all something enjoyable to her, and he was merely making her endure something unpleasant? Or if it was so much a part of her everyday life she didn't perceive it as being anything out of the ordinary?

Perhaps he was overthinking it. No, he knew; he *was* overthinking it.

Thank goodness Jamie spoke when he did. If only to save him from thinking so much. "What did she want the other night?" Jamie lowered his voice, even though there wasn't anyone within earshot.

"She wanted to ask me a question." Lasham spoke in a stiff tone of voice, one that would dissuade most people from asking more.

Of course that didn't stop Jamie. "What question? What could she possibly want at such a late hour?"

"I could ask the same of you. After all, I arrived home to find you in residence, drinking my liquor, and making yourself quite comfortable on my sofa."

Jamie stuck his elbow into Lasham's side. "You can't think you'll stop me from wanting to know just because you go on a counterattack, do you? And here I thought you knew me."

Lasham heaved an exasperated sigh. He did know Jamie, he knew full well that if the man wanted to know something, to find something, he would.

What could he tell him that wouldn't immediately make Jamie even more curious? Not *She treated me like a man, not an oddity.* Certainly not *She demanded to know why I'd arrived where she was*—that one would make Jamie ask even more questions. Nothing about embarking on mutual adventures, either.

And definitely not *I couldn't stop myself from kissing her.*

"She—damn it, Jamie, you know there's nothing I can tell you that won't sound improper."

Jamie clapped him on the back. "Precisely! She is just what you need, Lash. It is not as though I truly wished to know what she wanted—although if you want to tell me, I'll listen—but I wanted to see what you would come up with. Excellent, your being improper and all."

"I wasn't—" Lasham began, only he couldn't say that, could he? Especially with what they'd agreed to do? Not that ices and wine were improper, necessarily, but he hadn't ever done anything she suggested before, and since he was always correct, that must mean— "Never mind. Tell me, how is your mother?"

"Ah, resorting to the strongest counterattack in your arsenal! She is fine, she is delighted I am home, but she is already asking when I plan to leave." Jamie folded his arms across his chest. "Why is it that parents are always so inquisitive as to one's arrivals and departures? The minute I walk in the door she's asking me when I have to go, and then when I do go, she asks when I will be coming back. It is as though her questions are reversed or something."

Lasham shrugged. "I have no idea, I haven't had parents for a long time."

Jamie winced. "Sorry, that was thoughtless of me."

Lasham waved his hand. "It doesn't signify, it was so long ago." Although not so long ago it didn't still hurt. His parents had died of cholera, both within a week of each other. He'd been away at school, and hadn't been allowed to return home, not until the danger had passed.

Everyone had thought that people of his kind— the wealthy, titled ones—were immune to the types of diseases that devastated London's poorer neighborhoods like the ones he and Margaret had been to recently. But disease didn't care about wealth or titles. It just went where it wanted to.

Jamie had been there with him, helping him through it all. For that, if not for anything else, Lasham was entirely grateful.

Not so grateful he was sanguine about his friend being at his house at all hours drinking his brandy—there were limits—but enough that he would do whatever Jamie needed, ever, if called upon.

"It does matter." Jamie's voice was unusually solemn. "You don't ever get over that kind of thing, not when it was so sudden as it was. I apologize for being so careless."

Lasham turned to his friend, wishing he weren't in public, that it wasn't odd for him to be seen embracing his friend, that he could just put into words the things he felt once in a while. He couldn't even put his emotions into action, and so he was left with his simmering feelings, all bubbling around until he exploded. Or hit something. Or kissed someone. But not Jamie.

"Thank you."

Both men cleared their throats, suddenly nearly awkward, only not really. Lasham knew that Jamie knew what he was thinking, and he was grateful for it. If only he could know what he was thinking sometimes, that would make his life nearly perfect.

At least as perfect as it could be for a one-eyed duke with the inability to express his emotions and who wished, just once, he could be improper without consequences.

GEORGIANA AND THE DRAGON

By A Lady of Mystery

⁓⊶⊙⊸⁓

"Why would you stay?" The dragon didn't sound anything but curious.

Georgiana's fingers were starting to cramp from holding the arrow. He'd laid his head on the ground and had his eyes closed, clearly in pain. She shook her head, but realized he couldn't see her.

"I can't leave just because someone wants me to," she said in a broken voice. "You need me. I am here. I won't leave."

The dragon gave the most mournful sigh she'd ever heard. "Thank you."

"I'm not leaving, either," the princess announced, her hand on her bow.

Chapter 10

"Thank you, all, for a lovely game. I must excuse myself for a while." *Because a duke has asked me to dance, as though you are all not keenly aware of that already.* Margaret picked up her winnings and tucked them into her purse, relieved that her run of bad luck had ended. She had enough funds to pay her way for two weeks—not that that was all she had; she had money in the bank, but she felt she had to be vigilant about her balances.

Isabella would help her if she needed, of course, but the last thing Margaret wanted to do was ask for money from her sister.

No, actually, the last thing she wanted to do was marry someone she didn't want to, which was why she was in this situation in the first place.

And she did like cards—she liked the risk of it, the feeling as though she were diving off a cliff into unknown waters every time she placed a large bet. She liked being better than other players, knowing who likely had what card and how they played.

She couldn't ever stop being a writer—a person who observed people, and how they behaved, and what they were likely to do. At least she could make some money off her observational skills and ability to keep track of things.

"My lady, you have to give me a chance to win some of my money back!" Lord Gantrey said. He smiled at her, and she returned the smile. Lord Gantrey could not control his expression when he had a good hand, she'd discovered, so it was very easy to win against him. And he was so very good-natured about it, too.

"My lord, it is no longer your money," Margaret said. She glanced to where the duke still stood, in the corner with his dashing friend. "But I promise to give you a chance at my money later on this evening."

"I'll hold you to it, young lady," Lord Gantrey said. He, too, looked to where the duke was, and then a different kind of smile appeared on his face. "But meanwhile, I believe you have a prior engagement."

Engage— Lord, no. Not that. Never that. "Yes, thank you, and excuse me," Margaret said, nodding to all the players.

A young gentleman who'd just arrived in town—she wasn't sure what his name was, just that he was very young—sat in her seat, glancing around eagerly at the table's occupants.

Lord Gantrey would likely win some money from him, so she couldn't feel bad about vacating her position at the table.

She walked determinedly toward where the

duke stood. He hadn't seen her, since he had his blind side to the room. She was able, then, to stare at him without embarrassment, once again appreciating his sheer masculine beauty.

She hadn't realized before—not until she'd met him, in fact—that she appreciated a large gentleman much more than a smaller-sized one. There was just something so primally appealing about wide shoulders, great height, and a broad chest. Being enfolded in his arms must feel like—well, damn, she knew what it felt like, didn't she? It hadn't happened long enough for her to itemize just how it felt.

Which just made her want it to happen again. She'd say she was shocked at herself for such improper thoughts, but she wasn't. She knew who she was, and what she wanted to do.

And what she wanted to do right now was feel what it was like to have those strong arms wrapped around her while that mouth was on hers.

But, since they were in public, and he was the most proper duke of her acquaintance (not hard, since her brother-in-law was the only other duke she knew, and he was not proper at all), there was no chance of that.

She would have to reconcile herself to just feeling what it was like to dance with him.

"Your Grace?"

He started at her voice, then turned to regard her. There was something different about him now; something warmer. As though he weren't first thinking of what he should be doing. Perhaps thinking of something he'd like to be doing.

Was that why he had asked her to dance? Because she knew, even if he was not fully aware, that someone like him should not be dancing with someone like her.

She gave a mental shrug, then glanced at the duke's friend. She hadn't gotten to look at him too closely when she first saw him, at the duke's house; he'd removed himself too quickly. And, she had to admit, she was so irate she hadn't taken notice of her surroundings.

If the duke looked like an autocratic pirate, his friend looked as though he were the rakish ship's mate, the one who delivered all the pirate captain's orders, and then frolicked on shore with the ladies who couldn't resist a dashing pirate.

"Lady Margaret, may I present Mr. James Archer. Mr. Archer, this is Lady Margaret Sawford."

Warm fingers, warm even through his gloves, closed over hers, and a pair of mischievous blue eyes met hers. "I am delighted to make your acquaintance, Lady Margaret."

"Thank you," she said. His expression seemed to indicate that the duke had spoken to him about her, and she wondered just what he had said—that she had execrable taste in art, that she insisted on venturing into less savory parts of London, that— that he had kissed her.

He wouldn't have told her friend that, would he?

She wouldn't have thought so, but on the other hand, the gentleman was looking at her as though he knew something. Hopefully he just looked at everyone like that.

"The dance is beginning, Lady Margaret. Shall we?" The duke held his arm out, and Margaret curled her fingers around it, hoping she didn't audibly gasp at the strength she felt.

Thankfully, it was a waltz. Because if she was going to dance where she seldom danced, and dance with him, no less, of course it had to be a waltz.

A lesser dance—the quadrille or the schottische, for example—would have meant she spent less time in his arms, which would be . . . less optimal.

The music began, and he drew her into his arms, his hand at her waist, the other hand holding hers.

At first he didn't speak. He kept his gaze locked on her face, however, and she felt as though his expression was communicating something, if she could just figure out what it was.

He would make an excellent cardplayer.

"I do not dance often." That stiff voice again, only she didn't dislike it as much. It seemed as though his words were being pulled out of him, as though he didn't quite know how to converse all the time.

Perhaps she should write his dialogue after all.

"Neither do I," she replied. She glanced over his shoulder at all the whirling couples on the dance floor with them, ladies with enormous skirts that looked as though they were being tossed about by windswept seas. The gentlemen, most of them with enormous mustaches, were much drabber, but no less impressive.

It was a lovely sight. Although probably she only thought that because she was on the dance floor with him.

"Do you not dance because you prefer not to?" Now he sounded as though he was worried she really didn't want to dance with him.

If she were a different type of woman, she would tease him with the possibility that she didn't like to dance, and was doing it only because she felt obligated to. Because he'd asked her. But she could never be that cruel, especially not to someone like him.

Not that she knew him as well as that sounded. Although by now she could admit that she would like to. Know him better, that is.

"I do not dance, in general, because I do not want to dance with the gentlemen who ask me." She tilted her head. "But I find I very much like to dance with you."

He smiled—a real smile, not one of those tight grimaces that she'd seen more times than she'd cared to already.

"I find I wish to dance with you, also." He raised his eyebrow. "Does that mean I am behaving too gentlemanly for your taste?" The way he said it, in that low tone, made her stomach churn and tingles run up and down her spine.

"Well," she said, thinking it might be time after all to try that flirtatious tone, "I am not sure. What would ungentlemanly-like behavior look like if we were here, and not out where you had to look all frightening?"

He smiled almost wickedly at her, and the tingles burst into full-blown shivers. Oh my.

"Let's see what I can do to make me more ungentlemanly in your eyes then. We can consider this our first adventure."

And he took his hand off her waist, keeping a tight hold on her other hand, and strode toward the terrace windows, her following along behind, her heart in her throat, and other parts of her all shivery to find out what he might do.

This was likely the most spontaneous thing he had ever done, and it was all because of her. If he hadn't met her, he'd still be standing in that ballroom, a glass of wine in his hand, wishing he weren't there.

And now he wouldn't wish to be anywhere else.

He hadn't even known he'd had the thought to request her assistance with adventuring— whatever that might entail—until the words had spilled out of him, and as he'd said it, he had felt as though it was the most true thing he had ever said.

Of course, that was after she'd told him to stop being so gentlemanly, which had made him furious in any number of ways.

He wasn't furious any longer—that had subsided as soon as they'd struck their bargain—but definitely bothered. Wanting to tell her how he felt, but he couldn't find the words. As usual.

He led her onto the terrace, then pulled her to the far end. There was a surprisingly bright moon—for London, at least—and he could see her face, lifted up to his, her dark eyes catching the light. She literally sparkled this evening, little stars caught in her hair, her gown the deep blue of a late evening sky.

She was beautiful. She was alight with who she was, confident, and lovely, and radiant. He wanted to capture some of her light, take it home with him to draw out and look at in the darkness.

He saw her throat move as she swallowed. "Well," she asked in a soft whisper, "what ungentlemanly-like behavior did you wish to show me?"

He froze, not sure just what to do. That is, he knew what he wanted to do, but also knew he absolutely should not.

A moment. Another. And then—

Then she raised her arms, slid them around her neck, and raised her face, placing her lips on his. "Show me," she murmured against his mouth.

Lasham pulled her to him, a fierce charge of emotion, and lust, and want, and need coursing through him.

He slid his palms down her back, let his hands grip her waist, drawing her body in closer to his. It wasn't enough, it could never be enough, but he allowed himself to savor this, this moment, the carnality of their mouths touching, his hands on her body, her hands—well, she had hold of his arms and was digging her fingers into his muscles as though she, too, couldn't get enough.

He didn't know that a mere kiss could be so spectacular. He wondered if it was she, or they, or just that he was tired of being reserved, and measured, and finally was allowing himself to let go.

He licked at the seam of her mouth and she opened with a sigh. His tongue made entrance, and she tangled her tongue with his, giving as well as getting, an equal partner in the kiss.

He drew her in tighter, her breasts now pressed against his body, all soft and full and wonderful.

He drew his hand up her side, just there, just below the curve of her breast, stroking his fingers on the fabric of her gown, tasting her sweet lips, touching her body, wanting her.

She had moved her hands also, now reaching into his jacket and sliding her fingers down his chest, gripping the edges of his waistcoat to bring him closer.

The thought crossed his mind that if they were closer, she might be behind him.

She made a soft humming sound, deep and low in her throat, and his cock pulsed, wanting out, wanting into her, wanting, wanting, wanting.

This was going too fast, too soon, and he didn't know if he could handle the rush of emotions, of feelings that were sweeping over him.

He broke the kiss and leaned his forehead on

the top of her head, his whole body shuddering as he gasped for air.

"That was an excellent demonstration, Your Grace," she said in a soft voice before she drew away and left him, alone and hard and wanting, on the terrace.

Feeling as though the adventure had just begun.

GEORGIANA AND THE DRAGON

By A Lady of Mystery

❧❧❧

"The dragon is mine," the princess said, still in that same flat tone. Georgiana had to wonder if the woman had any emotion at all.

"He is not," she replied heatedly. "I doubt you even know his name!"

"And you do?" the princess replied. This time, her tone was more emotional, only the emotion was one of scorn.

"I—I do not," Georgiana admitted. "But that is hardly the point. If he is yours, as you say he is, then you should know more about him than that he is a dragon, and you have just sent an arrow through him."

The princess shrugged. "I am a princess, and princesses always have dragons. There is one here, so he must be mine."

"What can I do to make you leave him alone? To let him do what he wants, in his own dragon way?"

The princess smiled. Again, it was not a warm emotion, as it would be on another person's face, but more as though it was something she had been told to do, not that she actually felt it.

"That is a good question," she said slowly.

Chapter 11

"Hello?" Margaret called, Annie shutting the door of the Agency behind them as they entered the offices.

The open room was plain, but tidy. Paperwork was filed in an open bookshelf on one wall, while there was a battered desk on another. A few chairs sat at right angles in front of the desk.

Carolyn Ames, one of the Agency's proprietors, strode in from the back room, a warm smile on her face. "Margaret, and Annie, so lovely to see you!" She clasped Margaret's hands in both of hers and held them for a moment before shaking Annie's hand.

"Good morning, Carolyn," Margaret replied. "I stopped in to see if the Banner sisters had come by?"

Carolyn gestured for the women to sit, then went and sat behind the desk. She steepled her fingers and nodded. "Yes, and we were able to place both of them nearly right away. They do excellent work, thank you for sending them along."

Carolyn was older than Margaret, in her mid-thirties perhaps, and her engaging expression and confident manner made her seem so alive. She hadn't always been so vibrant, as Margaret knew; Carolyn had been taken in, as so many young ladies were, by a smooth-tongued gentleman who deserted her when she got into trouble. The Agency was a direct result of that encounter, with Carolyn determined to help women whose pasts might make it difficult for them to find work. They didn't take just anybody; all the workers hired out by the Agency were tested and proven worthy by the Agency owners. Margaret had sent a few women to the Agency whose skills were lacking, and so they were given training before being sent out for work.

"And how are you? You look tired," Carolyn said, narrowing her gaze at Margaret.

Annie made a harrumphing sound, which Margaret ignored. She couldn't very well tell either one of them that she hadn't gotten enough sleep because she'd been lying awake thinking about that kiss, out on the terrace where anyone could have seen them.

What was he doing, being so reckless? She knew what *she* was doing; she was already ruined, a scandalous woman returned to London and living on her own, with no chaperone beyond a busybody maid and a household full of people who'd been discarded. As she had been.

But he had so much more at stake, as he'd made sure to point out to her—yes, he was a man, so he could get away with far more than she could, but there were limits to what Society would tolerate.

And being caught kissing a scandalously reckless woman on the Purseleys' terrace would definitely qualify as something that would not be tolerated. A very bad sort of adventure, in fact.

She'd relived every moment of the kiss, from how warm his mouth felt on hers, to how hard his chest felt under her fingers, to how close he'd come to touching her breast as he held her side.

She wished he had touched her breast, come to think of it. She got fairly weak-kneed just thinking about what that would feel like—his strong, capable fingers on her, caressing her flesh, making her tingle all over with each touch.

"My lady?" Carolyn's voice intruded in her salacious thoughts. Of course, now was not the time to be having said salacious thoughts. That time would be, in fact, never. She couldn't risk it happening again, not for her sake, but for his. He was clearly over his head with what was happening between them, and she knew full well he had no wish to be married to her, given his reaction the first time they'd kissed.

But on the other hand, there'd been a second time. So perhaps she should just let him make his own decisions. She didn't have to manage everyone's lives, did she? Just the unfortunate women who couldn't seem to manage their own, at least for a short period.

Thus settled, she was able to turn her attention to Carolyn and the Agency and what she could do to help.

"You going to tell me, or what?" Annie asked as they left the Agency.

Margaret sighed. The woman would not stop until she knew, would she? No doubt she would take the credit for it, since she'd ensured Margaret was as lovely as it was possible for her to be.

"Can we wait until we are home again?" Margaret gestured to the sidewalk. "It is not as though we have privacy here."

"All I want to know is when you're going to see the duke again," Annie said in an aggrieved tone. "It's not a government secret or anything, is it?"

Was it possible for a heart to sing? Because if it was, Margaret's heart was doing some sort of glissando right now. Annie didn't know what had occurred between the two of them the night before—she was just concerned with when Margaret would see the duke again.

She realized she had no clue what the duke's first name was. He was the Duke of Lasham, yes, but was he a William? A Samuel? An Aloysius? She would have to visit Isabella and look him up in *Debrett's* to find out.

Although now that she thought about it, that seemed as though she were interested. And she didn't want to admit to anyone, least of all to herself, that she was actually interested.

So his first name would remain a mystery, for now, at least.

"We didn't make another appointment for an engagement, if that is what you are asking," Margaret said in as prim a voice as she could manage. Which was not very prim. "You know I only go to those neighborhoods when I've heard there is trouble, and I haven't heard of any lately. I assume there is some—there always is," she said with a sigh, "but I don't wish to put myself into danger stupidly, just so I can rescue someone who may not wish to leave."

"So you don't know when you're seeing him again?"

Leave it to Annie to get to the gist of the matter right away. Never mind that Margaret was set on helping unfortunate women, or that it wasn't appropriate for her to be spending time nearly unattended with the duke—Annie liked him, or more to the point, liked seeing him with Margaret, and so that was the purpose of her questions.

Thank goodness she had no clue about the kiss. Margaret could just imagine how little peace she'd get if her maid had that bit of information.

She would have to be discreet for her sake as well as for his, then.

"Your Grace, the stack of papers to your left are the ones which require attending. The ones on the right are those that are most urgently in need of being attended to."

Lasham leaned back in his chair and regarded his secretary. "So you're saying that there are no papers that do not require my attention." He spoke in a flat tone. He was grateful Mr. Meecham had gotten accustomed enough, both to his manner and to his visage, that he no longer started at anything his employer might do or say.

"Yes, Your Grace. That is what I am saying."

Lasham drew the top paper off the pile and placed it on the desk in front of him.

Having frequently stated our reasons for zealously espousing the great principles of Reform . . .

"And this one is the most important of the attention-requiring ones?" he asked, scanning the rest of it quickly.

"Yes, sir. This matter is to be presented in front of the House of Lords in a few days, and I thought you should be prepared."

"Prepared for the espousal of radical ideas, am I right, Meecham?"

"Precisely so, Your Grace." Meecham was deeply opinionated on the matters concerning land, farming, and a living wage, and Lasham found his advice invaluable. His peers might want to keep things the way they were because it was more convenient for them, but Lasham definitely did not.

Which spoke to his personal affairs as well, didn't it? Although he should probably not think of the word "affair" in context of Lady Margaret. That was too tempting a scenario.

But the truth was, he wanted a change. A change in his own life, a change in others' lives, change that would mean better things for everyone.

And, he had to admit, he wanted to change the circumstance of not having seen Lady Margaret in fewer items of clothing. Perhaps he could start by unbuttoning her gloves, one tiny pearl button at a time.

And then taking his button-undoing prowess to her gown, which he would unbutton not quite as slowly.

But he definitely should not be thinking on that, not with Meecham in the room. There was only so much a secretary would tolerate for the sake of his employer; having said employer getting lost in a lust-filled haze of imagination was definitely not within the bounds.

"What is the gist of it?" Lasham waved his hand at the taller stack of papers. "Unless you want me to be sitting here reading things for the next three years, you're going to have to summarize."

"In summary, Your Grace," his secretary began, "these people will be bringing some issues concerning their livelihood to you and your peers."

"Oh, is that all?" Lasham remarked dryly. "Well, let's put that one aside and get to work on the rest. I'll review the document later, it sounds as though it is an important one."

"It is," Meecham agreed in a vehement tone of voice.

Hours later, and Lasham was finally able to say he was done with all the papers Meecham had presented. For today, at least.

Tomorrow would bring another stack of papers, no less urgent, and Lasham felt the crush of his responsibility as though it were a weight placed on top of his chest.

He'd had the weight on his chest since he was fifteen. It had been his constant companion, except when he was with Jamie, and now when he was with her.

He'd known her for only a few days, and already he wanted to know her more. More intimately, yes, he was a man, but also just know her more.

He wanted to know just what made her so brave, brave enough to tell her parents no. He wanted to know why she was so determined to help those women. Not that they shouldn't be helped, of course, but it was usually up to people like him to make a difference, not single young ladies of dubious reputation.

He wondered when he'd see her again—they hadn't arranged anything the last time they'd seen each other. But since the last time they'd seen each other had been when they had kissed, out on the Purseleys' terrace, that hadn't left a lot of opportunity for rendezvous arrangement.

There was a knock on the door, and for a brief moment, Lasham had to wonder if his very thinking about her had conjured her here.

"Your Grace?" Williams, his butler, paused just inside Lasham's study. Not her, then. The butler for whom he'd rung. Why was he so disappointed?

"Yes, thank you, Williams. I would like a cup of tea."

"Of course, Your Grace." Williams made to leave the room, but the door opened wider, showing Jamie's face, and then his entire self walked into the room.

"Not tea, Lash." He walked to the server with the glasses and brandy, picking up a bottle, unstoppering it, and then pouring it, all in one fluid motion.

"Tea, Williams." Lasham made a dismissive gesture, and his butler withdrew.

"Here." Jamie handed him a glass half full of brandy, then made himself another, much fuller glass. He flopped on the sofa next to Lasham, crossing his ankle over his knee. "I missed you at the party last night. Last thing I saw of you was you dancing with the disreputable Lady Margaret."

"Don't call her that," Lasham bit out.

"I didn't mean it. I just wanted to get a rise out of you. And I did! Cheers to me," Jamie said, holding his glass up in salute. He took a healthy swallow and shook his head. "Damn, Lash, but being a duke has its privileges. This is the finest brandy I've had on this side of the channel."

Being a duke has its privileges.

If he were free—if he were able to do what he wanted, he would go to Lady Margaret right now and make some sort of indecent proposition. About buttons, and laughter, and impropriety.

"Lash?" Jamie's voice, less lively now, intruded on his thoughts. "You don't seem like yourself." Jamie took a swig from his glass. "Not that not being like yourself is necessarily a bad thing, mind you. If you were less like yourself you'd be doing something you shouldn't be."

That Jamie had come so close to saying what was on Lasham's mind was eerie. And thought-provoking. What would she say? How would he say it? What would it mean?

"What would you do if you were doing something you shouldn't be doing?" Lasham returned, taking a sip from his glass. The brandy was fine; it slid down his throat with a warm burn.

He should resolve to drink more brandy as well, if he was making changes for the better in his life.

"I always do things I shouldn't," Jamie said with a wink. He leaned his head back against the sofa and looked up at the ceiling. "But if we are talking seriously, I would want to create something." He sat straight up and looked at Lasham. "I collect and sell antiques, and antiquities, and basically anything anybody wants to buy." He crossed his arms over his chest. "I'd like to be the creator for once."

Lasham nodded, taking another sip, a larger one this time, from his glass. The warmth was akin to what it felt like to hold her in his arms, but it was much more acceptable in his Society.

And didn't that say something about the Society in which he lived, that it was far more respectable for him to get—well, drunk as a lord—than for him to hold a lovely woman in his arms for longer than the prescribed time?

He shook his head and drained the glass, setting it on the table beside the sofa.

The door opened, startling both Jamie and Lasham.

Williams entered, holding a silver tray. Tea.

"You know, Williams," Lasham said, standing to retrieve the glass, "I don't think I will need tea this evening."

"Excellent choice, Your Grace," Jamie said in a stentorian tone. Lasham shot him a warning look, then glanced back at Williams.

"Will you need anything more, Your Grace?" Williams asked.

"No, thank you." Lasham refilled his glass. "Thank you for bringing the tea, do go ahead and have some. It shouldn't go to waste just because I find I don't want it."

Williams bowed, at least as much as he could, given that he was still holding the tray. "Certainly, Your Grace. Good evening, Your Grace."

He walked out and closed the door behind him as Lasham sat back on the sofa, cradling his glass in his hand.

"Jamie, I want to ask your advice on something."

GEORGIANA AND THE DRAGON

By A Lady of Mystery

"What—what do you want?" Georgiana asked. The dragon had stilled under her hand, and she hoped he wasn't on his way to dying. She could feel his breath, hear the soft sigh of it, but otherwise, the dragon was absolutely immobile.

The princess tilted her head. "What any princess wants, I suppose."

Georgiana rolled her eyes. "Since I am not a princess, nor have I ever met one, you are going to have to let me know what a princess wants."

The princess's expression turned grumpy. Apparently princesses did not want to be asked to clarify things.

"I want a prince."

Georgiana's heart sank.

Chapter 12

Margaret slid the letter under her breakfast plate. It had been sitting at her seat when she arrived, and she hoped Annie hadn't been in and spotted it.

Of course it was from him. It had a ducal seal, and the paper was a lovely heavy weight that made Margaret envious. She wrote on cheap, flimsy paper, because it would be far too indulgent to get the more expensive kind—not when there were other places that needed her funds, plus she wrote a lot; it felt wasteful.

But as she ran her fingers over the stock, she felt a pang of pure envy. This was what it was like to be him—to use the best paper, the kind that felt sumptuous. To be able to just send someone around with a message, not wait for the post or anything.

She swallowed and glanced around the empty room. Just in case Annie was lurking nearby. Blessedly, she was not.

She drew the envelope out, and slid her finger under the seal to undo it. The paper within was a lighter cream, and his writing—because it had to be his, she hoped he wouldn't dictate a short note to a secretary, that would be ludicrous, even for a duke—was all black slashes, as though he were under the grip of some emotion.

Well, of course he was. As was she.

That second kiss—well, that had been splendid. Far better than any of the kisses she'd ever had before, not that they were numerous, and even better than the first one she'd had with him.

Would they keep improving, if they kept on? And would she just die of bliss by the eleventh one or so?

She shook her head at her foolishness. This was not getting the note read, was it?

> *Lady Margaret:*
> *I hope you will join me at the Royal Academy to view some paintings of real people. Perhaps around three o'clock again?*
> *Yours,*
> *Lasham*

That was—short but charming. Perhaps the opposite of him, since he was nothing but tall and somewhat brusque and, now that she knew him better, awkward.

It warmed her heart, that he'd been thoughtful enough to think about what she might be interested in seeing.

Even if what she was really interested in seeing was more of the duke. In many ways.

She shook her head at herself again. She really had to stop being so—well, so *lustful* when it came to him. She'd never viewed anyone with so much interest before, and it was aggravating, since it occupied perhaps a tenth of her brain at all times, and she knew full well that tenth would probably be put to better use with thinking about her next bit of writing, or how she could help more people who needed it, or anything but what he might look like with his clothing off.

It was hopeless. That seemed to be what she was set on thinking about.

She was just beginning to ponder if he would or would not have hair on his chest when the door opened. Annie bustled in, and Margaret quickly slid the note under the plate again.

Unfortunately for her, Annie's eyes were as sharp as her wit. "You got something from him, then?"

Why did Margaret even bother trying to keep a secret? And why wasn't Annie the one out there playing cards, when clearly she could ferret out any kind of mystery?

"Yes, I did." Margaret withdrew it from under the plate. She brushed a few toast crumbs off the parchment. "He's asked if we can meet at the Royal Academy again today."

Annie rolled her eyes and made a harrumphing sound at the same time. Her lady's maid was remarkably skilled. "More of those paintings, no thank you." Her eyes sparkled with mischief. "Of course I'll be waiting in the carriage, so you'll be alone with him."

"In a public place, Annie," Margaret returned dryly. At least she hoped neither one of them would get so swept away by their—whatever they were feeling—that they would make a kissing spectacle of themselves out in public.

Although that did sound rather fun, and exactly the opposite of what the duke would ever do. Just imagining his face if she even mentioned it was enough to make her laugh.

She was there early, of course. She spotted his carriage as she descended from hers. He was early also. That shouldn't have made her all warm inside, but it did.

She strode up the steps to the academy, her heart beating just a bit faster in anticipation of seeing him again. It was ridiculous that she had barely met him, and yet had this reaction to him.

It was just a momentary fascination, she reassured herself. *Just wait until you've known him for a month or more, his intrinsic dullness will trump whatever you think you see in him.*

Only a part of her—probably that part that was interested in seeing him unclothed—wondered if she would be even more fascinated the longer she knew him.

She walked into the building and spotted him right away. Her chest tightened, her breath caught, and she wanted to run right up to him and fling her arms around his neck.

Oh dear. She was in so much trouble.

"Lady Margaret." Lasham exhaled as she walked toward him, a wide smile on her face. How could she just demonstrate her emotion so—so exuberantly? He envied it, as he envied how she seemed to be able to act on what she wanted to do, and speak what she wanted to say.

"Good afternoon, Your Grace." Her brown eyes, like the rest of her, sparkled. "You promised to show me some people today, I believe?" She hooked her arm through his. "Shall we?"

Lasham nodded and began to walk, acutely conscious of her fingers on his forearm, her skirts brushing against his legs.

"It was very thoughtful of you to find paintings with figures in them." She laughed. "Although perhaps it is not so thoughtful as an act of self-preservation, given how derisive I was about those nonpeopled paintings."

"You weren't." He stumbled over his words, as usual. "That is, you expressed your opinion, and I expressed mine. That is how you think things should be, do you not? With people saying what they mean, and what they want, and all of that?"

What would you do if you could do anything you wanted?

"That is what I think." She sounded surprised. At what? That she'd thought those things? That he'd noticed?

"And I thought"—*oh, Jamie, I hope you are right*—"that it would be pleasant for both of us to view art together."

"View art?" she repeated, and he could tell she wasn't thinking about anything as innocuous as viewing art at all, but that other thing. The kiss.

"Yes, exactly." He tried to keep his voice as neutral as possible—he'd seen how she reacted when he withdrew, and he didn't want to do that with her, make her get that disappointed expression on her face.

"You are right, Your Grace," she said in a more natural tone of voice. "It would be pleasant for us to view art together. It is excellent that you thought of it." A pause. "It will be an adventure."

Something within him eased when he heard her words, as though a string had loosened, one he hadn't known was pulled tightly inside.

They walked to the gallery Lasham had been to only a few times—since, as he'd told her, he much preferred landscape paintings. Seeing people, even on canvas, far too often reminded him that he wasn't comfortable looking at people, and more importantly, that they weren't comfortable looking at him.

They walked into the room, a wide-open gallery with paintings hung one on top of the other, faces just staring out from their canvases. At him.

Which was a remarkably solipsistic thing for him to think, no matter who he was. These people were likely impressed with their own importance, what with having sat for a portrait and all, and were not concerned with impressing a duke who had but one eye to his name and a wealth of discomfort in the presence of others.

"Oh, she looks like fun, doesn't she?" Lady Margaret said, disengaging herself from his arm and going to stand in front of a painting. Lasham walked up behind her, noting how even her clothing was vibrant—he'd seen in her in a few shades of blue before, but today she wore green, the verdant green of the stalk of a crocus newly emerging from the cold earth after a long winter. As exuberant, as optimistic, and as wonderful to see as the brightest ray of sunshine.

If nothing else, his imagination was being awakened.

And thankfully, her bonnet was less grandiose than it had been the other time here, so he could see her lively face. He wished it were possible for her just to remove it entirely, but that was perhaps too shocking even for her.

"She does look like fun," Lasham said, only his gaze was on her, not the painting, and he smiled to share the compliment with her.

And then—then she blushed, but didn't look away from his gaze. Something in her eyes softened, and for a moment it seemed as though she were going to lift her head up to be kissed again, only of course they were in public, not to mention the hundreds of eyes gazing down at them from the walls.

"Thank you," she said in a soft voice, not bothering to pretend she hadn't understood. He found that so refreshing in her, that she could just understand things and then respond appropriately.

Too many people pretended ignorance if it meant they would have to do something unpleasant, or if they were being coy. Not her. She was as wide-open about who she was as—well, as he was not.

He turned to look at the fun woman, and had to smile—the woman in the portrait did indeed look as though she had a wonderful joke she was dying to share. Her lips were curved into an irrepressible smile, her eyes crinkled at the corners as though she were smothering a laugh.

She sat at a table, a book and a glass of wine in front of her, and the scene was so cozy and so precisely what Lasham wished for himself that he couldn't help but utter a groan of want. Of wanting.

"Did you just moan?" Lady Margaret asked, raising one delightfully arched eyebrow. Her expression mirrored the portrait lady's, her lips quirked up into a grin, her brown eyes sparkling.

"I—I might have," Lasham replied. He rubbed his jaw. "If I did, it was entirely unconscious, I assure you."

"Why?" She tilted her head and regarded him with frank curiosity.

He gestured to the portrait. "She just looks so pleased with herself and with her life. I think I have to say I am envious of her."

She didn't laugh, not as Jamie would have laughed to hear him say anything that would imply his situation was less than ideal. Because he knew full well it was ideal, ideal for someone, just not for him.

But since he was the one who had it, he knew he would make the best of it. As he'd always done. As he would continue to do.

"Perhaps she has a partner in adventure," she said in a whisper, one that shot straight to his groin. And his brain, but also his groin.

He concentrated on the brain part of the reaction. "I wonder if she has just eaten far too many ices." He frowned in thought. "Although I don't think they had ices then, did they?"

"They had the sixteenth-century equivalent, then." She leaned closer in to him, and her fresh, delightful scent tickled his nose. "It is easy to think of our ancestors as being dull as sticks, but they lived as we do. They laughed, and loved, and ate too much roasted rabbit, or whatever, and drank too much mead and likely didn't always keep their silly clothing on."

Lasham chuckled. "And here I thought my predecessors were all as proper and dull as I am."

She tilted her face up and glared at him. "You are not dull, Your Grace." Her expression eased. "You might be a bit . . . proper, but you are not dull, I assure you."

It would be disingenuous to ask himself why that warmed him so much.

She continued, "It is just that you should intersperse all the correct things with some things that are not *not* correct, if you know what I mean, but are more fun. Like an adventure," she said with a complicit look.

Now he had to shake his head for a different reason. "Not not correct? Perhaps I won't ask you to write my dialogue after all."

She chuckled. "I can see why. Not not correct is not a very good way to put it, is it." She rolled her eyes at herself. "Continue to do all the things you should, and add in things you would. That is all. Is that clearer?" she asked in a concerned voice.

"It is." He took her arm and walked to stand in

front of another painting. This one was much less fun, but no less interesting. It depicted a gentleman of some years standing in front of a horse wearing clothing from a hundred years previous, a proud expression on his heavy features.

"He appears to be inordinately pleased with himself for something, doesn't he?" she asked. She kept her arm in his. He felt his throat tighten at her nearness.

"He does seem to be one of those men who believes he has done everything right in the world, and no one would dare tell him otherwise." Lasham looked more closely at the portrait. "Although I believe I would have to quibble with his facial hair." He drew back. "He looks like a walrus."

She burst out laughing and clapped her hand over her mouth. "He does, doesn't he? So many men look just like that, I am so glad you do not have any kind of fuss on your face." She tapped her finger on her lips. "But why don't you? I mean, you do everything that is correct, and current men's fashion dictates that you have some sort of growth. Why don't you?"

He ran his hand over his jaw again, feeling the day's stubble under his palm. "I thought that with this going on already"—he gestured to his eye patch—"that having more on my face would be too distracting. I have enough people either staring rudely or looking away in shock to want to add another element there."

She seemed to be absorbing what he'd said,

processing it through what he surmised was her remarkable brain. "I know what that is like." She grimaced. "That is, not as much as you, obviously, but when my scandal first appeared, it seemed as though people either wanted to stare at me, or definitely not even look in my direction. Plus my sister is a duchess, and she is always getting stared at." She shivered. "No wonder you try to keep yourself from enduring that kind of scrutiny." She glanced around, then raised her gloved fingers to his face. Then glared at her hand and dropped it, removing her glove and bringing her ungloved fingers to his face. "I like how it feels far better than if you had something there."

He looked around, too, panicking that they would be seen, that there would be a scandal, that he would have to marry her, when she so obviously did not want that. Thankfully no one was in their room, and so he raised his own hand and placed it on top of hers.

"I like how it feels when you do that," he said in a low murmur, his entire body feeling as though it had been infused with energy.

"I do, too," she whispered, and he leaned to her, almost unconsciously so, his gaze fixed on her mouth.

Her lips lifted slightly, but she put her fingers on his mouth. "Not here, not where anyone could see." A moment as she thought. "Why don't you escort me home, Your Grace?"

"Didn't you arrive in your own—oh!" Lasham said, feeling as though he were possibly the slowest-thinking man in England. "Yes, I would be happy to."

He nodded to the gentleman in the portrait, made sure she was holding his arm, and walked swiftly to the exit.

GEORGIANA AND THE DRAGON

By A Lady of Mystery

"Where do you suppose I will be able to find a prince?" Georgiana asked. She waved her hand in the air. *"It is not as though one is always tripping over them or something."*

The princess shrugged. *"You asked what it would take, and I answered."* She crossed her arms over her chest. *"I want a prince. I suggest you go find one before the dragon dies."*

Georgiana wanted to hit the princess, but that would only get her into more trouble. *"Will you stay with him and get him water and make sure he doesn't die?"*

How she could trust this woman to do anything, she wasn't sure, but she knew that if she didn't do something to help, the dragon would die. And it would be her fault.

The princess considered. *"I will, provided you return with a prince within twenty-four hours."*

Georgiana blew out an exasperated breath. *"Of course you would have to give me a deadline,"* she said in an aggrieved tone.

"It wouldn't be any fun if there weren't one, would it?" the princess asked.

"I suppose not," Georgiana replied in a grumpy voice.

Chapter 13

She had really just suggested something so shocking. She knew she was scandalous, but she hadn't actually *performed* scandal that often before—besides spurning the man whom she didn't want, and who didn't want her, the most shocking thing she'd done was set pen to paper.

And that activity did not involve another person, a mad dash to a carriage, and the potential for some kissing.

But oh, she couldn't regret it. He knew how she felt, and what she expected of him, and vice versa, and so anything that happened now would just be—enjoyable.

He was walking so quickly she had some difficulty keeping up with him, but she did, nearly breaking into a run to keep up with his long-legged stride. She wouldn't have asked him to slow down, not when she was also so interested in reaching their destination.

Where something would happen. Something shocking, and scandalous, and that would involve skin. She appreciated the alliteration, even in the throes of committing some shockingly scandalous sin. Of some sort.

She couldn't slow down enough to laugh at herself, but she was feeling rather clever at the moment.

Clever and desirous, and desired, and intrigued, and all sorts of things a young single woman in the company of a not so proper duke after all should not be feeling. And yet, she was.

They left the building and descended the steps, the duke's enormous and impressive carriage right in front of them, Margaret's less grand carriage at the far end. She darted a glance at it, then reluctantly disengaged from the duke's arm. "I'll just go tell them to go home without me," she said. "It would be so impolite just to leave them here while you drive me home."

"I wouldn't have thought of that," the duke replied. "Should I escort you?"

Margaret was shaking her head even before he'd finished his sentence. "No, I don't want—that is, no. I'll return in just a moment."

He nodded, and she scurried down the street.

"Annie!" Margaret opened the door to the carriage before her coachman could descend from his seat. She poked her head into the interior and smothered a giggle as Annie woke from what appeared to be a sound nap.

"What? What is it?" Annie said, blinking.

"The duke is driving me home in his carriage, and so I want you two to return home without me."

That woke her maid up. "Driving you home? What a lovely idea, so grand for the duke to have thought of it."

Margaret didn't inform her maid that it was she who'd thought of it. The woman wanted things for her mistress, but she likely wouldn't approve of how forward she was being. Of how forward she was about to be, in fact.

"Yes, isn't it?" She smiled brightly, at which point Annie's eyes narrowed. Oh dear. She tried to dim her smile, so her maid wouldn't know she was planning on something entirely nefarious and delightful.

"I will see you at home shortly then," she said, giving a brisk nod before turning back to walk down the street to the duke's carriage. Walking very quickly, in fact, so that Annie wouldn't come barreling after her, determined to know what her mistress's intentions were toward the duke.

Because Margaret could safely say that they were entirely unrespectable. Whether he had the same intentions, she would be finding out shortly.

He stood holding the door to the carriage open, looking so entirely large, and gorgeous, and dangerous, that it gave her a chill. And determination.

"Can you drive me using the St. James's Park route?" she asked, conscious that his coachman was likely within earshot.

He frowned in confusion. "But that is in the opposite—oh!" he said, his expression clearing as he realized what she was saying. "Yes, excellent. I have been wanting to see some, uh, flowers," he added awkwardly. He looked as though he wanted to say something else, but just ended up shaking his head and glancing upward, as though he were exasperated with himself.

She thought he was rather adorable, if one could be adorable being over six feet in height with an eye patch and an occasionally intimidating manner.

"That's settled then," Margaret said, taking his hand as she got into the carriage. He gave instructions to his coachman, then vaulted up to sit beside her. Her insides got all quivery.

As was appropriate when one was in an enclosed carriage with a Piratical Duke.

The carriage was more than spacious enough for the two of them, but it did seem as though he were everywhere. His presence imbued the air, made her feel as though she were breathless, but in an entirely delicious way.

"Your Grace, I know this is—this is untoward," she said, gesturing vaguely in the air.

"Yes," he bit out.

"But I know you feel as I do, and a more permanent attachment isn't desirable." She paused, then took a deep breath and spoke before she could consider what she was about to say. Because she really wanted to say it, only she knew she shouldn't.

"But even so, it seems that there is something less permanent that would be . . . pleasant," she said, using the same word that he had when talking about viewing art together.

Only she wasn't talking about viewing art now, was she? This was something else, something so shocking even she couldn't believe she was suggesting it. And yet what was the point of being scandalously ruined if one couldn't enjoy it?

The duke didn't speak for a moment, and she wondered if he would just stop the carriage and toss her out onto the street for being so forward. For being so like her.

And then he turned to her, the intensity of his gaze making her shiver even more.

"Yes, Lady Margaret. That is a very pleasant idea," he said, before gathering her in his arms and placing his mouth on hers.

Her mouth was so warm, Lasham felt as though he'd been scorched as soon as he kissed her. That fire spread throughout his entire body until he felt enveloped in it, enveloped by her, her sparkle, her warmth of spirit, her beauty, and her humor.

It wouldn't have been the same if it weren't she—he had kissed enough women in the past to know the difference, and for a brief moment, he wondered if he would ever be able to enjoy kissing another woman again.

But he wouldn't think about any of that, not right now, not when her lips were opening, her tongue slipping into his mouth, her hands around his neck, her fingers in his hair.

And she was kissing him just as thoroughly as he was kissing her. As though she had an equal partnership in the kiss. Which she did; she'd asked for it, had wanted him, even though this situation was entirely inappropriate and improper and everything else he'd never been.

And why hadn't he done anything like this ever before?

Of course. The stakes were too high, the reward too low, only this, this risk was well worth whatever might happen. Because he had his palms on her arms, holding her to him, their bodies twisted in the seat but somehow connecting in all—well, most—of the places he wished to touch her.

His hand had somehow made it to her waist, and he gripped her tightly, feeling the soft curves of her underneath all her layers. Or so he imagined; it was difficult to feel just what was Margaret and what was fabric, only his now quite lively imagination knew that somewhere there was her body, and that was enough to make him harden and long for the chance to see her, to touch her as she deserved to be touched, with passion, and caring, and desire.

She had withdrawn her hands from around his neck and had placed them on his side as well, stroking up and down underneath his coat, close, but not close enough.

He broke the kiss and put his hands to his waistcoat, undoing the buttons as swiftly as he ever had, yanking his shirt from where it was tucked into his trousers, pulling it out so she—if she wanted—could place her hands directly onto his skin.

Oh, how he hoped she wanted to. He craved the contact, wanted to feel her fingers on him, to caress his skin, to honor his body with her touch.

She smiled, a joyfully wicked grin on her face, then slid her fingers under his shirt and ran them over his bare skin. "Just a bit of hair," she said in a low murmur as her fingers traversed his chest.

He couldn't help but gasp. She kept looking at him as she explored every inch of skin she could reach. His erect cock strained against the front of his trousers, but his shirt hung over so it was unlikely that she would notice.

Not that he would mind if she noticed; he was far past that kind of embarrassment, and he thought he knew her well enough to know that she wouldn't be embarrassed, either. Likely amused, or pleased, or curious. But not embarrassed.

She shifted in the seat so she was facing him more directly, then lifted her face to his in a clear signal.

And he kissed her again, drawing her tight against his body, relishing how her hands were touching him, enjoying the small noises she was making in the back of her throat.

This was very pleasant indeed, he thought with a rare burst of humor. This was definitely the most pleasant carriage ride he'd ever had.

My goodness, but when the duke was intent on something, he was absolutely and totally intent. The first two times they'd kissed, well that had been lovely, of course, but nothing in comparison to this. That first time he was likely just overset with emotion, and needed to show what he was feeling. The second time was on the terrace, and she'd tempted him into it, but this—this, when he knew full well what he was doing, and they were doing it together, and he was taking the lead, at least in terms of clothing removal, well—it was stupendous. And she was delighted that he had decided that it was crucial that she be able to feel her fingers on his skin, since she had just been thinking the exact same thing.

His chest felt as magnificent as she had imagined, and she wished she could peer under his shirt and take a good look as well. He was all ridges and muscles and firm skin with an intriguing trail of hair that led to where she knew things got even more intriguing.

She could tell he liked what she was doing also—not just because he was murmuring the occasional moan into her mouth, but because of the way he was moving his body, as though he wished he could be even closer, even though they were as close as two people could be to each other in a moving carriage with clothing on.

That thought brought a whole new range of possibilities to Margaret's vivid imagination. But if she thought too hard about all of that, she wouldn't be able to enjoy all of this, and she really, really wanted to.

So she told her imagination to wander away for a while, just for the time when she was kissing the most gloriously handsome, and handsomely rakish, man of her acquaintance and had the added bonus of having her bare hands on his bare skin.

"Mmph," she murmured, reaching around him to

the small of his back, which wasn't small at all, but just as large and solid and hard as the rest of him.

Goodness, men and women were really quite different in many more ways than she had even suspected. Her imagination had definitely not prepared her for what it might feel like to touch someone like him, nor had it even imagined that her breasts would feel full, her nipples would harden, and other parts of her would just ache with some sort of nameless longing.

They kissed for another few minutes, then the carriage slowed, and they pulled apart, not guiltily, but with the awareness that this—whatever this was—would by necessity (and carriage travel time) be over.

The duke's gaze was still intent on her, and she could see his eyelid droop over his eye, heavy-lidded with something she knew had to do with her.

That felt nearly as wonderful as the kiss itself, that she could have such an effect on him. On him, the owner of the driest, most bombastic tone in existence, to be so stirred up by the scandalous Lady Margaret.

And she had to admit he had stirred her as well. "I had no idea," she began, then shook her head, placing her fingers on her swollen mouth.

"No idea what?" he said in a ragged whisper. He was all disheveled, his shirt still untucked, his waistcoat hanging open, his usually immaculate hair rumpled where she—*she!*—had rumpled it.

"That it—that this—" She made an ineffectual gesture in the carriage.

One corner of his mouth quirked up. "Oh, so you're saying this doesn't just happen all the time to you?"

She wrinkled her nose at him. "No, Your Grace, it doesn't." She leaned forward and gave him another kiss, this one a soft one, just because his mouth was over there and hers was here, and she didn't like the distance. "What's your given name, anyway?" she asked in a whisper.

She could have sworn he closed his eye for a moment, as though embarrassed. "You don't know already?"

"No, I don't." She sniffed in mock disdain. "It is not as though I went through *Debrett's* just as soon as we met"—*even though I was tempted to*— "and you are just referred to as Your Grace, not Lord James or Lord Michael or Lord Aloysius. It isn't Aloysius, is it?" she asked hopefully.

He scrubbed his hand over his face, and then she knew that earlier look was embarrassment.

"Is it Mortimer?" she said softly. She picked up his hand and threaded her fingers through his. "Archibald? Silas?" Silence. "Uriah?"

"Vortigern." His voice was so low she wasn't certain she had heard it correctly.

"Pardon?"

He cleared his throat and dropped her hand. "Vortigern," he said in a louder tone.

She felt her eyes widen and the laughter start, and she tried her best not to laugh, but he was over there looking all rueful and sheepish, as though it were his fault he had a ridiculous-sounding name, and she wanted to poke him and tell him he could let himself relax every so often, it was only a name, and a title, and a position in Society.

In which case, no wonder he couldn't relax. No wonder he'd welcomed this interlude; it wasn't real, none of it was real, they would exit the carriage, and their lives would go on as before, and they would continue being acquaintances, because she knew that if she allowed it to happen again, she—and her heart—would be in so much trouble, because he could not be involved with her. He'd said as much, so had she, and they had agreed.

If only that didn't make her feel so forlorn, as though she'd found something wonderful and secret, only if the secret got out it wouldn't be wonderful, and it wouldn't be possible to keep it a secret, and so it all had to stop being wonderful right now. Before it wasn't.

"It means warlord. My father read history at Oxford, and Vortigern was some sort of leader in Wales many centuries ago. He thought it would shape me into who I needed to be. It is a stupid name, isn't it?" the duke said, apparently not realizing she was mourning the loss of whatever moment this was, and still focusing on his name.

"It is not a stupid name," she replied fiercely, reaching up to touch his cheek, again, as she had before, and as she wanted to all the time now, now that she knew there was a hint of stubble, and the hard planes of his face, and the softness of his lips.

That last bit she couldn't think too much on, or she would start to behave inappropriately again. And the carriage had definitely slowed, so she would be getting out soon and couldn't act inappropriately at all—at least not with him—ever again.

"Thank you," he replied, turning his mouth into the palm of her hand and kissing it.

Finally the coach stopped, and the door swung open, and she stepped down, giving him one last look as she left.

"Good night, Vortigern," she said softly.

"Good night, Lady Margaret," he replied, his voice huskier than usual.

GEORGIANA AND THE DRAGON

By A Lady of Mystery

Georgiana trudged through the forest, wondering just how she'd gotten herself into this situation.

Never mind. That wasn't worth thinking about. The concern was how she was going to get herself out of it.

She had to locate a prince, persuade him to return with her to the middle of the forest, and introduce him to the princess who wanted him.

The princess who wasn't shy about using her bow and arrow on someone who might not please her.

Georgiana froze, took a deep breath, and turned back around.

Chapter 14

She had been thoroughly, completely, and wonderfully kissed.

That wasn't entirely unexpected, of course, given how she'd been assessing him, and his gorgeous face and body, and they'd already kissed, but she hadn't been prepared for just how wonderful it was when he could put his full attention to it.

Was he remarkably skilled at it, or was it just because it was he? Either way, she had been unprepared for just how amazing it was. And she rather worried it was both that he was skilled and that it was he.

No wonder people liked to do it so often. She was surprised that people didn't do it more; after all, she'd only ever seen other people kiss when she turned a corner in her sister's house, surprising her sister and her husband in some sort of embrace.

She hadn't seen people just randomly kissing other people on the street, and given how it felt, that gave her much more respect for her fellow human beings. Because if there was that much pleasure out there, and people knew about it, it must take remarkable restraint not to engage it more frequently.

It was how Annie felt about plum pudding at Christmas. No pudding was safe during that time, and it had gotten to where they kept them locked up so Annie wouldn't devour all of them before the holiday itself.

But the duke was far more than a pudding. And it wasn't as though she could lock him away so she wouldn't eat him up.

Although that was an intriguing thought in and of itself.

She couldn't think about that. What she had to think about was her latest serial—she was seated at her desk, pen in hand, paper on surface, and no words were coming. None at all. Because all the words she had buzzing in her brain were things like "mouth," and "chest" and "arms" and "delicious."

Not appropriate for what she was writing. Not even appropriate thinking, not for a proper young lady, but thank goodness she was scandalously improper, because she just couldn't stop thinking about it all. About him.

She shook her head briskly, trying to shoo the images she had of her day—him drawing up his shirt, clearly desperate for her to touch him, him looking so uncertain when he told her his name. Him kissing her with a passion so definite it was almost tangible.

She shivered as she thought about it, clearly not doing a very good job of pushing the images away.

"You getting a cold?" Annie said, pausing to glare at Margaret, a stack of linen in her hand.

It had been nearly two hours since she'd arrived home, and she had a deadline, and all she had been able to write was the title of the serial and her byline. She didn't think her editor would accept that for publication. Because if he did, she'd been wasting much of her time before this.

"I am not getting a cold," Margaret replied in a peevish voice. "I never am, even though you ask me constantly. And even if I were, I still need to finish this, and I am not finishing it."

"Too distracted, are you?" Annie said in a knowing tone.

Margaret hoped she didn't know everything.

"Distracted? Of course not," Margaret replied. Even to herself, she sounded brittle and forced. Something Annie would be able to pick up on right away.

"Of course you are," Annie replied with satisfaction. "And who could blame you, with that duke squiring you home." She shifted the linen onto her hip. "And what did happen when the two of you were all alone?"

He kissed me, I kissed him, and I can now say I know that he has hair on his chest.

But of course she couldn't tell Annie that, even if her maid would no doubt also be delighted. Not nearly as delighted as Margaret was, but still rather pleased. It felt too—too new, too precious, to share with anyone, even a trusted friend. No wonder her sister hadn't wanted to tell her anything. It was all too much, and to try to explain it would take a better writer than Margaret was to do it.

She stared down at the blank paper—well, blank except for a few words—and tried to concentrate on her story, knowing she could at least write what would happen to her heroine and her dragon, even if she didn't have the slightest clue about her own life.

If only she could write her own life. Although she wasn't at all certain what she wished for.

A few days later, Margaret had successfully written not one but three installments of her serial, placed the Banner sisters in full-time positions, visited with her sister and niece, won a fair bit of money at a card party at Lord Gantrey's, and gone over her accounts to gauge just how much she needed for the next six months.

She did not contact the duke. Nor did she go anywhere where she might see him. She didn't visit the neighborhoods she had promised she wouldn't visit without him, and she hadn't sent any kind of suggestion for where they could go adventuring. She hadn't even gone out to social events where she might run into him.

And that bothered her, quite a lot. Nearly as much as it bothered Annie. As Annie's question proved.

"What are you doing, hiding away from him like that?"

Margaret had just finished her breakfast, eating without quite realizing she was eating, too engrossed in not thinking about him, not at all, to pay attention. A stack of letters lay to her right, but none had his distinctive handwriting, and she wasn't certain she would be able to comprehend what was said, given her current state of mind.

Margaret shrugged, unwilling to pretend any longer she wasn't doing precisely that. And why was she, anyway?

"I don't know," she replied, her voice sounding hesitant, nearly fragile. She never sounded that way.

There is a first time for everything, a voice said in her head, *from the most divine kiss ever to hiding out because you're cowardly.*

I am not cowardly, another voice said in a forceful way.

Am too.

"Well, it seems to me that you should just go find him and settle whatever it is you have to settle. You never did tell me what happened the last time you saw him," Annie said with a significant sniff.

"It sounds so simple, when you say it," Margaret replied.

Annie picked up Margaret's breakfast dishes— not that Margaret didn't have staff to clear the table, but Annie always found occasions to do things and fuss around Margaret, even though that wasn't her job. The clearing the table, not the fussing part. The fussing part was absolutely Annie's job.

"It is simple." Annie let out an exasperated sigh and raised her eyes to the ceiling as though having lost patience. No doubt she had. "What is the alternative? You hide out here forever?" She tsked. "The Lady Margaret I know wouldn't be so craven."

Oh, that smarted. More so because it was true.

She was being craven. But she was also being protective—she was a good enough writer to forecast what was very likely to happen: She would see him again, she would find herself filled with inappropriate thoughts for him, she might even act upon them, she would get to know him, and then she would eventually fall in love with him, which would even more eventually lead to a broken heart.

She should just cut it off now, while her heart was still intact. No matter how wonderful it had felt to be held in his strong arms, and feel the warmth and strength of his chest under her fingers, and how he'd kissed her as though he were showing her how he felt, since she knew well he couldn't say anything aloud. Not just because that would lead to other discussions involving marriage and lifetime and things neither one of them wanted, but just because she knew by now he wasn't always able to find the words.

But he certainly was able to find the actions.

Goodness, how he had found the actions.

She stood so abruptly and awkwardly she slammed her hip into the breakfast table. She had not accounted for the weak knees engendered by her current thoughts. "I need to go work," she told

Annie. "And can you go through the invitations and see what event might be the one I am most likely to see him at this evening? And then lay out my yellow gown."

Annie nodded in satisfaction. "Yes, my lady. If I may say so—"

"And when has that ever stopped you," Margaret cut in.

"—you are acting more like yourself," Annie finished.

"Thank you, Annie."

Good evening, Your Grace.

Margaret regarded the words on the paper. That was a reasonable start.

"Good evening, Lady Margaret," she said aloud, deepening her voice to mimic the duke's tone.

That would also likely be what would be said.

"Your Grace, might I speak with you in private?"

And he would probably regard her with horror, since it had been a week since they'd seen each other, and what if he was mortified at having behaved so, and was glad to be rid of her presence?

Maybe not in private then. "Your Grace, might I speak with you?" Which was asinine, since by saying the words to him she was speaking to him, but hopefully he wouldn't point out how redundant she was being.

"Yes, of course, Lady Margaret." And he would just look at her, waiting. Because that was what he did. And she would have to figure out what to say.

Margaret swallowed and laid the pen down. "Your Grace, I wish to relieve you of your duties toward my forays into the disreputable neighborhoods. I do recognize I require some protection, and so I have"—and at this Margaret frowned, because she would have to have an alternate plan, "I have hired the services of a Bow Street Runner to accompany me." It would be an additional expense, but it would be worth it, if she were able to rid herself of this inconvenient obsession. Of the possibility that he would have to say something along the same lines, later on, when Margaret's heart was inextricably engaged.

And then he would bow, to acknowledge his understanding, and then she would go find an enormous glass of wine somewhere.

She picked the pen back up and wrote it all down, changing a word or two, saying it aloud a few more times to ensure it sounded reasonable.

All the while wondering if she was being cowardly, or making the biggest mistake of her life, or frightened of her own feelings, or making more of the situation than it was.

Or all of it.

"Could I ring for tea, Your Grace?" Meecham sounded almost desperate. Lasham looked up from his desk at his secretary.

"Certainly, yes." He rubbed his temple between his thumb and forefinger. "What time is it, anyway?"

"Nearly five o'clock, Your Grace."

Five o'clock. So he'd been sitting here in this chair for nearly six hours. As he had the day before that. And the day before that. For a week after the last time he'd seen her, when he'd kissed her, and wanted her to touch him, and told her his name, and she hadn't laughed at him.

And he still hadn't been able to get her out of his mind.

"Go ahead and order tea, Meecham. It will be good to have a break." He would have laughed at the relief on his secretary's face if he had had an iota of laughter in him.

What was he doing, anyway? It wasn't as though he could forget. Not that he wanted to forget. Not that he didn't want to do it all again, and more.

It was just—it felt too real, too close to an emotion, too close to making him wonder if he let go here if he would just let go everywhere, and he couldn't have that. And more than that was that she hadn't sent him a note, or anything, nothing to indicate that she was interested in having him continue to escort her anywhere, much less engage in adventuring.

Although if he did find out she'd headed to those places by herself, he'd be livid. He would take several afternoons' worth of awkward silence over having her be in danger.

But he trusted her enough to know that if she had promised she wouldn't go there without him that she wouldn't. And now he started every time he heard the door open, or the low murmur of his butler speaking with someone, or when he received letters in an unfamiliar hand.

Given that he had an enormous household filled with staff and his duties required correspondence and there was always bustling going on somewhere, he started frequently.

Eventually he'd just been forced to immerse himself so thoroughly in his work that he neither thought nor started, hoping to banish all that unwanted emotion. All that unwanted . . . want.

And it wasn't working. Not at all.

He was getting a lot done, however, so perhaps there was something to be said for trying to push away an obsession.

He grimaced at his foolishness and picked up the papers on his desk. More money for improvements on the land, another bill to discuss in the House of Lords, various letters from distant relatives asking for help.

All legitimately requiring his attention, and yet he couldn't stop a part of his brain from thinking about her.

It didn't seem like such a good idea after all to try to forget all about her, not when he knew she didn't expect anything of him, and that perhaps being with her could cool his ardor. Although he very much doubted that.

He'd nearly gone to the National Gallery the other morning, desperate to catch a glimpse of her, but had stopped himself at the last moment. Was he a coward? Or afraid of revealing just how much he did want to see her?

He wished she *were* here, so she could supply what he should say, if only to himself, to explain what was going on in his brain. Because he certainly couldn't figure it out, and maybe he needed the help of a writer.

Or maybe he just needed her.

Meecham returned, sitting down at his desk. "Tea will be here soon, Your Grace."

Goddamn it. He might as well go ahead and do what he wanted to, the other way was definitely not working.

"Are there any events this evening? Something for which I received an invitation?"

Meecham's eyebrows lifted, but that was his only reaction. "Yes, several, Your Grace. You had told me to decline everything," and he picked up a stack of paper, "but if you have changed your mind . . ."

"Yes, I have." Lasham leaned back in his chair, placing his palms flat on the desk. "Find which one appears to be the most well-attended, and I will go."

"Certainly," Meecham replied, looking as though he wished to ask a question, but pausing at the last moment. Good thing, too, since Lasham couldn't answer what he was going to do. Or why he was going to do it.

"Now, what do you think about this bill regarding the textile tariffs?" Lasham said, drawing the relevant paper from the stack.

If she wasn't going to find him, he was damn well going to find her. She owed him an adventure, at least.

Georgiana and the Dragon

By A Lady of Mystery

Georgiana shook her head at her own foolishness, even as she strode furiously through the forest to where the dragon lay.

How could she possibly go up against a princess? A beautiful princess armed with a bow and arrow, no less?

She was just the daughter of a blacksmith, one whose grandest triumph thus far had been to fetch water without spilling too much of it.

But if you don't, who will?

Exactly. The dragon would die, all just because he was a dragon, and the beautiful princess would triumph, and Georgiana would be haunted by the dragon's mournful tone and desolation at having been betrayed by his beautiful princess.

She stopped dead when she returned to where they were.

And launched herself at the princess, who was tugging on the arrow in the dragon's side.

Chapter 15

"The Duke of Lasham," the majordomo intoned. As usual, heads swiveled toward him, but now he wasn't as uncomfortable with the regard.

They weren't she, after all.

He scanned the crowd as he descended the staircase, knowing his usual impenetrable mien would keep most people from approaching him.

"Your Grace." It was Lady Dearwood, the head of the amateur daubists. Who met monthly, once a month.

"Good evening, Lady Dearwood." He gave her a nod, and then fell silent. He didn't have to work at being unapproachable, it just happened naturally. And when it didn't, and someone did approach him, he just fell silent and waited for them to grow more and more uncomfortable with it.

"Your Grace, the ladies and I are eager to hear your opinion on the new works hanging at the gallery. Would you be able to join us? It is perfectly respectable, I assure you," she said with a titter, putting her hand up to her mouth.

That was the last thing he wanted to be, was it? Perfectly respectable. He'd done that for over thirty years of his life, and look where that had gotten him—awkwardness in Society, a profound sense of duty, and one friend. Not much to say about a life.

There was the truth that he had helped people, many people, people who depended on the dukedom for their livelihoods. But he could continue to do all of that and still have fun, couldn't he?

He hoped so.

He bowed. "Thank you, Lady Dearwood, for the invitation. I will speak with my secretary about my engagements and see if I can manage it." Which was as oblique a refusal as he could muster.

It seemed the lady did not speak Oblique Duke. She positively beamed at him. "Wonderful! We meet next Wednesday at ten o'clock."

He bowed again. Still not speaking.

She blinked a few times, then patted her hair in a self-conscious motion. "And so if you will excuse me, Your Grace, I must go check on the refreshments."

Thank goodness. He didn't bother about watching Lady Dearwood make her departure, he was far too busy seeing if he could see Margaret.

And felt his heart rate speed up when he spied her.

She was literally glorious, wearing a gown that appeared to be sun-drenched, the most vivid yellow he'd ever seen, her whole presence seeming to truly sparkle.

His eyes drank her in, from the top of her lustrous brown hair to her feet, clad in cream-colored slippers with some sort of embroidery.

Spending more than the allotted time on her figure, the curve of her upper breasts showing above the gown's neckline. His mouth went dry as he realized that, depending on what would happen that night, he might actually touch her there.

Later on, when they were alone. What would her breasts feel like in his hands? How would they taste?

He took a deep breath, trying to control himself. It was one thing to be seen calmly appraising the gathering—he did that every time he went out—but to be seen regarding a lady with what was clearly desire was not to be, in fact, *desired*.

But he truly wanted to touch her, as she had touched him. She'd seemed to like what she'd felt, as well—he hadn't mistaken her soft sigh of satisfaction when her fingers trailed over his skin.

And how she had pressed her body into his as they kissed.

This was not helping him gather his control.

He swallowed and made his way to her.

She owed him an adventure, after all.

He was here, approaching her. She could feel it, even though she didn't see him. She'd heard him announced, and her chest had immediately tightened, but she hadn't turned around to see him, not yet. It would hurt to do what she knew she had to, and she didn't want to get swept up in just how damnably attractive and intriguing she found him.

"Lady Margaret." Even his voice—well, especially his voice—made her shiver.

She turned around to face him, taking a deep breath as she did.

Yes. Still remarkably handsome. And tall. And large and imposing and altogether making her feel weak-kneed. Until recently, she hadn't realized her standing was so dependent on those two somewhat knobby items.

"Good evening, Your Grace." Excellent. So far they were following what she'd written, only he spoke first, and he hadn't said good evening, so maybe not so close to what she'd written.

A tremor went through her as she realized that life, unlike her writing, was unscripted.

And they were both still here, just looking at each other, not speaking. Maybe if they never spoke she wouldn't have to say anything. Since that would be the literal embodiment of not speaking, wouldn't it?

She was so foolish. And so far gone.

How could she have thought it wouldn't hurt, seeing him? Knowing what she was going to say?

Her heart was not irretrievably lost, but it was definitely in need of a map in order to return home to her chest.

She cleared her throat. "Might we speak, Your Grace?"

His lips twisted. "That is what we are doing now, is it not?"

Damn him and his intelligent observational skills.

"Yes, but perhaps you might accompany me to get a glass of . . . something?" Not that enormous glass of wine, not yet—she had to be clearheaded to do what she was going to do, and she didn't trust herself not to launch herself at him if she was the slightest bit disguised.

"Of course." He held his arm out, and she placed her fingers on it, squeezing to feel the strength in his arm before remembering she absolutely should not be doing that. Not now.

They walked to the side of the room, a few curious glances cast at them. She lifted her chin, as much to keep from meeting anyone's eyes as to announce she, for one, was not frightened by the Piratical Duke.

Intrigued, attracted to, and wanting to know so much more about, yes, but not frightened.

Those thoughts were absolutely not helping.

He stood by her side as she asked for a glass of punch from the footman, then plucked the glass from her hand and held his arm out again, all without a word.

How odd was it that she was intensely attracted to someone for whom words were not his primary way of communicating?

He walked purposefully to the doors leading out to the garden, waiting as she gathered her skirts and stepped over the threshold.

She stopped and let go of his arm, still in view of the partygoers, but not within earshot. He glanced back into the room and took her elbow in his hand, pulling her to the side so they could not be easily seen.

She licked her lips, which were suddenly dry. His gaze tracked the movement, and she felt her knees buckle. Again.

He put her glass down on the ground. Where she might end up if she didn't try to wrestle control of her heart, and her knees, and all the parts that seemed to want to . . . do things with him. Which were all of them.

"You haven't sent a note." His expression tightened. "I would have expected you would have contacted me, given how we last parted."

Oh, you mean how I had my hands on you, and you were kissing me as though you wished to devour me? That last parting?

"And you could not send a note to me?" Margaret hadn't realized, not until she said it, that she had been hoping for something from him, some indication that what happened was not only wonderful but important.

He straightened. "It would not have been appropriate, my lady."

She burst out laughing, but not in humor. "Because what happened was so appropriate, Your Grace?"

He shook his head, as though in frustration. "You see, this is precisely why I did not send a note to you. I cannot adequately explain myself, not even in conversation." He stripped off the glove of his right hand, then did the same to hers. And took her hand in his, their bare skin touching.

She wanted to swoon, but swooning would mean she was unconscious and couldn't enjoy this moment.

"I've missed you."

That was not in the script.

Margaret stared down at their entwined fingers. "I've missed you as well," she said in a soft voice.

Neither was that.

His hand tightened. "So will you still accompany me on adventures?" He sounded so—so wanting, it made her chest tight.

Definitely not in the script.

This was why she needed an editor. And at this moment, the editor was she. And she wasn't sure these words were what should be said, but they were what felt right.

"Yes, I would," she said, then stepped closer and lifted her face to his.

He wasn't sure what she wanted to speak with him about, and now he didn't want her to speak, not now when they were kissing. Her speaking and their continuing to kiss would be at odds with each other, and right now he would have to say he preferred the latter.

She sighed into his mouth, and he licked her lips, at which she opened and he thrust his tongue inside.

Her tongue met his, with as much enthusiasm he could wish for, and she seemed to inch forward so that they were touching at several crucial points of their bodies—mouths, hands on arms, chest against chest, and of course his cock pushed up against her skirts, the slight pressure made more delicious because it was all so forbidden.

And then her hands crept under his jacket, slid along his rib cage, her fingers touching and pressing and caressing.

In the past, when he'd kissed a woman, it had felt as though she were surrendering to him, allowing him to make advances while she remained stable.

But Margaret, as he knew she would, was not surrendering. She was attacking, each glide and press of her mouth another maneuver, her hands now going to his back, pulling him closer into her, so close it almost felt as though they were one—albeit one who wore far too much clothing for the occasion.

If they weren't in the company of no fewer than two hundred of their peers—literally—he would ask her to remove some.

God, she felt good. Her curves pressed softly into his body, and every place of contact sent a ripple of pleasure through him. His hands were now at her waist, holding her to him, and he could feel how her breath was coming faster and faster, her breasts pushing into him with each ragged inhale.

And then she broke the kiss, pulling away from him, her eyes as sparkling as the candles from inside the ballroom. "We should leave," she said in a low, husky voice.

"Yes, we should." He didn't even think about

propriety, or how they would manage to leave without anybody seeing them, or how he'd just arrived and the Duke of Lasham never failed to stay at least half an hour for such events, and that he was with her, not only A Lady of Mystery, but also apparently A Lady of Scandal.

He just wanted to go somewhere with her where he could remove some of her clothing, and then she could remove his. A very equitable arrangement, he thought.

"I'll go first and collect my wrap. Meet me in front in about ten minutes? I'll send my carriage home and you can take me." She glanced up at him, not coyly, but with frank desire in her gaze. She was remarkable. He had never met a woman who was just so—so honest. So determinedly and assuredly her.

"Yes, I'll—take you." He felt himself wince at just what he'd said. Because it was entirely what he wanted to do, and yet not at all what he should be saying to a woman, even this remarkable one whose gown was nearly as bright as her eyes.

She didn't seem to notice, however, just gave him a knowing smile and glided back into the ballroom.

And now what was he supposed to do? He glanced around the now empty terrace. Should he just wait here? What if someone walked out and engaged him in conversation, making him late, and then she'd think he wasn't coming to meet her? Or if someone started talking to her while he was delayed, and then he made his escape only to see her with someone who shouldn't know they were—well, whatever they were going to do together.

And when had he become this awkward thing who didn't know what to do with himself?

Ah, of course. He could answer that, even if he didn't know where he should be standing at this exact moment. Forever. He had been this awkward for as long as he could recall, from first being sent off to school and then at his family's various homes, and in the House of Lords.

Always wondering just where he fit in, knowing he did, of course, because of what he was, but never because of who he was.

Was that changing? Was she changing him?

Likely not questions he was in any condition to answer, given that all he wanted to do was to be alone with her where perhaps they could continue what they'd started out here.

He took a deep breath, smoothed his jacket, and strode purposefully to the front door.

GEORGIANA AND THE DRAGON

By A Lady of Mystery

At first, Georgiana wasn't able to move the princess, not at all. It seemed the princess was as much strength as she was beauty, which made Georgiana wonder at the fairness of it all.

But then Georgiana felt the princess's grip slipping, and she gritted her teeth and dug her heels in, pushing the princess with her shoulders.

She had to ignore the gasps and groans of the dragon, for fear she would get distracted by his pain, which would then result in worse pain for him. Better to ignore him and try to get the princess away.

At last the princess made a very unprincesslike groan and fell onto the ground, releasing her hold on the dragon.

And the blood started to spurt from his side while Georgiana frantically tried to find something to stanch the wound.

Chapter 16

She had not said anything from her carefully written script after all, with the exception of "Good evening, Your Grace."

Instead, she'd told him she'd missed him, of all things, and then she had told him—using her actions, and not her words—that she wanted to be kissed again.

What was she thinking?

Well, she couldn't answer that, but she knew what she was not thinking—anything sensible. Because thinking sensibly would mean not going to gather her wrap, smile at the footman as he helped her put it on, then walk calmly to the door as though she were not about to leave with the Piratical Duke who couldn't Express Himself Except Through Action. Capitals inferred.

Once outside, she glanced down the long line of waiting carriages, spotting hers nearly at the end.

"Might I go call your carriage, my lady?" a footman asked.

She didn't want to put the poor servant into the

position of having to listen to Annie's reply if she sent the message that she would be making her own way home.

"No, thank you, I will just step down there for a moment." And she gave him a quick smile, then marched off as though it were customary for ladies to walk unescorted to their carriage several hundred feet away.

It was not customary. Not at all. But nothing about this was, nor had been, since she'd told her parents she would absolutely not be marrying the Collingwood, and that furthermore she was the author of that serial that pitted fantastical dangerous creatures against averagely fine heroines.

So perhaps she should grow . . . accustomed to the uncustomary. Such as leaving a party early to take a very large, very handsome duke on an adventure.

She smiled to herself, picked up her skirts, and ran down the line of carriages until she reached hers.

"Where are we going?" he asked. She'd spoken to his coachman as he'd entered, and then she'd darted around to the other side so that no one would see her entering.

So he had no idea where they were headed, or how long it would take, or anything about it except that they were in the carriage together, alone, and he couldn't stop playing the scenarios of everything that could possibly happen between them.

And he'd thought he had no imagination. He

had plenty, especially when it came to picturing her in a bed, eyes warm with desire and passion, a sheet wrapped carelessly around her naked form.

Her running her hands over him, her fingers touching his skin, his muscles, his cock. Especially his cock.

He strangled a groan in his throat as he thought about it. He didn't think they would be ending up there, no matter how much his imagination truly wished for it. There was a limit to just how scandalous she could be, wasn't there?

Maybe there wasn't. Oh Lord, what if there wasn't?

"It is an adventure, Your Grace," she replied in a mischievous tone. "And isn't the anticipation of such a treat, the not knowing just what will happen, nearly as fun as the adventure itself?"

She spoke as though he had experience with not knowing exactly what would happen, when, and how. He did not.

The last time he hadn't anticipated something was when his parents had died, and that was not something he wished to discuss.

Since then, he had been in command. In charge. It felt . . . odd, for him not to know precisely what was to occur, but it did not feel unpleasant.

It felt freeing, actually. He couldn't recall any time when he had been able to just let go, to give over the chore of responsibility to someone else.

"Thank you." He reached over and took her hand, lacing his fingers through hers. But then he didn't want to rest their hands on her thigh, for fear she would think he was being too presumptuous, and he certainly didn't want to put their clasped hands on his thigh, not when that area was so close to his erection, which hadn't subsided since they'd entered the carriage.

So for a few moments, their hands were suspended in the air between them, until she gave a soft laugh and tilted her face up to his as she put their hands on his thigh after all. So close to there, and yet not close at all, at least not close enough.

"Why are you thanking me?" she said in a whisper. She punctuated her question by placing a soft kiss on his jaw.

Lasham swallowed. How to explain it, when he wasn't sure himself?

"It's—it's that you didn't laugh at me."

She drew back, her brows knitting together. "For telling me what your name is?"

He shook his head and held her hand more tightly. "Not that. Well, yes that, but that is not what I meant." He exhaled. "That you didn't laugh when I asked for an adventure."

And didn't he sound lonely?

Although he was, wasn't he? That was what part of this was all about—that with the exception of Jamie, who was seldom in England, he didn't have friends. Nobody to laugh with, to talk with, to look at art with.

Nobody to kiss, either. That he wanted to laugh with, talk with, look at art with, and kiss her was stupendous.

Even if it couldn't last more than a few weeks, maybe a month, before the gossips started talking and they would have to make an irrevocable break.

"I would never laugh at you," she said in a fierce tone. "Unless you were to tell a very funny story." She paused. "Do you tell funny stories, Your Grace?"

He had to laugh at that, ironically, because no, if there was a person who was least likely to tell a funny story it was he. "Not as far as I know, Lady Margaret. I might have inadvertently," especially when out in company when he felt stupidly uncomfortable, "but I assure you, not on purpose."

"We will have to introduce you to the art of telling amusing anecdotes, then," she said. "Consider it to be a future adventure."

"We're here," Margaret said as she glanced out the window of the carriage. The coachman had looked startled when she told him where they wished to go, but thankfully—and probably understandably—a duke's coachman did not question anything, not even when it was not the duke issuing the orders.

They waited until the coachman opened the door, then Margaret stepped down onto the pavement and waited for the duke—Vortigern—to alight as well.

They stood in front of a large, shabby building that was ablaze with lights, a few people standing in front of it, rousing, lively music leaking out.

"This is a—a dance hall?" It was understandable that he was confused. She doubted he'd ever seen a dance hall, much less ever gone to one.

"Yes." She took his hand and drew him forward. "This is Caldwell's, my favorite one." And the one that was respectable for a lady to go to.

"You've come here before?" Now he sounded shocked. Although why he would be, when she'd just brought him here, didn't make sense. Because why would she take him somewhere on an adventure when she didn't know in advance that it would be an adventure?

He probably hadn't thought it through enough.

"I have." She turned to look at him. "The women I help, they like to have fun, and I have attended with some of them." She couldn't help the defiant tone that crept into her voice—what if he judged her harshly for going somewhere no female of her station would?

But that was true of the neighborhoods he'd promised to accompany her to, and he hadn't balked at that. It just must be his propriety emerging at precisely the wrong time.

"Come in, then," she said, then stopped and frowned at him. "No, wait, first we must muss you up a bit."

She reached for his cravat and undid it, sliding it from around his neck. His throat was strong, the base of his neck sprinkled with a few dark hairs. She swallowed at the sight, wishing she could just lean up into him and lick him there, right at the hollow of his throat.

She squelched that impulse—there was only so much adventuring he was likely able to handle, after all—and put her hand up to his head, running her fingers through his hair and making it less tidy.

Then she returned to his collar and tugged at it so it was slightly askew.

She stepped back and surveyed him. "You look more appropriate for where we're going." She tucked his cravat into her pocket. "And if anyone asks who you are, just growl. Anything but actually speak because your voice will give the game away."

He arched his eyebrow at her. "So this is a game?" The way he said "game" made her shiver. As though he were looking forward to playing.

"Yes," she said with a decisive nod. "A game to have fun without anyone finding out who you are, and what it might possibly mean"— she lowered her voice and tried to sound serious—"for the Duke of Lasham to be seen patronizing a dance hall where anyone could see him."

He gave her an appraising glance. "And what about you? Do we need to muss you as well?"

She felt her cheeks start to burn. "Ah, no. They will all just assume I am your—your"—and then she waved her hands in the air until finally she was able to say it—"your mistress, and you are very generous to clothe me so well."

"My mistress," he said in a flat tone. Was he upset? Had she pushed him too far into adventuring?

After a moment, another, of fraught silence, he spoke again. "Well, then, let us go in and play this game."

He held his arm out for her, a nearly roguish smile on his lips, and she felt her insides relax as he escorted her into the building, dropping a few coins into the hands of the man selling admission at the entrance. All without saying a word.

The music was of course a lot louder inside, and it was almost impossible to hear one another. Likely a good thing, given that she thought he shouldn't speak at all. He nodded to the dance floor, then back at her, lifting his eyebrow in a silent question.

She smiled back and nodded, taking his arm and leading him right into the middle of all the dancers.

The music was lively, and boisterous, making up in energy and volume what it lacked in precision. It seemed she knew the dance, since she took his hands in hers and began to move, laughing as he attempted to follow along.

As he'd told her, he did not enjoy dancing. It was far too likely that someone would come along and smash into his blind side, and he was so much larger than any of his partners it wasn't very pleasant for him to dance with anyone. He danced when he had no other choice—an excess of debutantes, for example, or some woeful spinster he felt sorry for—and gritted his teeth throughout the exercise.

But this was different. Entirely different.

For one thing, they were not waltzing. Or, it seemed, performing any kind of choreographed dance. Instead, they were moving to the music along with all the other couples on the floor, bumping into one another, smiling, laughing, and continuing on.

Then there was the fact that she smiled up at him, nonstop, her expression one of absolute and total joy.

As though there was no other place she'd rather be, and nothing else she'd rather be doing.

And he found to his surprise, once he thought about it, that he felt the same.

The song went on for a few more minutes, and Lasham discovered there were some sort of steps being performed, although not with precision. He found himself navigating the crowd better than at the beginning, and her approving expression made him warm all over.

Never mind that the vigorous dancing was making her cheeks flush and her bosom move interestingly. And that their hands—bare, again, since wearing gloves would have made them stand out from the crowd—were clasped. He gripped her tightly, enjoying the moments when their bodies brushed against each other in a movement of the dance, enjoying when he could see how happy she was, flinging her head back at times and laughing, or otherwise just meeting his gaze with a mischievous grin on her face.

The music stopped, and they stood on the dance floor, just looking at each other, him knowing he was smiling like an idiot. But not caring.

The music began again, a different tune but similarly lively, and they started to dance again, both now grinning at each other. They were better moving together already, anticipating each other's movements and dancing more or less in time to the music.

Had he ever had so much fun?

He didn't think so. Not so much undiluted fun, unsullied by anything other than what this was—no alcohol, or bets, or sexual congress.

Although that last item was something he should not be thinking about. Because if he started to think about how much fun sexual congress with her might be, he would embarrass himself in front of all these people he didn't know. And who didn't know him.

With that thought, he maneuvered them to the corner of the room, finding it a lot easier to avoid collisions with others than when they'd first started dancing.

And stepped behind a row of chairs, next to a pillar, relatively unseen.

At which point he tucked her into the corner, grabbed hold of her waist, and gathered her to him so he could kiss her senseless.

GEORGIANA AND THE DRAGON

By A Lady of Mystery

⸎⸎⸎⸎⸎

"It won't work, you know." The princess spoke in that same flat tone.

Georgiana merely shook her head. She drew up the skirt of her gown and tore a strip of fabric from the bottom. She crumpled it all up into a ball and placed it against the wound, hoping to help the blood clot.

Did dragons' blood clot, anyway?

"He'll need more than what you can give him." Now the princess's tone was downright scornful. At least she was exhibiting some emotion.

"Well, if you know so much, why aren't you helping him?"

The princess shrugged. "I told you, I need a prince. None of the dragons I've encountered have produced one."

Georgiana glared at her. "You don't need a prince. You don't need anybody. You're strong, beautiful, and probably not terribly stupid. You just need yourself." She gestured to the dragon, whose eyes were shut. "And you need to help him, because helping others is what makes us human. Even if it is helping a dragon," she muttered.

The princess's expression froze, and her eyes widened.

"Oh. I see," she said slowly, wonderingly, "maybe I don't need a prince after all?"

Chapter 17

*H*e was kissing her. Again. But this time he was in total command, and she just . . . surrendered to the kiss, reveling in how he seemed to want to devour her. His hands started at her waist, but quickly slid up her ribs, his thumbs extending to just below the curve of her breasts.

Please, move them up, she sent a silent plea.

And he must have heard her, because he drew his thumbs over her nipples, just there, even as he pressed closer into her, pushing her back against the wall, his entire body touching hers, his fingers just where she wanted them, his lips on hers, his tongue deep in her mouth.

It was all-consuming, and entirely wonderful, and she never, ever wanted it to stop.

She put her hands on his side, rubbing her palms up and down, then sliding around to his backside and then, far more tentatively than she wanted, she put her hands there, on the firm round globes of his arse, pulling him into her even more.

That must have done something to him, since

he groaned, low and deep in his throat, almost the growl she'd told him to display if asked any questions.

But she wasn't asking any questions now, not only because her mouth was otherwise occupied—thank goodness—but also she was, for once, not sure what she'd want the answer to be.

Shall we go somewhere so you can ravage me thoroughly was not quite what she wanted to ask. Not quite.

Shall we go somewhere so you can remove all of your clothing and I can see precisely what you look like underneath, thereby ruining all viewings of marble statues—and any future husband—for me forever?

Or just please take me, now, make me forget everything but your skin, your kiss, and how I feel when you touch me.

The thoughts catapulted in her mind, making her start, and she shoved his chest, pushing him away, feeling how her heart was racing.

He gazed down at her, his expression intense and dazed. "I—I am sorry," he said in that terrible stilted way he had.

And she felt sorry for him, and angry that he could get her so wrought up, and upset with herself for wishing to succumb to everything with him, when she absolutely shouldn't, and for bringing him here in the first place, not to mention making him look even more ridiculously handsome by mussing him up and removing his cravat.

Making her want to lick his throat.

"Do you want to leave?" he asked, still in that odd tone, and it hurt to hear him like that, to know, as she thought she did now, that he was stunned and hesitant inside all that grand dukeliness of his. That he was as unsure of himself as anybody who wasn't a duke, who wasn't tall, and handsome, and wealthy, and intelligent, and who didn't appreciate art.

Who wasn't he.

What had happened to make him so unsure? The writer in her wanted to know, but the woman in her—the one whose mouth was bruised from his kiss, whose body shook with longing of some sort or another—wanted to persuade him that he was valuable, that he was deserving of lo— No, not that, she thought quickly, she couldn't allow herself even to think that.

"I don't want to leave." Her hand was still on his chest, and she watched as her fingers slid down, sliding over the buttons of his waistcoat, feeling his chest rise and fall with his rapid breathing. "I just"—*never want to stop kissing you, and that frightens me, so I stopped kissing you, since apparently I make no sense whatsoever*—"I like this," she said, gesturing between them, "quite a lot, but I don't want you to be put into a position where there is scandal, and this"—she gestured again—"is scandalous."

He regarded her for a few silent moments, and even though the music was still loud, it felt as though she could hear him thinking.

"You're scared of this," he said. Did he sound

angry? She couldn't tell. She opened her mouth to argue, only to snap it shut again because he was right.

He glanced away, over her head. "I don't blame you. I'm scared as well." He looked back at her. "I've never had this—this intensity with anyone before." His lips twisted into a rueful grin. "Except with my friend Jamie, the one you met, and I definitely do not engage in this sort of activity with him."

"The thing is," she said, taking his hand in hers, "it does scare me. You scare me," and then she raised her head to look at him, already knowing what he'd likely be thinking she meant, only she didn't mean that, not at all, "but not because you're a duke and have an eye patch and are generally tall and large and intimidating."

"Why do I scare you, then?" he asked in that low, velvet voice. The one that made her shiver. The way he seemed to always make her shiver now.

"You scare me because I know we cannot, that this cannot, continue, and I'm already devastated that it can't. We both know that our . . . friendship can't be forever. I don't want you to risk anything because of this."

"What would I be risking?" he asked, again in a voice so low it seemed to send a rumble through her chest.

"The chance for happiness," she replied, dropping her gaze to the floor.

The chance for happiness.

Until she said it, until it dangled in the air between them, he hadn't even thought about happiness as an attainable goal.

What was happiness? Was it knowing that the world, the tiny corner you inhabited, was marginally better because of your actions? Was it spending time with a good friend drinking whiskey?

Was it discovering the hidden joy in dancing among a group of strangers at a place you would never have gone to on your own?

Or was it kissing someone so thoroughly that you forgot who you were, even as you were acutely aware of every single thing about her?

That wasn't happiness, none of it. It was—well, it was satisfaction, and comfort, and desire, but it wasn't happiness.

He knew, as his throat tightened, that he had no clue what happiness was.

She was still regarding him, allowing him to process the thoughts her words had triggered in his brain. He appreciated that she didn't rush him, didn't make him say something when he wasn't ready yet to say it.

"I don't know if I know what happiness is," he said, lowering his mouth to her ear so she could hear him. He had his hand on her bare shoulder, the other hand on her arm, and they were nearly embracing again. He felt the warmth and vibrancy and sheer sparkle of her as though it were a tangible thing, nestled among the skirts of her gown and spilling out with every one of her movements.

He felt her swallow, he was that close to her. "That is so sad," she said, then added, "Vortigern."

He hadn't heard his name spoken by anyone but

her in years. For so long, his name had sounded ridiculous, and he'd actively dissuaded anybody from using it, but now it didn't sound ridiculous. Not at all. It sounded as though it meant something special to her, as though saying it meant more than what she could say.

Like him, he thought ruefully. He couldn't say what he meant and he had to rely on actions, on gestures, on what he didn't say to convey what he meant.

And now he was glad he hadn't let anyone use his name. It was hers to use, hers alone, and he wanted to hear it more often on her lips.

"There is a difference between not knowing what happiness is and not being happy, though, you understand," he said, gripping her shoulder more tightly to punctuate his words. "I might have been happy. I am, I suppose, sometimes." *When I am with you.* "I just am not certain what it is, precisely. Or how to recognize it when it occurs to me."

She drew back from him, her mouth curling into a warm, soft smile. "That is why we are adventuring, is it not? Happiness is an adventure. Does this," she said, gesturing to the hall behind them, still filled with dancing couples and loud music and chatter and common folk, "make you happy?"

He glanced over her head at the hall, then returned his gaze back to her and slid his hand down her arm to take her hand in his. "It does," he replied, hoping she understood precisely what he was trying to say.

Even if he wasn't entirely certain.

GEORGIANA AND THE DRAGON

By A Lady of Mystery

Georgiana looked at the princess, knowing her mouth was hanging open, and she probably looked exceedingly dim-witted.

"Did you not know that before?" Georgiana rolled her eyes. "Because I am just a smithy's daughter, and I definitely know I don't need anyone What did your princess training consist of, anyway?"

The princess shrugged. Now Georgiana could see that her flat mien was likely born out of a taught sense of superiority, of a discomfort with the world that wasn't princess-ish, and Georgiana wasn't in quite as much awe as she was before. Not quite.

"I learned what we all learned—how to tell if a pea is under your mattress, how to discern a prince from a pauper, how to sniff in disdain."

"Ah." Georgiana tried not to show how appalled she was. "So your treating this dragon as you did—that was just part of your training?"

The princess nodded, absentmindedly stroking her bow. "We were told to shoot dragons and wait for princes."

"I think it's time for a new lesson," Georgiana replied.

Chapter 18

She was in so much trouble. His expression as he admitted he didn't know what happiness was, the exuberant way he'd let himself move during their dance, and the way he'd taken her, steered her, to the corner of the room so he could kiss her senseless—well, all of that made her more than weak-kneed. It made her heart weak. Or strong, depending on how you looked at it.

Damn it, she could not allow herself to fall in love with him. She knew, as she'd told him, that whatever this was had a finite end date, a time when it wouldn't be possible to continue, no matter what she felt about the matter.

And yet—and yet she couldn't resist him, not when his mouth twisted into that vulnerable curl, and his hands touched her in places that made her shiver, and how just being with him made her feel as though she were more alive than usual, as though his presence gave her an excess of oxygen. Or a loss, since she found she couldn't quite breathe properly in his presence.

"Should we go be happy some more?" Margaret said, rising up on her tiptoes to speak into his ear.

He looked startled, then blinked and looked down at her, a slightly embarrassed expression on his face. "You mean resume dancing?"

His voice was rough, and she felt a thrill move through her, knowing that she was the cause.

"Mm-hm," she replied, a sly grin on her face. "For now, that is."

She turned, taking his hand, and led him back onto the dance floor, feeling the strength of him at her back, nearly a palpable force that made her knees, once again, pleasurably weak.

Not helpful for dancing, having weak knees, but she supposed she would figure that out once they started to move again.

The music was playing already, slower than before, but not quite a waltz. But it seemed he thought it was a waltz, since he drew her into his arms and held her closer than he normally would have at a Society party.

And they paused there, both gazing at the other, not moving, even as the other couples on the floor floated about beside them, some in the same sort of embrace they were, while others continued just to hold hands and dance together.

"I will enjoy taking the lead, my lady," Vortigern said with a sly curl on his lips. Margaret knew he wasn't just talking about the dance, and she shivered in response, her nipples hardening under her gown. She moistened her lips and he inhaled, his hand tightening on the hand he held.

"I look forward to that, Your Grace," she said in a whisper, knowing she spoke the truth and could not wait to find out where he might lead her, beyond this dance, this dance hall, and his carriage.

She couldn't quite believe she was being this— this daring, even she, who had flouted the match made by her parents and didn't give a tinker's dam what people thought about her.

She'd caused scandal, to be sure, but she had never courted it. Never longed for it, not the way she longed for him. But since they were both well aware of their actions, and what would occur—both in the short term and the longer, more heartbreaking term—she couldn't pretend it wasn't going to happen.

And when it did, her knees and heart would be strong again, and she could move past whatever this was. But not until she explored every inch of what this was, and him, and found out as much as she could about him in the process.

Suddenly, she didn't want to dance.

"Can we leave?" she said in a low voice, just as it seemed he was about to start guiding her around the floor.

She saw him swallow. And felt her whole body react as profoundly as though he'd actually touched her somewhere improper, not just his hand on hers, his other hand at her waist.

"Yes," he said, his voice nearly a growl. "We should."

For once, Lasham wasn't the observer. Or the ob-served. Instead, he was the participant, drawing

Margaret through the crowd toward the exit, his arm wrapped around her shoulders in a way that he would never have done under normal circumstances.

But these were not normal circumstances. They were here, together, alone, unchaperoned, unnoticed, and they—at least he hoped this to be the case—had just agreed to do more with each other. To spend time together, outside of what Society deemed was proper.

He would have to find out for certain, despite his usual inability to speak properly, which was exacerbated by how little he wanted to talk and how much he wanted to just feel.

They stepped out into the night air, and he felt her shiver. Whether it was from the cold or something else, he couldn't say, but he took the occasion to draw her in closer to his body. He felt her all along his side, the skirts of her gown tangling with his legs.

His coachman nodded at them, his expression bland.

"We are going home," Lasham said, and the coachman nodded, as though he routinely took ladies home to his house during evening hours. Or anytime, actually.

Because he never had. He'd spent time with certain ladies, or women, but never in his home. Never where anyone could know.

The coachman shut the door behind them, and he felt his chest tighten with the anxiety of it. What if he'd misunderstood? What if she were about to demand he propose, or slap his face, or tell everyone they knew how he'd made an improper advance?

"Well?" she said, an amused tone in her voice. She reached over and took his hand.

And something within him eased.

"Well what?"

Not that he was suddenly the most articulate man in the world, much less London; there was only so much intense attraction, the potential for happiness, and a shared sense of humor could do.

"Well, we are going to your house." She paused, and he heard her inhale. "And we will likely be alone, and so I want to remind you that you are under no obligation to me, no matter what happens."

No matter what happens. Which means that something would happen. Not that he didn't know that already, she was the one who'd asked if they could leave, after all, but her saying it, confirming what he thought he knew, was a welcome reassurance.

"Thank you," he replied. Because how else would one reply to a lady who'd basically just told a gentleman that she was going to do things with him that would normally require a commitment of some sort? From both of them? And yet would expect nothing.

This was adventuring of the sort he never would have imagined when he'd first asked her, and yet he knew this was precisely what had been missing in his life—passion, desire, touch, closeness, and a secret that felt as though it were even more precious because it was a secret.

"Margaret," he began, only to stop when he realized he'd called her by her name, and not her title. Although keeping to formalities felt foolish, given what was happening between them. So he would just continue. "Margaret, have you ever—"

And she interrupted, yanking her hand away from his, leaving him bereft.

"Have I ever done this before? No, I haven't." Her voice shook. "It is not as though I have embarked on ... adventuring with gentlemen before, I just, with you, it just—" and she stopped, seemingly as at a loss for words as he normally was.

"That wasn't what I was going to ask," he said, retrieving her hand from her lap. "I was going to ask if you had ever felt this sort of connection with anyone else before. I haven't myself." He heard how his voice practically vibrated with emotion. He'd never spoken this way before. Much less said anything like this before. "With my friend Jamie, yes, but not to the same extent. As though I could say something—or not say something—and have you understand what I mean."

She gave a shaky laugh. "Oh, I see. I apologize, I assumed you—well, I assumed you thought I was as scandalous in my behavior as my reputation." She laughed again, this time stronger. "But since I completely misunderstood it might mean your point does not entirely stand."

"It does." He drew her hand to his mouth and placed a soft kiss on her wrist. That this strong, vibrant, passionate woman could be so quickly felled by gossip meant he would have to ensure their discretion. He would not have her further ruined by anything they would do together. He had to say it, even though he didn't want to. "We don't have to . . ." and he paused, because now he really was at a loss for words, since if he assumed something that she hadn't meant, then he was bound to break this delicate moment, this feeling he had that he'd never felt before.

"No, we don't." She sounded fragile as well. "We should just do what feels right."

He laughed. "That is what you said to me the first time we met, isn't it? *If it doesn't feel right, you can stop. But you should at least have tried.*" He drew a deep breath. "We should at least try."

GEORGIANA AND THE DRAGON

By A Lady of Mystery

❧❧❧❧❧ ❀ ❧❧❧❧❧

"What lessons will you teach me?"

The dragon raised his head as Georgiana was thinking. "Excuse me, but I am still in trouble. I need help."

Georgiana clapped her hand over her mouth and let out a yelp. "Of course! I am so sorry." She took hold of the princess's arm and brought them both down to sit on the ground. "The first lesson is compassion. Help him," she commanded, bringing the princess's hand to the dragon's side.

"Help him," the princess repeated. "I can do that," she said in a wondering voice. "I can help him."

Chapter 19

We should at least try.

Margaret felt her breath hitch as he spoke, the deep rumble of his voice resonating through her whole body.

They should try. It sounded so innocuous, trying; as though it were just a matter of attempt, not of possible failure.

But they had to try, didn't they? If they didn't, she knew she, at least, would regret it. She was guessing he would also. That he was daring to try something so beyond what she knew he was ever likely to do made her feel special. That he was willing to try for her sake.

She clasped his hand more tightly and leaned against his shoulder. It felt so right, so comfortable to be there, alone with him in his carriage, that it felt as though they'd always been this way.

And yet they had not. And could not always be this way.

But she couldn't think about that, couldn't write the ending to her own story, not until she knew where the story might go. And since she wasn't the only one writing it, she wouldn't know until they tried.

"Thank you." He spoke softly, and she raised her head to regard him. It was hard to see his face in the dimness of the carriage, but she could make out the dark place where the patch was, and then catch the glint of his eye. He shook his head. "It seems I am always thanking you."

"What are you thanking me for now?" she asked. She placed her hand on his abdomen and fiddled with a button on his waistcoat.

He covered her hand with his. "For trying with me, I suppose. For agreeing to this," and then he paused, "whatever this is."

"Should I also be thanking you?" She drew back to look at him more clearly. "You showed me I was in need of adventure, too. And doing it together," and her whole body reacted, knowing what "it" she was referring to, "makes it that much more worthwhile. Doesn't it?"

"Then we are both thankful," he said. He reached his hand up to her chin, then lowered his face to hers and kissed her. A soft kiss, one that was no doubt meant to be gentle, but turned into something more within seconds.

She clutched his arm, bringing his hand to her waist, turning into his body so she could feel it press against her. His mouth opened, and he licked her lips, making her let out a little moan, low and deep in her throat. She thrust her tongue inside his mouth, meeting his, and wriggled in her seat, longing for more closeness, but not sure quite what to do.

It seemed, however, he did know what to do. He grabbed hold of her and raised her up off the seat and onto his lap, all without breaking the kiss.

She would have complimented him on how smoothly he finessed the motion if she hadn't currently been far too busy cataloging just how it felt to be this close to him, her bottom resting on his thighs, his erection—because that was what it was, she knew that, even though this was her first encounter with one—pressed against her hip, his hands anchoring her to him, as though she would wish to escape.

She leaned into his chest, pressing her breasts against his strong, hard body. Well, that felt wonderful also. Who knew her body was capable of so many simultaneous sensations?

He definitely was not awkward or at a loss when it came to this.

His hand curled around her breast, holding the weight of it as his palm caressed her. He reached up and tugged at the neckline of her gown, making an impatient sound as he pulled it down. She thought she probably made an impatient sound as well, since she really wanted to feel his skin touching hers, with nothing between them.

She hadn't forgotten how it had felt to touch his bare chest. She wanted to touch more of him, and have him touch her in return.

His fingers slid below the neckline and then his palm was cupping her breast, his thumb rubbing over the nipple, making her whole body tingle. She felt a warmth creep over her, spreading from her lower belly, and if she were being honest, lower than that, all throughout herself.

And they were still both clothed, and still just kissing. She could not wait to discover what other feelings she might have when they did other things.

The carriage rolled to a stop a few minutes after that, just as Margaret was busy calculating just what else they could do inside its confines. She slid off his lap and onto the seat, yanking her gown back up and making a halfhearted attempt at smoothing her hair.

He was likewise smoothing and tugging and such, and she recalled she had his cravat in her pocket. But she didn't want to return it; not just because she had an odd yearning for a memento, but also because he just looked so compellingly handsome and rather dangerous without it.

But it was scandalous enough that he was bringing her home with him; for him to have a bare throat would be tantamount to admitting just what they'd been doing.

Not enough, Margaret wanted to say. She wanted to do it all with him, explore every plane and length of his body, to find out what it meant to be with someone so intimately.

She was honest enough with herself to admit it. She wanted him. She could not and would not marry him. But she still wanted him, and it seemed he wanted her.

So she would continue on this path until she got what she wanted.

The coachman flung the door open and Vortigern got out, holding his hand to her to help her descend. It was so late the streets were nearly quiet, although the duke's butler was at the door, the soft candlelight streaming onto the steps from behind him.

"Would you like to come in?" he asked. He didn't sound hesitant, not now; perhaps his awkwardness just extended to his words, because his actions—especially when inside a carriage—were confident enough.

She felt herself start to blush thinking about it.

"Yes, thank you," she murmured, taking his arm and walking up the steps. The butler looked momentarily surprised, but quickly schooled his features into a noncommittal expression.

"Tea in the library, please," Vortigern said as they walked inside. He waved the butler off and led her to the same room she'd burst into a few weeks ago. Demanding to know why he'd followed her. And that was the first time he'd kissed her.

He shut the door behind them, then gestured toward the sofa she'd sat on before—where she'd seen his friend Jamie lounging.

"Is this where you spend your time?" she asked, glancing around the room. A large desk was at one end of the room with bookshelves in back of it, filled to the ceiling with books of all colors and sizes. The ones within the easiest reach also looked as though they were the most read—the spines were worn, and some of the letters had rubbed away.

She didn't sit, but walked over to the bookshelf, running her finger on the leather of the book bindings. "I wouldn't have thought you'd have time to read, what with being so busy with your duties." She glanced back at him, a smirk on her face. "Because I know you do not neglect your duties. You do everything that is proper, isn't that what you said?"

He smiled, a wolfish grin that made her shiver. "I said I always do what is right." He strode toward her. "There is a world of difference between proper and right."

He stepped behind the desk with her, crowding her against the bookshelf with his body. His large, solid, entirely masculine body.

She leaned back against the books, folding her hands in back of her and looking up at him. "I hadn't realized you were such a stickler for meaning, Your Grace," she said in a teasing tone.

He put his arm up over her head, bracing himself against the bookshelf. She could feel the warmth and strength of him, of his body, just inches away from hers.

"It is not something I had thought of, until recently," he replied, his gaze on her mouth. She shifted and licked her lips, which were suddenly dry.

"And has your recent interest in meaning revealed anything . . . interesting?" She shook her head at her own redundancy.

"It has, indeed." It seemed he didn't notice her poor word choice.

"Ah." She reached up to touch his face, the

rough stubble on his cheek, just below the eye patch. She wanted to ask how it happened, how he'd lost his eye, but she knew, somehow, that revealing that—since nobody seemed to know— would be an even more profound secret than his name, which anybody could look up.

The door opened, and he quickly snatched a book from over her head, opening it and running one long finger down a page. "This is where you will find what you are looking for, my lady," he said in a reasonable tone, as though locating information in his library was precisely why they were there.

"I don't think so," she replied in a whisper. His cheeks reddened, and she wanted to laugh, but not in earshot of the butler, who was setting up tea things on a low table in front of the sofa.

"Is there anything else, Your Grace?" The butler's voice gave no indication that there was anything out of the ordinary going on. And perhaps there wasn't; Margaret didn't know for certain that the duke wasn't in the habit of inviting young ladies over by themselves in the evening. And then serving them tea.

"No, thank you," Vortigern replied.

He turned his head to watch as the butler left the room, then let out a deep breath as the door shut. "I have the most remarkable staff," he said. "I have never had—well, this," he said, gesturing toward her, "and yet they are behaving as though everything is entirely normal. Remind me to give them an extra bit of Christmas cheer this year."

So not only was he not in the habit of bringing

ladies home, he was perhaps imagining that they would still be . . . acquainted in December.

Those two things shouldn't have made her so pleased, but they did. They absolutely did.

He took her hand and guided her to the sofa, making sure she was comfortably settled before sitting himself. She turned to regard him, then let out a noise that she muffled quickly. "We should switch sides." She was on his left, which meant his blind side.

He looked embarrassed, although why he should be was beyond her. After all, they both knew he had a missing eye. He had already made mention of it being something people noticed—as of course they did—so why it should startle him when she said something didn't make sense.

But then again, there were more layers to the Impenetrable Piratical Duke than she had ever imagined on first meeting him.

They swapped seats, and Margaret leaned her head back—scandalously, no lady would ever be seen in such a relaxed position—and turned to look at him, feeling herself smile as she caught his eye.

"Would you like some tea, my lady?"

As though they were having a proper visit at a proper time with proper chaperones. As opposed to all this, which was the most improper thing she could think of.

No, wait, she could think of many more improper things. She shouldn't do that, not now, not when he just wanted to serve her tea.

"Yes, please." He reached for the pot and poured, then set the teapot back on the table.

"Milk? Sugar?"

"Mm-hm," Margaret said, relishing what a novelty it was to be waited upon by a man. This man, in particular.

Because of course she'd been waited on by men before, but always by servants. Certainly never by a gentleman, much less a duke.

Knowing that he wanted to please her—to make her happy in how he prepared her tea— gave her a flutter of excitement entirely unrelated to the beverage in question.

"Thank you," she said, taking the cup.

He made quick work of his own cup, but instead of drinking, he placed the cup on the table and leaned his head back, as she had done. She mirrored his action so that they were both resting their heads against the back of the sofa, just looking at each other.

"Tell me more about your work in Soho and the other slums of London." He raised an eyebrow at her. "I didn't get many of the details since I was too focused on you not getting beaten by that drunkard."

"And hiring the Beecham girls. Are they here? How are they doing?" Until he'd mentioned it, she'd entirely forgotten that he'd told those girls to come to his house for employment. What did that say about her, that she'd neglected to ask about their welfare, too engrossed in what the duke might look like naked and if there was hair on his chest?

She didn't think it said anything good, that was

for certain. And she still hadn't gotten the answers to all her questions.

Which definitely didn't say anything good, either, that that was the first thing she thought of.

"They are fine," he said in a soothing tone. "They are both working as scullery maids; my cook is likely browbeating them at this very moment."

Margaret popped up on the sofa, her eyes wide. "Browbeating them? That will not do," she exclaimed, starting to rise.

He put a hand on her arm. "You cannot solve everyone's problems. When I say browbeating, I mean Cook is demonstrating her sympathy for the girls by worrying about them." He grimaced. "I wish I could speak what was in my head at times."

Margaret relaxed again, feeling her mouth widen in a grin. "If you could speak what was in your head—if anyone could, actually—Society would be a much harsher place." She tilted her head. "More honest, but definitely harsher." She looked at him, raising one brow. "What would you say if you could speak whatever was in your head?"

He had to be expecting her to ask that, but judging by the expression on his face, he absolutely wasn't.

So perhaps he didn't quite mean it himself when he said they understood each other. She didn't think she would point that out at this particular moment.

"I—I don't know. I should rephrase that, as usual," he said in an irritated tone of voice. "I think I mean I should like to know what I think, definitively, about something. Rather than weighing all the sides, considering all the possibilities. Imagine how easy and wonderful it would be if I could just know."

She rolled her eyes. "If you just knew, you would have made up your mind before even hearing something. It says just what an intelligent, considerate person you are that you are so conflicted about things."

He looked doubtful. "So you are saying that my inability to make up my mind is a representation of my intelligence?"

She poked him in the arm. "You can't tell me you are unable to make up your mind. Of course you decide things, you make myriad decisions every day. What bills to support in the House of Lords, what to spend on certain expenditures, whether or not to follow young ladies who might get into trouble into dangerous neighborhoods of London . . ." She paused, waiting for his retort,

"And a very good decision it was, too," he said, folding his arms over his chest.

"Precisely. What you are saying is that you wish you were so stupid you could just make a decision with no information. But you really don't wish that."

"I suppose I don't." He edged closer to her on the sofa. "But I was also honest when I said I didn't wish to be entirely proper anymore. I want to do what is right." He took her hand in his and bent his head to regard their hands. "This is right."

And then he looked up, with an expression that blended hope, and desire, and want, and a fierce strength that made her knees buckle all over again, no matter that she was seated.

"It is," she replied. "Whatever this is, it is right."

GEORGIANA AND THE DRAGON

By A Lady of Mystery

"First I'll need you to cut me." The princess produced a knife from somewhere about her person and held it out to Georgiana.

"Why?" Georgiana asked, even though she thought she knew the answer.

"Only the blood of a true princess can heal me," the dragon said softly.

Georgiana rolled her eyes. "Of course. A beautiful princess, no doubt?"

If dragons could shrug, this one would have. "The princess can be beautiful or not beautiful. She just has to be a princess."

"Here," the princess said. She'd rolled her sleeve up and held her arm out. "Just there. I'll hold it over the wound."

"I have a bucket," Georgiana said, looking around wildly. The bucket had to still be here, didn't it?

"Never mind the bucket. Just get the blood."

Georgiana shuddered at just how gruesome it sounded, but took hold of the knife and slashed the princess's arm.

The blood started to flow immediately, bright red drops falling onto the wound.

The dragon cried out, as though in pain.

Chapter 20

Lasham swallowed, his throat thick with the wanting. The needing. But more than that, he felt—welcomed. Odd, not to always feel welcome, but he didn't. Hadn't ever, as far as he could remember.

He was tolerated. Wanted at events because of his prestige, but not truly welcomed.

And even in his own home, which they were obviously in now, he wasn't welcomed, because he was the only one who could welcome anybody. The rest of the people who lived here were here merely on his sufferance, and couldn't welcome anybody at all.

But she could. She sat on his sofa, in his library, in his house, and he felt as though she had let him in, and not the other way around.

He wanted to touch her, of course, but he also wanted to gather up everything about her he could, every tiny drop of knowledge sucked into his brain like the most intoxicating beverage. He would get drunk on it, on her, finally able to forget—as wine was not able to make him do—what it felt like not to be him, at least not what he was, for a few moments.

"What are you thinking about?" She sounded as though she were truly interested, not as though she wanted to hear he was thinking about her, as many women would have wanted.

The irony, of course, was that he was thinking about her.

He shifted, picking up his teacup and taking a sip. The tea was lukewarm now; he'd let it sit too long. He shook his head and returned the cup to the saucer.

"I was thinking about you."

She blinked. "Really? I hadn't meant—"

"I know," he said. He smiled at her. "I do know." He put his right ankle on his left knee and slumped down farther on the sofa. A posture he knew was shocking even if he had been alone, but with her it was downright—well, whatever was worse than shocking. Perhaps a word so scandalous it had never been uttered.

He would have to ask her what that word might be, given that she was a writer and all.

"What were you thinking?" She raised her eyebrow in challenge as well as flirtation. The quintessential Margaret, he was coming to understand.

He shrugged. "Just that I am impressed by how you've taken it upon yourself to try to make a difference. It is not often that anybody from our world pays attention to what happens in those kinds of neighborhoods, at least not without a speech to make in the House of Lords."

"If I could go speak in the House of Lords," she replied quickly, "I would." Now it was her turn to shrug. "Only I can't, and I also can't just leave them to suffer there."

"Why not? Why is it so important to you?" He held his hand up as her mouth snapped open. "Not that it is not what should be done, what people should do, but I haven't seen any ladies doing what you're doing. With or without my fearsome presence." He paused, hoping he could explain himself. "I—I admire what you're doing. Initially I thought it was foolhardy, and it might still be, but at least you're seeing a problem and doing something about it." Like me, he thought, only his problem wasn't that people in the world were suffering, but that he wasn't happy. Far less important in any context, but it felt important to him. He already knew he was doing his best to help ease the world's suffering, or at least the part he could affect, and now, perhaps, it was time to focus his attention on himself.

What would it be like if he were truly happy?

She seemed to understand him, since her expression changed into a thoughtful one. "I think it is because those women could so easily have been me." She waved her hand in a dismissive motion. "Not that I would have ended up there, not really, because my sister would look out for me. But those women, they have the barest support, and still they survive. When I was away from London, I thought a lot about the difference between living and survival. I want people to be able to live, no matter who they are."

He reached for her hand, feeling impossibly tender, as though he were standing on the edge of a precipice, but one where he would fly if he leaped, not fall to the ground, shattered. *I want people to be able to live, no matter who they are.* That could apply to a duke as well as a chimney sweep.

He took a deep breath. Knowing he would say this right, at least. Because it was so full in his heart, he had to let it out, or burst. "We talked earlier about happiness, and what it is." He swallowed, keeping his gaze locked on her face. Watching the shifting of her emotions as she listened to him. "I think I was just surviving before. I think," and here he paused, because it felt too much, "I think with you I might live a little."

She bit her lip and nodded, and it looked as though, for once, she was speechless.

He didn't want to kiss her at that moment. Well, he did, but he didn't want her to think that was all this—whatever it was—was. So he just held her hand, stroking her skin with his fingers, tracing the calluses where she held her pen. Touching the inside of her wrist, the skin so soft there he wanted to rub his cheek against it.

"I want to live also," she said at last. She lowered her gaze and her voice got quieter. "Living is more than just existing." She'd existed while she had been away from London. But now that she was back, and feeling useful, and seeing her sister again, and meeting her niece, and helping the women who needed help—that was living.

And then there was he. His mere presence in her life shouldn't make her entire life more meaningful—that would be to pin her life's work to a man, and not doing that was what had brought her here in the first place, ironically enough. But somehow he did, he twisted her all around, he made her want to do more than live, even. But even as she thought it, her brain shied away from it, because the next thing up from live was love.

She could not fall in love with him.

Because even she couldn't write a happy ending if that happened.

GEORGIANA AND THE DRAGON

By A Lady of Mystery

"What is it? Is it worse?" Georgiana cupped her hands under the princess's arm, trying to catch the blood. Of course that didn't work, and the blood spilled through Georgiana's fingers onto the dragon, who was still moaning.

"He's recovering," the princess said, pulling Georgiana's hand away. "This is just part of the process."

"How can you be so certain?" Georgiana asked, rubbing her bloody palms on her gown.

"This is not my first dragon rescue," the princess said. She frowned in thought. "As I think about it, in fact, I believe this is my twelfth dragon." She glared down at the beast. "And none of them have been princes."

But even as the words emerged from her mouth, the dragon's shape started to change, the hidelike skin shifting into something softer, the scales falling away to reveal—

A man. A naked man lying on the ground, curls of steam coming from his skin.

The princess smiled as Georgiana shrieked.

Chapter 21

Margaret hadn't expected this, any of this, to be as . . . intense as it was. Although she should have expected it, once she'd realized the Piratical and Proper Duke was full of layered depths, a fathomless well of feeling and repressed emotion. Likely so repressed he wasn't even aware it was there. But she was. She could feel it every time he touched her, or kissed her, or regarded her with his burning gaze. It was almost a palpable thing, his emotion, and she wanted to bring it out, expose it to both of them, see what it would look like if they examined it closely.

And wasn't she fanciful? Likely as not he would shut down, as he had before, if she even mentioned it. He'd barely been able to tell her his name, after all. How could he show her what he was feeling?

Although—although he had, hadn't he? Shown her through his actions, if not his words.

She swallowed. "I would very much like you to kiss me," she said in a soft voice. His mouth lifted in a half smile, and she saw a familiar gleam in his eye.

"I could do that," he murmured, lowering his mouth onto hers.

It was splendid, of course, because it was with him, and by him, and for once Margaret's mind was stilled, entirely focused on what it felt like to be kissed. More importantly, to be kissed by him.

His hands were cupped around her jaw, holding her softly, tenderly, but also as though he were in command, that this was what he wanted, and was going to make happen.

He coaxed her mouth open—not that it needed much coaxing—and thrust his tongue inside, licking and savoring and generally making her feel as though she might just collapse under the deliciousness of it all.

It was a good thing she was seated, since she knew her knees could not take the pleasure.

They kissed, just kissed, for what seemed as though it were forever as well as just a blink in time, and then he took his mouth away and leaned his forehead against hers, breathing heavily.

"I never thought," he began.

"Nor did I," Margaret said, lifting her fingers to his lips. He sucked her index finger into his mouth and licked it, sending shivers through her entire body.

"Oh." It was all she could manage to say, not without begging him to do something entirely outrageous. Not that they hadn't tacitly agreed to outrageous behavior, but it was one thing to have it in one's mind, and another entirely to just say it.

He moved his hand to her neck, running his fingers along her skin. "You are so soft," he said in a wondering tone. "So lovely." He drew his head back and met her eyes. "I want to savor this. Savor you," he said, trailing his fingers over her skin. "So that even though there is nothing I wish more than to draw your skirts up and push my way inside, I won't this evening."

"You won't?" Margaret couldn't keep the note of disappointment from her voice, although she also appreciated that he was taking care with her. As though she were something precious, not a walking scandal. Which would explode into something far more scandalous if their behavior got out. She couldn't risk that for him. For her, she didn't care, but she knew his title, and the respect it commanded, was important to him, made it possible for him to do what he thought needed to be done. Whereas her very lack of propriety, of reputation, made it possible for her to do what she knew needed to be done.

He chuckled. "No, I won't." He gathered her in his arms, then positioned them so that he was leaning against one end of the sofa and she was leaning against him, her back to his front. He did it so easily she felt a thrill at just how strong he must be. And then she thought about what it would be like to feel all that power surrounding her, and—

"Are you all right?" he asked in a tone of concern.

Yes, I was just imagining you displaying all of your magnificent masculinity to me. "I am fine, why do you ask?"

"You let out a noise. A groan or something."

Margaret felt her cheeks heat. "It's nothing." She drew his arms around her so they were crossed over her chest. "Tell me about yourself. Why did your father choose Vortigern, anyway?"

Now it was his turn to groan. "He thought his son should have the name of a ruler. Why he didn't just choose George or William or even Arthur is beyond me."

"I like it. It's different."

"That it is. You can't imagine what young boys can do to turn your name into an insult."

Margaret laughed. "I can't imagine. Tell me."

His arms squeezed her, and she snuggled closer into his chest. It felt so right, so comfortable, it was hard to believe that if anyone saw them they would immediately say it was wrong. How could something that felt so right be wrong, just because they didn't want this forever?

And she should not be thinking about any of that, not when this right thing had barely just begun. Thinking to the end was an unfortunate side effect of being a writer; she always had to forecast the final pages.

"Wartigern was one of the most popular ones. Fartigern was also a big favorite. Gern, a few times. Then Gernie, for some reason. That one didn't make sense, but it got used, nonetheless."

"Gern sounds as though it is a boulder or

something—'The trees are just a few paces past the gern.' Like that." She hoped he would laugh.

Thank goodness he did. "Or something that is unpleasant, like an illness—'The gern was responsible for three farmers' illnesses; hopefully it is cleared up now. That gern can be a nasty business.'"

She laughed, delighted he was comfortable enough with her to join in with the joke.

"You can't gern here, you have to go over there if you want to," she said, adopting a broad London accent.

"That almost sounds real. I wonder what 'gern' would be." He lowered his mouth to her ear. "Probably nothing as fun as this."

She felt her whole self shiver again. Thank goodness he was wealthy enough to have a roaring fire, or all this shivering would make her catch a chill. Maybe a gern, even.

She looked up at him, so close she could see the gold lights in his dark brown eye. The eye patch reminded her she hadn't asked yet, but she caught herself before she did. What if he was only able to share one intimate thing a week with someone? She would have to bide her time. "My sister calls me Margie, but that's all anyone has ever done with my name. Of course I didn't go to school, so I didn't meet many other young ladies."

"Your sister is married to the Duke of Gage, isn't she?"

How odd was it that they were having this

quite normal conversation under such extraordinary circumstances? And yet it felt—right.

Margaret nodded. "Yes, and it's turned out remarkably well. Nicholas hadn't expected to inherit, but he did, and he loves Isabella."

"I wonder what that would feel like."

To love someone? she thought. But he couldn't mean that. Of course she would have to ask.

"What what would feel like?"

He made some sort of hmphing noise. "To be raised without expectation. I am surprised I wasn't born with a ducal coronet of strawberry leaves. I have never known what it is to not be a duke, or at least in preparation for being a duke."

That explained a lot. "Your parents didn't encourage you to have fun? Or just be a child?"

He shook his head. "No, that was for other children. For me, it was all about preparing for the awesome responsibilities I'd have. To be the Vortigern I was meant to be. And then I came into them at fifteen, and was completely unprepared." He paused. "Not for the work of it, I knew that, but for losing my parents and then having to be so responsible."

"That must have been very difficult."

A shrug. "I didn't—I don't know any differently, so I suppose it might have been. I simply can't know."

Her heart clenched at that, hearing the plain fact of his reality stated so baldly. No wonder he wanted an adventure, and no wonder he had no clue how to have one. He simply didn't know.

"What about you? Were you raised to be A Lady of Mystery?"

She snorted. "Hardly. My parents were so focused on Isabella they barely acknowledged my existence." It hurt, it always had, but the pain had ebbed. "And then when they did acknowledge me, it was to try to force me to marry someone entirely unpleasant."

"It was brave of you to decline."

"It wasn't. That is, thank you, but it was what should be normal for women, to be able to say no. It's terrible that some women have no choice but to say yes. I was able to find another way, but other people aren't so lucky."

"And that's why you're back, because you said your parents are not here?"

"Yes, apparently they are traveling." Unable to stay in London because their daughter the duchess was never more than icily polite when she saw them, and her husband was even more dismissive. "And I have a niece, I had to return to spend time with her. She's the most adorable little thing ever. Her name is Victoria, so unless anyone wishes to insult the Queen, it's unlikely she'll have to suffer as you did." She turned to look up at him. "Is school where you met your friend? The one I met?"

"Jamie." He smiled. "He and I met at school, yes, and we've been able to stay friends, despite his frequent travels."

"He seemed nice. Not quite as—as—"

"—stuffy as me?" Vortigern said.

She laughed and leaned up to kiss his jaw. "That is not what I was going to say. For someone who claims to know what we mean even before we speak, you are doing a terrible job."

He chuckled ruefully. "You're probably right. What were you going to say, then?"

"Not as serious. You seem to walk around with the weight of the world on your shoulders." She paused. "Of course, your doing that meant that you came to my rescue, even though you had just met me, and—I thought—wanted to have nothing to do with me. And I am guessing that is not the first time you've done something similar." An unpleasant emotion coursed through her. Jealousy, that's what it was. "Are you in the habit of rescuing young ladies?" And who else had he rescued?

"No, I am not. You are the first."

That eased her mind, although she was annoyed with herself for even having those feelings. He wasn't hers, he never would be, and this was just—this. Whatever it was.

"So what else do you involve yourself with? Do you do anything besides all your duke work?"

He snorted. "My duke work, as you call it, keeps me busy most of the time. Which is why I require someone to take me adventuring."

"What do you think you would like to do if you could do anything you wanted?" It was an echo of the question she'd asked him the first time they met—*What would you do if you could do anything you wanted?*—but he hadn't answered yet. She would just keep asking until he knew. Then, she thought, he might be able to find, if not happiness, at least contentment.

"I wish I knew." She could tell, from the honesty in his voice, that this was why he'd begun this whole thing in the first place. To know. To know what happiness was, to discover things by "adventuring," to do things that would spark some delight in his soul, even as he continued to do what was proper most of the time.

She swallowed against the lump in her throat, the one caused by how lonely it must be to be him. "That is why we are together now, isn't it?" she asked, patting his hand with hers. "To figure out what we want?" She turned in his arms and slid her fingers along his jaw. "Right now, at this very moment, what I want is you."

The intensity of his gaze, the way he took a deep inhale, made her quiver. And then he closed his eye and sighed, his lips pressed together.

"I want the same," he replied in that low, resonant voice. "At least I know that much."

GEORGIANA AND THE DRAGON

By A Lady of Mystery

~~~~~~~∞○⊃C○~~~~~~~

"Is that the dragon?" Georgiana asked, even though she knew perfectly well it was.

The princess's eye roll indicated what she thought of Georgiana's question.

"Yes, it is." She leaned over the former dragon/current naked man as she wrapped her sleeve around the wound. "The question is, is he a prince?"

Georgiana frowned. "Did you know this might happen? Is this why you helped?"

The princess shrugged, then knelt down on the ground and leaned into the man's face, so close she could have kissed him. Not that she did.

She sniffed, then drew away with a jerk. "Not a prince." She stood and brushed her hands together. "Well, thank you for teaching me that lesson."

"What lesson? I didn't teach you anything."

"Oh, you did. You taught me not to waste royal blood on random dragons in hopes of finding a prince. I don't need one after all."

And she walked determinedly out of the forest, leaving Georgiana alone with an unconscious naked man.

Chapter 22

"Well?"

Lasham looked up as Jamie walked in, of course not even bothering to knock. The same room where, not twelve hours before, he'd lain on the sofa with her in his arms. Talking, touching, *being*.

He didn't think he'd ever felt as relaxed as he had been for those few hours. It was remarkable how—how calm he felt, how right it felt to be with her.

And something in his expression must have revealed his thoughts. "It went that well, hm?" Jamie said, a knowing grin on his face as he flopped down into the chair on the other side of Lasham's desk.

"It—what?" Lasham was terrible at prevaricating. He'd never had to before, actually. Dukes seldom had to lie about anything, and Lash prided himself on being as truthful as possible.

Except now, when his closest friend was reading his activities just from his face.

Jamie flung his head back and laughed, clearly enjoying Lasham's awkwardness. *That makes one of us*, Lasham thought sourly.

He and Margaret had made arrangements to meet the following day, since she required his presence to go back to Soho or some other London slum again. He had been relieved to hear she hadn't gone there while they'd not seen each other, but now, as she said, "who knows what might have occurred, and who might need me?"

I need you, was what he wanted to say, only that felt too—too much, even given what they'd shared. And he couldn't be that selfish, not when there were people who could benefit from her attention, and not just because they'd found it was the most spectacular thing in the world to kiss her.

But meanwhile, Jamie was here, and was asking questions and commenting on every facet of Lasham's life, as he usually did.

"You and this, and her." Jamie leaned forward, clasping his hands in front of him. "You did see her, did you not? I thought I spotted you both last night, and then all of a sudden you were both gone."

"Yes, well." Lasham cleared his throat. "It is what it is." Whatever that meant.

"Whatever that means," Jamie said with a smirk. Apparently he and his closest friend did understand each other better than Lasham had assumed.

"Listen, Jamie." Lasham glanced around, feeling even more awkward than usual. "I have some other things to ask of you." A pause. "Things about ladies."

Jamie raised a quizzical eyebrow. "Ah, so it is to be that, then?"

Thank goodness he and Jamie did speak a similar language, because if Lasham had to say it aloud, he would no doubt mangle it entirely. Hopefully he and Jamie were actually talking about the same thing, because now that he thought about it, he wasn't sure what he would say.

Dear God, let them be talking about the same thing. "Yes, it is to be that."

Jamie smiled and laid a hand on Lash's shoulder. "Then we have plenty to discuss. I am definitely the expert in these matters."

They were talking about the same thing. Thank God.

"Good afternoon, Your Grace."

Lasham turned at hearing her voice, acutely aware of the other members of their world who were nearby in the museum. None of them precisely paying attention to them, but on the other hand, who could fail to notice an eye-patched duke over six feet tall and the sparkling woman to whom he was speaking?

"Good afternoon, my lady." He drank in the sight of her, even though he had seen her just the night before. She wore relatively nondescript clothing, compared to the yellow sunburst gown of the night before, but somehow the simple gown managed to inflame his desire.

But who was he fooling? He would want her no matter what she was wearing. He'd never paid much attention to ladies' clothing before, but now he could state for an absolute fact that ladies wore far too much of it. At least, this lady did.

She dipped into a brief curtsey, as befit his rank, but the sly smile on her face as she rose befit who she was to him now. Who he was to her.

They had become more than duke and lady, even more than a do-gooder and her protection. They weren't yet lovers, but that was only a technical matter. For all intents and purposes, in his and their Society's eyes, they had behaved inappropriately.

And since Lasham had never done anything inappropriate in his life, he wanted to do all of it. With her. And soon.

But he couldn't start thinking about that now, not when they had plans to go into one of the rougher areas of London. She'd told him she'd received several notes from various young women in that area that some outsiders had recently arrived and were fomenting political revolt—which didn't bother Margaret, although it did bother Lasham—but were also taking advantage of some of the women, since they were traveling in an organized group, and there was nobody to stop them.

Lasham had asked his butler for his pistols, making that imperturbable gentleman almost perturbed. Not surprising, given that most people assumed he'd lost his eye in a duel. Probably the man was sitting back at the duke's house wondering how to serve a master with no eyes.

"You're thinking about where we're going, aren't you?" she said in a whisper. She nudged him in the side with her elbow. "It will be fine, don't worry so. Let's go view some art, since we're here." She took his arm and led him to stand in front of a painting that seemed to depict a moldy piece of cheese and a half-empty bottle of wine.

He ducked his head to speak as close to her ear as he dared. Hoping nobody else was in the mood to view a portrait of the most unpleasant meal ever. "Oh, since we are heading into a potentially dangerous situation, you armed with just me and your fractious maid."

She laughed so loudly a few heads turned in their direction. And covered her mouth with her hand, but her eyes were dancing.

He was glad one of them could find humor in the situation.

Wait— "Have I just told a humorous story?" he asked in a low voice.

She shook her head, her hand still over her mouth. So he hadn't told a humorous story, but she was amused enough to still be laughing.

"Annie is not fractious, she is just—a bit high-handed." She gestured to another painting. "Let's look at that one."

This painting was far more pleasant—it depicted a group of people out in the forest somewhere having a picnic. It seemed entirely improbable, to Lasham's eye, that these people would actually be keeping company with one another, but at least the wine bottles were full. Maybe that accounted for their conviviality.

"Where is your maid, anyway?" Not that he wanted her there, but he knew enough to know that maids seldom left their unmarried ladies' sides.

Margaret raised an eyebrow and rolled her eyes. A remarkable trick, actually. If he had had two eyes, he might have tried it; if he did it as he was now, he would likely look even more frightening than he did already.

"She refuses to come look at art with me. She says life is too short to watch people not moving about. And," she said, speaking in a lower tone of voice, "I didn't think she was necessary today. After all," she continued, shrugging her shoulders, "the scandalous thing that everyone thinks might happen if a lady and a gentleman are together has happened, so there's not much she can do to staunch that particular flow."

"We're a flow?" he replied, bemused by her turn of phrase.

She grimaced. "Bad choice of words. I have no excuse except that I was up late."

"Did you mean the damage has already been done?"

Now she was rolling her eyes at him. "We are damage? That's even worse."

She folded her arms, glaring at him for a few heart-stopping moments, then she snickered, her mouth in a wide smile. "You are far too serious, Vortigern," she said in a whisper. "And we should be on our way, so we don't have time to discuss what has already been done."

"Fine." He couldn't pay attention to what he

was viewing anyway, not with her here, and him thinking about the night before, and also thinking about the pistols in his carriage, and what they were about to venture into.

That he would be the only protection she had.

An awesome responsibility, far more serious than whether he had seen her unclothed.

He had not, he thought with some disappointment.

"And the men are gathering in The Mongoose's Tail? Hideous name for a pub," she said in an aside.

The woman to whom she was speaking nodded. "Yes, ma'am, they are there most afternoons into the evening. Planning their things and accosting some of us that live nearby." The woman looked frightened, and Margaret's heart hurt for her.

How lucky she was to have a maid, even if she could and would leave her at home? These women had no such support, nobody to help them if they were harassed. If the men were as many as the woman had said, likely nobody could stand up to them.

Except her and him.

She glanced to her left, where he was standing, just slightly behind her as though he were a menacing shadow. He was following her reminder not to speak, no matter what was said, since his speech would reveal that he was far more than just protection. She was able to modulate her accent so as to seem more like them, even if they

could still tell she was different. She didn't think
he would be able to do the same. Not that she'd
asked him; perhaps he was a remarkable mimic,
but now was not the time to test that.

His eye was flickering back and forth between
her and the lady, and his hands were crossed over
his chest, with one hand tucked into his jacket.
She knew, since she'd seen it, that he had a pistol
in there. It frightened her to think that perhaps
a pistol was necessary, but she didn't argue. Because it might be necessary.

She couldn't yet go speak to anybody in authority about the situation, since she didn't know if
there was a situation, and she was only one scandalous woman. He could have done something,
certainly, but she didn't want him to become con-
nected to all this since their activities together—
the nefarious ones and the farious ones, not that
that was a word—would come to light, and he did
not deserve that result, not when they'd gone to
such lengths to keep their acquaintanceship quiet.

"Acquaintanceship" was definitely too mild a
word for what they had, but her brain shied away
from naming what it truly was.

"Let us go there, then, and speak to whomever
seems to be in charge." She spoke decisively, as
though she absolutely believed in what she was
saying, even though she had no such confidence.

This was more than just rescuing some down-
trodden or worse women—this was challenging
a group of men, men who were no doubt pushed
to their limits.

He grabbed her arm as she began to walk. "Are

you sure this is a good idea?" he said in a low voice. "If you are hurt . . ." He paused, and she saw his throat work.

"It will be fine. I have my fearsome protector, don't I?" She patted his hand. "Come along and look frightening. You do that so well."

He opened his mouth as though to argue, settling for some sort of unintelligible growl before running his hand through his hair.

Good, things were nearly normal. She could do what she had to.

GEORGIANA AND THE DRAGON

By A Lady of Mystery

Georgiana stared down at the naked former dragon, not sure what to do.

How did one rouse a naked former dragon? Should one even try?

Thankfully, he groaned and rolled over, but then Georgiana remembered he was naked, and now he was on his back, and she shouldn't be looking, only she was.

He opened his eyes as she felt her cheeks start to burn. She turned her head to stare somewhere other than at the supine naked man.

"What happened?" His voice was rough, probably because he'd just been a dragon and still had smoke in his throat.

"The princess changed you, and then she left," Georgiana replied.

He glanced down, his eyes widening in surprise. "I didn't think this could happen." He frowned as though puzzled.

"Do you mean—do you mean you weren't a human being before?" That would explain why he wasn't very concerned about his nudity.

He shook his head. "Not precisely. I've always preferred being a dragon. This is a big change." He glanced up at her. "You'll have to help me learn."

Chapter 23

Lasham walked after her, the stubborn woman, wanting to clench his jaw and drag her back to his carriage, but knowing she would not accept that. And he couldn't let her do this on her own.

The woman who was guiding them to their destination seemed to have discovered a friend in Margaret, since she was chattering to her about all sorts of things, most of which Lasham didn't understand. He heard mention of daily work, scuttles, darning, and tea being dear. Margaret, however, seemed to comprehend entirely, and respond appropriately. He knew if he were speaking to the woman, not only would he not understand, but he would likely reply in some poor way.

He was usually grateful for his position, but even more so when he realized that he didn't have to work to make himself understood. That was other nondukely people's jobs.

Meanwhile, they were heading for what sounded as though it might be a difficult situation, so he couldn't be thinking about how his communication skills were lacking.

He touched the handle of the pistol in his pocket. It was both reassuring and terrifying that he had it. He certainly did not want to have to reveal it, much less come close to using it.

Despite what the gossip might say, he had never used a pistol to defend or attack anyone. He didn't want to start now.

"Here we are," the woman announced, pointing to a plain wooden door with a weather-beaten sign hanging overhead. "And if you don't mind, ma'am, I'll leave you here. My girls should be getting home soon, and I have to get supper ready."

Margaret nodded in understanding. "Thank you, Sally. I will be returning to find out how you and the girls are doing. Do go see Miss Carolyn at the Quality Employment Agency, as I suggested. She has work for women such as you and your girls."

The woman nodded. "Thank you, ma'am, I will." She glanced at Lasham, but averted her gaze quickly when she caught his eye.

He was both pleased and annoyed that he continued to frighten anybody who saw him.

But he didn't have time to ponder that, since Margaret was already pushing the door open and walking inside. He followed after her, hoping he wouldn't be called upon to do more than look scary.

"Goodness, it is dark in here," Margaret said over her shoulder.

It was. It was also redolent with smoke, and

burning coal, and what was probably years of dust. Lasham's vision cleared, and he saw the long wooden bar to the left, with an assortment of mismatched tables and chairs taking up the floor. A group of men were seated to the right and back of the room, while only a few of the other tables were occupied. Margaret nodded at the barkeep, whose mouth was agape, likely at having someone that looked like them walk into his establishment, then she proceeded to where the men were seated, Lasham close behind.

"Excuse me," she said as she approached. All of the men looked up, their faces registering varying degrees of surprise, which increased as they saw who was coming toward them.

One man, of course the largest of the group, rose, a belligerent expression on his face. Wonderful, Lasham thought, reaching inside his pocket again to touch the pistol.

"What do you want, lady?"

Margaret did not appear daunted by the man's general appearance, which both frustrated and impressed Lasham. Did nothing intimidate her? Not wandering into dark rooms with grouchy dukes she didn't know were dukes, or facing ladies intent on art viewing, or challenging large and possibly revolutionary men?

She was remarkable.

"I would like to speak to you gentlemen about your activities here."

The man folded his arms over his chest, making him look even more impressive. Lasham took note of that, thinking he might try it one day himself.

As though he might ever need to look more impressive.

"What activities? Ain't nowt wrong with us being here, is there?"

Margaret shook her head in what appeared to be a conciliatory manner. "Of course not. It is just that I concern myself with some of the women who live in this area, and they have mentioned that you gentlemen might not realize just how you appear to these women. I wanted to ask you to behave like gentlemen around them."

"Who's saying we ain't been gentlemen?" Another man, this one smaller than the first, but with a more pugnacious expression. Lasham stepped forward so his legs brushed against Margaret's skirts, trying to keep his expression neutral and yet also still intimidating.

"Nobody. That is, a few of the women are concerned for their daughters. If I could ask you to be cautious. You don't want to attract the wrong kind of attention, do you?" she said, making a quick gesture behind her toward Lasham.

Wonderful again, he thought. Now she was using him as a potential cudgel. He hoped he wouldn't have to be an actual cudgel.

The smaller man nodded, glancing at the other man, whose arms were still crossed over his chest. "We don't want that attention, do we? We have plenty to do here. If those lords hear of it before we're ready . . ." He paused.

Oh, so what they were engaged in was something he and his world would want to know about. Probably one of the things Meecham was always discussing. And if they knew who he was, they would be very much displeased. He would definitely be keeping his mouth shut, no matter what happened.

The larger man didn't seem convinced. He walked to stand just in front of Margaret, not even bothering to look at Lasham. "What business is it of yours how we act here?" His expression hardened as he looked her up and down. This was not good.

Margaret shrugged. "It is my business as someone who is female, and who has interest in the women who live in this neighborhood, and others like them. That is all. If it seems as though I have interest outside of that concern, let me reassure you that I do not. I simply want these ladies to feel safe where they live. And many of them work, which helps their husbands feel more secure and perhaps able to think outside of their next wage. That is what you need, isn't it, for your plans?"

She tilted her head to the man and put her hands on her hips, waiting for his reply.

His eyes narrowed as he thought. Behind him, the men were urging him to relax, and sit down, and not to make more of a fuss than was needed.

Lasham's fingers were on the pistol.

The man gave a quick nod, then turned and sat back in his chair. "We'll be cautious, like you said, lady," he said in a grudging tone.

"Excellent," Margaret replied. "Thank you."

She turned to walk away, and Lasham could see she was shaking. Hopefully the men wouldn't have noticed it.

He took her elbow and walked her through the pub, holding his breath until they had made it outside.

He glanced down the street to where he'd told his coachman to wait with the carriage. It was still there, with only a few people gawking at it. Hopefully they could return without being noticed.

How had she thought this made sense at all? It was one thing to go help able-bodied women to find work, but another thing entirely to confront a group of men clearly bent on societal disruption with a plea to treat the women in their immediate area properly.

A conversation he would be having with her as soon as they were in his carriage.

She could tell he wasn't happy. Mostly because she wasn't happy, either; she had assumed she could just go in and take care of things, as she always had, but this situation was substantially different from what she had ever done before.

He walked beside her, quickly, and she had to trot to keep up with him. She knew that the sooner they were out of there, the better, but she also suspected he was just—angry, and walking quickly was an outward result of that anger. But was he angry with her, or just upset about what they had just gone through?

The coachman leaped down to open the door for them, shooing a few gawking children away, and Margaret sat, finally feeling as though she could breathe properly.

He sat opposite her, not beside her, and her heart sank. He was upset with her. A fact that was eminently obvious when he spoke.

"What did you think you were doing back there?" He raised his gaze upward, exhaling as he did so. "Did you even think through what you were doing? What you had gotten me into?"

An answering anger flowed through her, and she spoke before she even thought about it. "You don't have to be into this, as you say. I can do it on my own." Even though she knew he was right—she'd had no idea what she was doing, and she was definitely in over her head.

But she was too angry to admit that to him.

"Do it on your own?" He leaned forward. "Do you even think that is a possibility, now I see what foolhardy behavior you are capable of? To go into a place like that, being who you are, and to tell those rabble-rousers how to behave?" He shook his head. "I understand why you started doing what you do, but this—this is beyond what you should be doing."

Her anger unfurled. "What I should be doing?" Even as she spoke, she knew she was wrong, at least partially, but she couldn't stop. Not when she'd been forced into situations because of her gender. "Helping these women out is more than just finding them positions so they can keep their husbands in beer. It is about giving them a sense of purpose, of safety, of—"

He cut her off before she could continue. "I know that. You've explained it. I believe in it as well. I just cannot have you in danger, Margaret."

His voice was rough, nearly breaking, and she felt as though her heart turned over in her chest.

"I know." She leaned forward as well, putting her hand on his knee. He immediately curled his fingers over hers, gripping them tightly. "I—I did not think it through, entirely."

"At all," he said.

She bristled, but had to admit he was right. "At all. I—you just don't know what it means to be as helpless as some of those women are." She looked away, blinking as she felt the sting of tears in her eyes. "If I were not willing to be a scandal, I would have ended up like one of them. Dressed in more elegant gowns, but still subject to a man's whims, dependent on his fortune to keep me fed and housed."

She looked back at him, fierce desperation coloring her speech. "Those women deserve as much of a chance to—to cause a scandal, as I did," she said, wiping the tears away with the back of her hand, "if they want to, or be free of men who would control them, or to kiss a duke, if they feel like it."

"I'm sorry." He spoke so sincerely she couldn't help but believe him, but—

"Sorry for what?"

He grimaced and resumed looking to the ceiling of the carriage again. "I'm sorry that you feel under so much pressure to right the wrongs done to you and to other women in your situation. I'm sorry that that problem exists, that we—people like me, in my position—haven't done enough to fix it." He shook his head, as though trying to figure out what to say. "You don't have to do this alone, though. That is," he added, looking rueful, "you're not, and I am sorry I even suggested that you should. I want to help you in this so you can continue to refuse to marry unpleasant men and kiss the occasional duke. Hopefully me," he said with a smirk that told her he knew she would not wish to kiss any other duke.

And she didn't. What was more, she didn't want to kiss any other man, ever, and wasn't that a depressing thought?

Because, damn it, she'd fallen in love with him. And she'd sworn she wouldn't get too involved, had promised him as much, and yet here she was, absolutely in love with him.

She was disgusted with herself.

Something of her thoughts must have changed her expression, since he was now looking anxiously at her. "Is something wrong?" he asked. "Should I have not made light of kissing a duke?"

He was so adorable. Not something one would normally say about a very large, very tall, occasionally frightening-looking aristocrat with only one eye, but then again, none of this was normal, so she supposed thinking he was adorable was now the norm.

As well as the norm that she was now in love with the Absolutely Unattainable, Not to Be Wanted Anyway, Piratical and Awkward Duke.

She was very glad she was not writing the story of her life, because she had no idea how to continue it.

But she could write the next few hours, couldn't she?

"Are you up for another adventure?" she asked.

He looked at her warily. "As long as it's nothing involving rabble-rousing men in dusty pubs. I've had enough of that kind of adventure."

She laughed. "No, it's nothing like that. Can you tell your coachman to head toward Cremorne Gardens?"

Lash rapped on the roof and the coach slowed. When it stopped, he opened the door and told his coachman where to go; thankfully, the man seemed to know where it was, since Lash himself had no idea.

He settled back inside and nodded to her. "On our way. A garden, you say?"

"Much more than that," she replied. "It's got restaurants, and balloon ascents, and dancing pavilions. It will be too early for dancing, but we can wander about for a bit, perhaps find something to eat, like oysters or an eel pie." Her eyes sparkled in delight, and he found himself smiling in response, even though he most definitely did not want an eel pie.

"It sounds enjoyable," he replied, trying to keep his voice from being stiff.

"It is, Gernie," she said, her face alight with anticipation.

GEORGIANA AND THE DRAGON

By A Lady of Mystery

Georgiana hadn't the faintest idea how to teach a man to be a man, much less teach a naked man how to join the world without causing comment.

"Here," she said, taking her cloak off and draping it over him. "The first thing we need to do is get you clothed. Dragons can go about with nothing on, but people frown on men doing so."

He sat up and drew the cloak around his body, thankfully covering some of the more . . . human parts.

"And next we should go back home, to my house." She swallowed as she thought of what her father and sisters would say. But the alternative—leaving him here—wasn't an option. "We can get you more clothed, and possibly fed, and then figure out what to do."

He nodded as he rose. "Lead on, not a princess."

Chapter 24

If there was anything more fun than watching the duke wander about bemusedly at a pleasure garden, Margaret didn't know what that was.

Well, she did know, but at least this they could do in public.

"And that is where people go to dance?" he said, pointing to one of the raised stages in the open area of the gardens. "Outside and everything?"

She smirked. "Yes, outside and everything. Perhaps one day, or rather night, we will come to dance under the stars." And then she had to laugh at how dumbfounded he looked. Yet also feel a pang that he was so far removed from real life that this kind of possibility seemed so distant.

"Lady, over here!" a voice called, and she and the duke both turned to look. A young man, likely no older than seventeen, stood behind a cart, smoke pluming out of the top. "I've got sausages to keep your stomach from growling," he said.

She looked at him, one brow raised. "Is your stomach growling?" she asked.

"Most definitely," he replied, and took her arm to lead her toward the cart.

After the sausage, and consuming some ale from another vendor, they wandered about the gardens, nodding at the various people they encountered, but were mostly just silent, both of them lost within their thoughts.

The adventure had distracted her for a little while, but now she was left with the reality of her situation—spending time with someone she'd stupidly fallen in love with, who made her happy, who had been quite clear about where he saw any of this going.

And it was only a matter of time before people started to talk—yes, it was unlikely that anybody they knew would be here, or at Caldwell's Dance Hall, but she knew the possibility existed.

But thus far she hadn't been very successful in breaking off whatever this was; in fact, she'd only found herself more immersed in it when she did try, so perhaps she should just try not to think about it.

Which she well knew would be impossible for her.

"This is delightful," he said, breaking into her thoughts. They were standing in front of a flying balloon, now deflated, but they could see the balloon's brightly colored stripes and examine the basket that would hold the hardy travelers.

Not that Margaret wanted to be of their number; she was adventurous, but not foolhardy, at least not in terms of going aloft.

"I wonder if we could take a ride," he continued. Apparently the duke had no such concern about the possibility of falling straight out of the sky, as she did.

"You might take a ride, if you wish," Margaret replied. "I cannot even contemplate going up without feeling shaky." Which was also what she could say about having fallen in love with him and confronting those gentlemen at the pub—all of it made her shaky, and anxious, and worried, although definitely not for the same reasons.

"You and yer lady wish to go up, then?" A man in a striped suit, nearly matching the balloon, stood up as he spoke, having been directly behind the basket. Margaret jumped at his voice.

"My lady does not wish to, but I do," the duke said.

She couldn't help but be surprised at how excited he sounded. This, from the man who'd never done anything as exciting as dancing outside, now he wanted to ascend into the clouds?

That gave her hope for him, but also despair for her, since she would not be a part of his ascent, either literally now, or later on, when he was able to find happiness.

Writers should not fall in love, she thought sourly. *We are always to come up with the most gruesome metaphors for our own lives.*

"You fell in love with him?" Isabella asked, her voice full of amazement. A day later, and she could still see how thrilled he'd been to ride in that balloon. And how sadly real it had been to watch him drift out of sight.

Margaret nodded. She'd arrived at her sister's town house nearly thirty minutes earlier, but had spent that time cooing over baby Victoria and eating all the biscuits that were served for tea.

Margaret had even swatted her sister's hand away when she was about to reach for one. Isabella leaped back, then burst into laughter, and had begged Margaret to talk about it. The falling in love part, not the biscuit part.

They were in Isabella's sitting room, adjacent to her bedroom. It was very quiet, especially because Isabella's husband was out at the boxing gym "pummeling someone," Isabella had said with a wave of her hand.

Isabella had recently done renovations, changing the room's colors from a mélange of pinks to pale greens and blues. It was lovely, and Isabella was rightfully proud of what she'd done.

Plus, she'd informed a surprised Margaret, she didn't like the color pink.

"What do you want me to tell you?" Margaret said through a mouthful of biscuit.

"Everything. From the beginning, please."

So she had. Victoria had gone to sleep, since her aunt's romantic travails weren't enough to keep her entertained, and Isabella had just let Margaret talk, only interrupting to ask the important questions.

"He went ballooning? That sounds so reckless. Is that how he lost his eye? Not ballooning, but something equally reckless?"

Margaret froze, a biscuit—maybe her seventh?—halfway to her mouth. "I don't know! I haven't asked him yet. He hasn't told me, either." She returned the biscuit to the plate and dropped her head into her hands. "This is hopeless. I am hopeless." She raised her head and stared at Isabella. "I did the one thing I specifically knew I should not do. And now what?" She shook her head. "Pathetic."

Isabella leaned forward and patted her sister's hand. "Not pathetic, Margie. If there is one thing being in love has taught me, it is that it is never pathetic." Her mouth twisted up into a half smile. "Hopeless, perhaps. But not pathetic."

Margaret couldn't help it, her sister's words made her laugh, although she still felt as though she'd been punched in the heart. Sadly, she could not blame that feeling on all the biscuits she'd consumed.

"What are you going to do about it?" Her sister sounded so—so practical, as though being in love meant you could do something about it. Of course, when you looked as beautiful as Isabella, chances were good that you could do something about it.

Margaret was nothing close to Isabella in looks. *But*, she thought, *he does think I am attractive*. He said so, and she knew full well it was difficult for him to say things, so if had said it—well, it must be doubly true. If having an opinion could be doubled, that is.

But more than his possibly wanting her was the reality that she did not want to be a duchess, much as she loved her sister and her irascible brother-in-law. Especially the duchess to a duke whose responsibilities required him to stay out of gossip's way, and definitely not have a wife who had caused scandal in the past and would likely do so again, despite any of her best efforts.

She would never curtail her work among the women she helped, nor did she particularly want to give up writing. Yes, it could feel as though it were a chore at times, but she did love doing it, and she got great joy out of having done it, and by making people happy.

Even she knew a duchess couldn't continue to write a serial for a vulgar newspaper. At least she didn't think so, not without scandal. What would the Queen say about something like that, anyway?

She didn't think the Queen would be in favor of it, that was for certain.

And it wasn't as though he showed any signs of being in love with her; he was concerned for her, he did admit to wanting to kiss her, but that wasn't love. Because if it was, gentlemen were in love with a different woman nearly every day, if not every hour.

There was nothing for it but to keep her feelings to herself. Not something she was normally accustomed to doing.

Speaking of which, her sister was still waiting for her reply. Her feelings.

"I am going to do nothing about it." She glanced over at the sleeping Victoria. "You'll have to endure your spinster aunt, Lady Victoria." Because while she could keep her feelings from him, it wasn't as though she could easily swap them over to anyone else.

"Don't assign yourself to spinsterhood too quickly," her sister said with a pointed look. "Even you cannot predict the future, much as you might like to."

The idea that things might not end up as she thought they should made her shudder, and shiver, in two entirely contrasting reactions.

"It is your deal, Lady Margaret."

Margaret nodded as though she knew that already, and picked up the cards, shuffling them with a practiced hand.

She'd come to the Dearwoods that night to make up for being so . . . distracted of late. She still had funds for what she wanted, no *needed* to do, but going to that pub and seeing those men had made her see that there was more to her mission than just helping some women escape their circumstances.

If she wanted to make a change, a real change, she would have to engage the men of the households also. And that would mean placing more people with the Quality Employment Agency, or finding another place that could help them, if the men weren't trained for the types of positions the Agency generally had open.

The Dearwoods were pleasant people, and the company they kept was generally pleasant as well. It was unlikely she would run into Lord Collingwood, for example, who seemed to be running with a racier crowd since losing his ducal title to her brother-in-law. That was a relief.

But the duke wasn't here, either, even though he absolutely did not run with a racy crowd, unless she was a racy crowd. Perhaps she was. And it was getting late, so he likely wasn't going to be here. She should be relieved at that as well, since she didn't want to have to pretend she wasn't in love with him to his face. She'd rather just pretend at home, to Annie, or to herself when she was looking in the mirror practicing looking not in love.

She looked very much in love, unfortunately. It was only when she'd thought up a terrible story about a great herd of vultures coming to rip out her heart if she kept loving him that her expression changed.

But at least that gave her an idea for her next piece of writing.

She frowned, and shook her head.

"Is something wrong, Lady Margaret?"

Nothing falling out of love wouldn't fix. "I am fine, Lord Gantrey, thank you."

Lord Gantrey patted her hand, leaning forward to speak in a stage whisper. "Is my favorite card-sharp distracted by something?"

Margaret forced herself to smile, not that it was too difficult, since Lord Gantrey was such a nice person. She nearly felt bad about always winning when they played, only he could afford it, and she knew it brought him joy, especially on the very rare occasions he won a hand or two.

But she was distracted. And being distracted by love was no way to acquire enough funds to keep on with her endeavors. And since she was not interested in marrying money, she would have to keep on supporting herself, which meant she couldn't get distracted.

Even she didn't think she could write herself successfully out of this one. Especially not within a reasonable period of time.

"The Duke of Lasham."

Well, that was not going to help her distraction. She did not look up at his arrival, instead sorting her cards—again—as though they would have a different result if she went by suit, not number.

They did not. She had a bad hand in reality, and what was more, she had a bad hand in life. Although that sounded ludicrously dramatic, as though she were starving on the streets or something.

She was not. She was lucky, truly lucky, to be born into her station in life. It was just unlucky that no matter what station a woman had been born into, she was constrained by her gender.

Men could do what they wanted. They could offer and expect to be accepted by a lady who had no wish to marry them, they could make their living at gambling if they wanted without being derided for it, they could go wherever they wanted to without fear of assault.

"Does anyone know how he lost his eye?" The woman to the right of her, a Miss Simpson, asked in a low voice. "He looks so fearsome, I swear he looks like something out of a nightmare."

Margaret opened her mouth to protest, but snapped it shut again. That was the common perception of him, and she had even had it herself, back when she thought his fearsome appearance was the most interesting thing about him.

Now she knew better. Much better, unfortunately for her, not to mention her heart.

"I heard it was a duel over a lady," Lord Gantrey said. "But he's never spoken about it."

A duel over a lady. She had always assumed it was a wartime injury. What if it was over a lady? What if he'd never gotten over her?

She should be happy, then. It meant he wouldn't go fall in love with her as ridiculously as she had fallen in love with him. It should make her happy.

But it absolutely did not. Instead, it caused a churn of emotions inside her, primarily jealousy, and she wanted to simultaneously demand he tell her the lady's name and also go punch the lady herself for not staying by his side.

"No wonder he hasn't married," Miss Simpson said with a sniff. "Who could stand to look at him? Imagine what is under that eye patch?"

Now Margaret just wanted to punch Miss Simpson.

Really, she was getting to be as bad as her brother-in-law the duke, who seemed to like going around hitting people.

She glanced at her hand, knowing there was no way she could win anyway. She nodded and smiled at everyone around her—with the exception of Miss Simpson—and laid her cards down on the table. "Excuse me, everyone. I must be on my way, I have promised to see my sister, the Duchess of Gage, this evening."

A total lie, but no one would call her on it, especially when a ducal title was invoked. She felt her mouth twist into a sour smile at the thought. A duke was so important that every move he made, every eye he happened to lose, was discussed and debated and nearly held as a public forum.

Why couldn't she have fallen in love with a plain mister? Even a lower-titled aristocrat might have been doable. A baronet, or an earl's third son.

But no. She had to go and fall in love with a duke. If she had fallen in love with Prince Albert, she couldn't have chosen any worse. Although if she had fallen in love with Prince Albert, she would have had Queen Victoria to contend with.

As it was, she just had to contend with her scandal, his responsibility, her responsibility, and the minor fact that as far as he knew, they were just adventuring together. Not falling in love. Not doing anything more than whatever they were doing, in fact.

GEORGIANA AND THE DRAGON

By A Lady of Mystery

❧❧❧

"You should be able to wear some of my father's clothing, you are of a size," Georgiana said, glancing back at him as they walked through the forest.

"Won't your father wonder why you are bringing home a man who has no clothing of his own?" Little puffs of smoke accompanied each word, and she wondered if they would eventually dissipate, or if she'd have to come up with another lie—something not involving the words "former" and "dragon" to explain the oddity of his breath.

Georgiana gave a rueful laugh. "My father has long ago accepted that I am, as you so succinctly said, not a princess. I have done many odd things in the past, although I have not as yet brought home naked strangers."

"I am not naked," the man pointed out. He drew her cloak more tightly around himself. "I am wearing a garment now, which is much more than I've ever worn before."

Georgiana halted in her steps, turning around to face him. "You were a dragon before; I don't believe dragons wear any clothing. Men do." She looked him up and down. "And you need more than you have on."

He shrugged. "If you say so, not a princess. If you say so."

They kept walking, Georgiana's chest getting tighter and tighter with each step.

Chapter 25

He couldn't stay away from her. Even the day before, when he'd been up above her, in the sky in the balloon, he'd kept his eye on her, watching as she became a dot on the ground.

The feeling of flight had been wonderful, but couldn't compare to what it felt like when he was holding her. When she was holding him.

He'd thought she might be in attendance here, and he'd felt his chest ease when he spotted her in the crowd—tonight she wore green, a dark, jewel-like hue that looked black in certain angles of the light.

Not that he was studying her from all angles, or anything.

Even though he absolutely was.

She had those star things pinned in her hair again tonight, and a necklace that sparkled as well. But nothing to compare with the sparkling essence of her, the thing that made him want to go to her and capture it, and her, in his arms, never to let her go.

That was very dangerous thinking.

"Your Grace, we are so grateful you could make it," Lady Dearwood said. The woman was so tall she could look him straight in the eye, which made him feel even more awkward. Most people had to crane up to look at him, so they weren't confronted by his lack of sight so directly.

But Lady Dearwood didn't seem at all bothered by it, judging by the self-satisfied expression on her face. Of course, he thought she had a few daughters lying around, and a duke, even a duke with one eye, would be a good catch for one of them. One wife, one eye. A good match.

"Thank you for the invitation," Lasham replied. "It is a lovely night for a party, isn't it?"

Lady Dearwood's expression faltered. In truth, it was raining quite hard, so much so that Lasham's feet were squeaking because of the water that had gotten into his shoes on the short walk from the carriage to the house.

"It is, Your Grace," she said firmly. Apparently she'd decided it was better to agree with the duke than debate how "a lovely night" would be defined.

"And this is a lovely party," he continued, deliberately using the same word so as to make his entire opinion suspect in her eyes.

When had he gotten so devious? And more to the point, why hadn't he started before? It was fun to watch Lady Dearwood wrestle with the information that he had just provided—that he categorized a rainy evening and an evening party into the same description, which must mean . . .

He saw when she gave up parsing it. "Your Grace, the beverage table is over there, and of course I can summon someone to fetch a glass, if you could tell me what you prefer."

"Thank you, my lady." He glanced over to see Margaret had gotten up from the table she'd been sitting at, and was making her way through the crowd, looking as though she were heading toward the terrace.

Even though it was raining. Did she think it was a lovely night also?

"Excuse me, I do think I will go get something to drink." He didn't wait for whatever she was going to say next because it wouldn't be anything that would enable him to reach Margaret faster.

He cut her off just before she arrived at the table with all the beverages. "Lady Margaret."

He saw her swallow before she looked at him. What had he done? Had something changed?

The look in her eyes made him want to take her in his arms immediately, despite all the people here, despite the scandal, despite the fact that he didn't know what she was feeling. Except, it seemed, hurt.

"What is wrong?"

She shook her head, biting her lip. Up close he could see the signs of strain in her face, the flush of emotion staining her cheeks.

"Nothing." She heaved an exasperated breath. "A few things. But nothing I cannot take care of myself."

"Something to drink, my lady?" The footman in attendance at the table interrupted what he had been about to say. Which was probably good, since he didn't know what he was going to say. As usual.

"Yes, thank you, I would like a glass of champagne."

"I too," Lasham said.

He nodded to the terrace. "Were you going outside?"

She blinked and looked in that direction. "Isn't it raining?"

He shrugged. "That just means there won't be anyone else out there."

She laughed, and he felt something ease as her expression lightened. "You have a point, but I don't wish to get rained on."

"But I want to know what is bothering you. Perhaps I can help you." He spoke in a gruff voice, unaccustomed to saying precisely what was on his mind. Usually he mangled it somehow, but this time, what he'd said was what he meant.

"Thank you." She took a sip from her glass, then eyed it, shrugged, and downed the whole thing. "Let us go where we can talk in private."

He drank his glass down as well, then winked at her. With his one good eye, which just probably appeared that he was twitching, so perhaps he hadn't thought that through entirely. "Can you go to my house? Say in ten minutes?"

She arched a brow, looking as though she were planning an adventure, which made his body react in ways that were not appropriate for a public setting.

Which made it even more imperative that he

get her alone. Besides which, he had some of Jamie's advice rattling around in his brain, and he wanted to test his newfound knowledge.

"Yes, Your Grace. I will see you at your house very soon."

She placed the empty glass on the table, dipped a curtsey, and made her way through the crowd to the exit.

Lasham watched her go, resisting the urge to accompany her, since that would not be avoiding the gossip they needed to avoid, especially now that Lord Collingwood was sniffing around.

It didn't feel right that they had to pretend, but the alternative—not pretending—was something she'd adamantly said she was against. And he was, too, wasn't he?

Maybe he wasn't after all. Maybe he should think about what might happen, should try to write the ending to this story himself.

If she were writing this story, she would have the duke take her into his arms, profess his undying love, and offer marriage to her.

But this wasn't a story, it was her life. And while the fairy-tale ending sounded good, it wouldn't help what would happen afterward—the scandal, the responsibility, the eventual disappointment when neither one of them could do what they truly wished to.

This was a better solution, she told herself as she got into her carriage. Something with an end, not a happy end, necessarily, but a finish. A finality. A close to this period of her life.

Annie was seated inside, doing some sort of knitting, although Margaret suspected she just borrowed some of the work from any of the young ladies whom Margaret had helped, since Margaret had yet to see Annie actually produce something.

"We going home so early?" Annie said, straightening in the seat.

And here is where it would get . . . difficult.

"You are. I am headed elsewhere." She tried to speak in as firm a tone as possible to dissuade Annie's questions, only she knew, even before Annie spoke, that it would be no good.

"Elsewhere?" Annie's tone was arch. "Elsewhere like to a certain duke's house? That kind of elsewhere? And you won't be needing your maid there, will you?" She leaned forward, her gaze locked on Margaret's face. "What have you two been doing, anyway?" Her expression became outraged. "And what you have not been telling me?"

"I will tell you when I can. Right now, I don't even know, it's just—it's just that he is kind, and has been helping me with the women, and I know you wanted me to have more protection, and he has been splendid. And all he asked for in return is that I show him some adventure."

Annie's eyebrows rose up so much on her face they were in danger of getting lost in her hairline. "Show him some adventure? Is that what the young gentlemen are calling it these days?"

"Oh my gosh, no, not that," Margaret replied, feeling her cheeks start to burn. "I took him to the dance hall," *where we kissed*, "and we've been to the museums," *where we almost kissed*, "and he makes sure I get home safely in his carriage," *where we frequently kiss.*

"Ah." Annie seemed somewhat assuaged by all the details. But her next words made Margaret speechless for once in her life.

"So you've gone and fallen in love with him, haven't you?" She shook her head as she folded up her knitting. "You know that there aren't very many happy endings in life. Your sister had one, but it was a close call. And the chances of you finding love with your own duke are even more reduced. You know the odds, you gamble against them enough."

Margaret sighed, wishing Annie weren't quite so perceptive. And likely correct. "I have, Annie, and I know that nothing can come of it. But I do like him, and he does enjoy my company, and I need his help, at least until we get more assistance for those women."

Annie narrowed her gaze at her mistress. "So you're going to keep on doing what you're doing, feeling what you're feeling, until you have to give it all up, aren't you?" She sighed. "It's not as though I can say anything to change your mind. Just be careful, mind."

It was the same admonition she'd given Margaret a few weeks ago, and it still held true. But how could Margaret be careful when she was too busy being in love?

GEORGIANA AND THE DRAGON

By A Lady of Mystery

＊＊＊

"Did you want to be a man?" she asked after an hour or so of walking. He followed along behind, but not so far behind she couldn't see his bare leg from the corner of her eye.

It was very disconcerting.

"No," he said plainly.

"Oh." There wasn't much more she could say about that, was there?

"Did you ever want to be anything other than you are?" he asked.

She heard herself snort. "Besides someone who didn't have to go into the forest where she might encounter strange and possibly deadly creatures? No."

"Then why did you ask me if I wanted to be a man? Isn't being a dragon enough?" He didn't sound as though he were offended, just as though he was curious.

She considered it. "I suppose it is."

"So why do you want something else?"

That was a very good question.

Chapter 26

"Your Grace, the lady is here." The butler didn't sound precisely approving, but then again, he didn't sound disapproving, so perhaps he was just neutral.

And why did she care about what the butler thought, anyway? Oh, of course, because she cared what people thought in general, which was why she was currently gambling her way through the best houses in London Society to give lower types of people a better chance at life. So being dismissive of a mere servant would be hypocritical of her.

Vortigern was waiting for her at the door to his library, where so many wonderful things had happened. She felt a shiver of excitement as she walked in after leaving her cloak with the potentially disapproving butler.

"Tea, please," Vortigern said as he closed the door behind them. He didn't pause, he just drew her into his arms and held her. She immediately felt calmer, and yet also more apprehensive—

because if this was what she needed to be calm, then what would she do in six months? Or three? When whatever this was was over?

"You're shaking," he said. He withdrew his grasp of her, but took her hand and led her over to the sofa. Their sofa.

Margaret sat down, still not looking at him. Not because she didn't want to see his face, because of course she did, but because she wasn't certain she had mastered the I-am-absolutely-not-in-love-with-you expression she'd been working on, and she didn't want to ruin the evening with that revelation right away.

"I am fine." She smoothed an errant piece of hair behind her ear. "I think it is the delayed reaction to confronting those gentlemen, and realizing there is so much more to be done." A lie, but she couldn't exactly tell the truth, could she?

"Not by you," he said in a fierce tone of voice.

That startled her enough to look directly into his eye. "Why not me?"

He took her hands in his, holding them firmly as though to emphasize his point. "Not entirely by you, I mean to say. I am working with my secretary to craft some new bills that might ease some of the suffering in those places. Make it easier for mothers to find work and not have to abandon their children." He shook his head. "It's easy to be discouraged, there is so much to do, but it has to be done. You've shown me that."

"Thank you."

They sat silent for a few moments, him still holding her hand. A knock at the door made them leap away, and Margaret regretted the feeling of commonality, of companionship, she'd just felt.

"Come in," Vortigern called.

The butler entered, bearing a silver salver with all sorts of tea things. He laid them on the table in front of the sofa, adjusting a saucer here, a sugar bowl there, until he rose and nodded. "Will that be all, Your Grace?" he asked, not looking at Margaret.

"Yes, thank you," Vortigern replied.

The butler nodded again, then left, only pausing to ensure the door was thoroughly and shockingly closed.

"Tea again?" Margaret said. "And here I thought all unmarried dukes sat about drinking liquor a lady should not even know about when they were on their own. You are disabusing me of my exciting notions, Your Grace."

His hands froze over the teapot, and he looked up at her, a knowing smile on his face. A smile that, if she was not mistaken, meant that there would be touching and more happening very soon.

And she was all in favor of it.

Still watching her, he removed his cravat with one hand, tossing it to the ground. Her eyes drank in the bare expanse of his throat, the way his body seemed poised to pounce. Preferably on her.

"Come here, Margaret," he said, leaning back against the sofa. His eye was on her mouth and she knew in that moment that he was going to kiss her, and what was even more wonderful was that she was going to kiss him as well—kiss the man she loved.

She'd always wanted to know what that would feel like, and had resigned herself to having to imagine it. Imagine the flutter in her heart, the quickening pulse, the overwhelming rush of emotion that would flood her when she was in the arms of the man she loved.

But now she could find out for herself, a writer's most direct way of figuring out how to convey it in prose, and she wished she were doing all this for the sake of her writing, only she wasn't. That was just a lovely side effect, one that would hopefully impact her sales in the future.

He waited for her, as though he could read her mind and see the tumult of thoughts therein. Only she hoped he couldn't, or he might not wish to kiss her at all—they'd agreed, this was part of the adventure, not part of a life plan.

She leaned into him and pressed her mouth against his. And knew immediately it was entirely different.

This was something special, something new and fresh kindling inside her. They were alone, they were well aware of what they were doing, were going to do, and it was spectacular.

She reached up to his neck, putting her hand on the bare expanse of skin where his cravat normally was. It felt strong, and smooth, and she slid her fingers around to the back of his head, pushing them into his hair.

His hands were on her shoulders, but his

thumbs were on the top of her chest, the part not covered by her gown, and they were stroking her skin, creating fiery trails wherever they touched. All of a sudden she felt consumed by it, the burning need for something more, no matter what that more was.

And she was fairly certain she did know what that more was.

Was she really contemplating doing that more?

She would have to say she was.

His fingers were sliding over her upper chest now, and then he stopped kissing her mouth, instead lowering his head to her neck and kissing her there, then moving to her collarbone, then farther down, and then, oh then, his fingers were sliding the fabric of her gown aside, and then her chemise, and he plunged his hand down into her bodice, his fingers finding her nipple and rubbing.

She twisted, arching to get her body closer to his, although any closer and he would be behind her, but she wasn't thinking logically. Wasn't thinking at all, not with his clever fingers pulling and stroking her nipple, his mouth sucking on her skin, her hands holding him to her.

She pushed at his legs so she could ease herself down the sofa, wanting to be beneath him, to feel all of his largeness on top of her, making her unable to move, unable to see anything but him.

He obliged, sweeping his hand over her hip and arranging her on the sofa, then easing down on top of her. He raised his head and met her gaze. "I am not too heavy, am I?" he asked, that tender hesitancy in his voice.

"No, please," she said in a pleading voice. "Please." She wasn't quite sure what she was asking for, just that she wanted him, all of him, on her and around her and—and yes, inside her.

Dear Lord. This might happen.

His gaze was focused on her gown, his expression considering. Was he thinking she was forward? Well, she was, so she couldn't argue with him there. Was he thinking they were making an enormous mistake?

Dear Lord, she hoped not.

"I am wondering how best to remove your gown," he said at last. He looked up at her. "Because if I don't remove it properly, I might just rip it, and then how would you explain that to your very inquisitive maid?"

She shivered at the forcefulness of his words. Odd how she loathed being told what to do, and yet she was willing to do whatever he wanted.

Well, provided whatever he wanted was more of this.

She turned onto her side, trying not to think of what they must look like now—her underneath him, but not entirely, with a leg sprawled out from the sofa, her arms waving in the air now that she wasn't holding him to her. "You can unbutton me," she said, turning her head toward the back of her gown.

"Oh, I can," he said with assurance. Where had the Awkward Duke gone? This duke looked and sounded utterly confident, his fingers going to the top of her gown and beginning to undo the buttons.

A few buttons down, and then his mouth was there, kissing her back through her chemise. And then he was finished with the unbuttoning—but hopefully not the kissing—and rose, pulling her with him.

They stood facing each other, she knowing her cheeks were flushed, seeing the same flush on his cheekbones. His eye blazed with the same fire she had felt sparking through her, and his mouth—God, that gorgeous, lovely, absolutely kissable mouth—just seemed to beckon her. She leaned up and kissed him, then bit him very softly on his lower lip.

That seemed to surprise him, but not in a what-have-you-just-done way. More like "Well, that was fun, and now that has given me all sorts of interesting ideas," judging by the way he was looking at her.

"Turn around," he said in a growl, not waiting for her to react, but putting his hands on her waist and moving her so her back was facing him.

He put his hands on her shoulders and slid the gown down, drawing her arms from her sleeves and guiding the fabric so that it ended up in a pool at her feet. She followed his actions by undoing the laces of her corset, allowing it, too, to fall to the floor.

She felt totally exposed, of course, given that she was now standing only in her chemise, but also absolutely safe. She trusted him. And what's more, she wanted this. All of it, no matter what the consequences.

No matter what the consequences? a voice chimed in her head.

Even that.

Really?

That voice again. And why did it sound so much like Annie?

Yes. Really.

Fine, then.

Margaret turned back around, instinctively holding her arms crossed over her breasts, but then lowered them slowly as she looked at him.

His gaze was devouring her, traveling from her face to lower down, then back again. The room was absolutely quiet, except for their breathing.

His breathing was a lot louder than hers. Somehow that pleased her in a self-satisfied, feminine way.

And in the spirit of wanting to undo him entirely—literally, not figuratively, since he was still entirely clothed, save for his cravat—she undid the tie of her chemise, then began to gather the fabric up from the bottom, drawing it up slowly but steadily.

"Shouldn't you do something about your clothing?" she asked, the chemise now just at mid-thigh. A few inches more and he would be able to see there, that place that felt as though it were throbbing.

He swallowed, his gaze not wavering from her lower body, shrugging his coat off and flinging it behind him, then beginning to undo the buttons of his shirt.

She closed her eyes for a moment and drew the chemise up, up over that spot, to her waist. Pausing there as she opened her eyes to see him drawing his shirt over his head, revealing his (as she knew it would be) splendid chest.

Now her whole body felt as though it were ablaze, and wanting, and she knew very well what she wanted—a cessation of this ache that seemed to be centered there, at her core.

She glanced down to that spot on him, feeling her eyes widen at seeing just how his trousers were tented out from his erection. And her mouth got dry at thinking what it would be like to see him, to touch him.

"Hurry up," he said in a rasp. He jerked his head toward her waist. "Get that thing off or I'll tear it off."

At some point—not now, she had far too few brain cells to spare on the question—she would ask herself why hearing him say those things made her even more excited.

And then she would ask him to talk that way some more.

She licked her lips and brought the chemise up over her head, tossing it to the floor as he had done his clothing.

And now she was entirely naked. She panicked for a moment, aghast at herself, but then he knelt down on the rug in front of her and placed his hands on her knees—those same shaky ones—and then drew them up so his palms were at the crease of her leg, and his thumbs—well, his thumbs were nestled in the curls of her sex.

He glanced up, a knowing, confident smile on his face. "You're beautiful," he said.

It was on the tip of her tongue to argue with him, because she'd never thought of that particular area as having beauty or not, but then he did something that made her completely speechless.

He leaned forward and kissed her there, his hands holding her in place, drawing her legs apart so he could reach everywhere.

Which he did. He licked her, drawing his tongue down through the folds of her sex, finding a spot that made her jump, only she couldn't because he was holding her firmly in place.

He kept licking and kissing her there, teasing her with his tongue, making her feel as though every single thought she'd ever had had flown out of her head, all her focus on there, where he was— where he was sucking and licking her.

She heard a moan, and knew it was she. And felt her knees get shaky all over again, but knew that he wouldn't let her fall, no matter what happened.

And it seemed as though something were happening—it felt as though there was a gathering storm whirling inside her, focused on that spot, right where his tongue was, so blissful and yet so urgent she didn't know what to think.

Until—"Oh my," she said as the first wave of pleasure hit her, spiraling through her body, every bit of her immersed in the feeling, the waves continuing to roll through her body until she felt as though this was all she'd ever felt.

When it finally stopped she looked down at

him; he was regarding her with a very satisfied look of masculine pride.

"That was—that was—" she stammered, and he smiled even more. His mouth was moist, from her, from there, and if she were in the least bit embarrassed, that would make her turn scarlet, only she wasn't. There was no room in her head for embarrassment; it was completely filled with what he had done, how she felt, and—well, that was about it.

He stood and gathered her in his arms, her skin against his chest, the hairs tickling her. That meant, too, that his erection pressed against her waist, and she felt herself start to blush as she thought about what might happen next. What she thought might happen next, although since she had had no idea that what he'd just done was possible, maybe other things were possible she'd never even imagined?

And here she thought she had a fairly vivid imagination. Now she couldn't wait to discover what she hadn't known about before.

Lasham tried to steady himself as he held her, still shaking, but it was difficult to concentrate when she was so very naked and he was so very aroused.

He was also, if he were to admit it, rather impressed with himself for what he'd just done. If he could figure out how to thank Jamie without complete embarrassment, he would.

But he didn't have time to swell with pride—so

to speak—because she began to unbutton the fall of his trousers, her eyebrows drawn together in concentration.

He couldn't help but let out a groan as her hand brushed his cock.

She looked up at him with a look of concern. Which was ludicrous, given that she was entirely naked, he had just brought her to climax, and they were still standing. Why were they still standing? That he could do something about.

"Let's lie down," he said, pushing her gently toward the sofa.

"Oh, you mean . . . ? Oh yes, of course," she said, going to lie on the sofa. She turned on her side and beckoned for him. Or, more specifically, beckoned to his trousers. "You really have to get those off, that looks painful," she said, an amused tone in her voice.

If it weren't so actually painful he'd have laughed. But she was right. It was.

He undid the rest of the buttons and yanked his trousers down his legs, now standing only in his smallclothes.

It felt exceedingly odd to be so unclothed in front of her. Although he'd already come close to baring his soul, hadn't he? These were just the trappings of the body, not what was really important.

Even though it seemed as though this were the most important thing right now, at least according to some of his body parts.

She patted the sofa, grinning at him. "I am enjoying this, you know."

He snorted. "I should hope so, given what I just did."

She arched a brow. "Oh, aren't you cocky," she said with an emphasis on the last word. He couldn't help but groan.

"Did I ever say you were good with words?" he asked as he lay down beside her. "Because I rescind that compliment. That was terrible."

She snickered. "I know, and that is why I said it to you. So you wouldn't feel so bad about not being as good with words as you might want to be. Not that I've had any complaints," she added, in a serious tone. "You don't give yourself enough credit for saying what you do say, or what you don't say. Too many people just talk and talk and ta—"

At which point he had to stop her mouth with his, wrapping his big hand around her waist, pulling her to him so nearly every surface of skin was touching hers. And it still wasn't enough.

She kissed him eagerly, the hand that was pinned underneath her body coming up to reach behind his neck, the other hand on his waist.

Still not enough.

He let go of her enough to take her hand and put it on him, right on his cock. "Now who's cocky?" he murmured as he squeezed her hand to show her what he wanted.

"It's still you," she said, but he didn't—couldn't—say anything in reply because she had slid her hand into his smallclothes and was grasping him, sliding her palm up and down the shaft, from the base to the tip.

It took a bit of fumbling for him to convey to her just what felt right, but eventually she found a rhythm, working her hand up and down, until it felt as though he were going to explode.

Which of course he was.

He buried his face in her neck, breathing in the scent of her, the womanly warmth of her skin, feeling how her breasts pressed against his chest. His hand was on her waist, then slid down her hip to her arse, which he ran his palm over, relishing the soft curves. He slid his hand down farther, between her legs, picking up her thigh and placing it over his leg so they were entwined, her hand still between them, still working his shaft.

It felt so perfect, and he didn't want it to ever end, only of course he did, because then it would mean he'd had an orgasm at her hands, and he'd never wanted anything so much in his entire life.

He felt it building, and building, the softness of her skin seeming to permeate his entire being, her hand and what she was doing with it the only thing he could focus on until—"Aagh," he said as he climaxed, spilling his seed into her hand. His cock pulsed, and he shook, dropping his forehead to her chest, wrapping her leg more fully around him.

"Are you all right?" she asked after a few moments.

Of course, she likely—at least he hoped she hadn't—had never experienced this firsthand, so to speak.

"I'm fine," he said. "I'm wonderful."

She wiped her hand on his smallclothes, chuckling, then ran her hand on his abdomen. "You are, aren't you," she said in a husky voice.

He kissed her collarbone in reply, then took a deep breath.

"I suppose we ought to consider getting married," he said at last.

Georgiana and the Dragon

By A Lady of Mystery

⁓⟡⟡⟡⚬⟡⚬⟡⟡⟡⁓

"Georgie!" Her sisters burst out from their cottage, shrieking, nearly tumbling over one another to reach her.

And stopped short when they saw him. Because while Georgiana had come home with many things, usually water or some sort of foodstuff, she had never arrived home with a man.

Much less a barely clothed man.

"Georgie, is that you?"

Georgiana suppressed a groan at hearing her father's voice from inside. In only a few moments he would come out as well, and see what she had done. Only what had she done?

He walked out, shielding his eyes from the sun. "Well, girl, and what—?" His mouth dropped open.

"It's not what it looks like, Father," she said hurriedly, trying to ignore her sisters' equally agape mouths.

"What is it, then?" he asked, in a mild tone.

"It's much, much worse," she replied.

Chapter 27

She felt as though there were nothing else she wanted, not now, perhaps not ever.

Only—"What did you just say?"

She jerked away from him, which was near impossible, given that he was already pressed in against her on the sofa, which hadn't been designed to fit two people, at least not one of whom was he, with all his largeness.

"Married." He was still speaking somewhere in the vicinity of her neck, but she knew she'd heard him clearly enough.

"Why?"

That seemed to snap him out of his post-whatever stupor, since he jerked back as well, nearly falling off the sofa, only clinging on because her leg tightened instinctively around him as he began to move.

"Because of this," he said, gesticulating toward their nakedness.

Her heart fluttered, but didn't quite sink. Not yet.

"And besides, it seems as though it'd be good for both of us. I know we spoke about not doing that, but now that this has happened, shouldn't we?"

Now her heart sank. Because all of a sudden he'd returned to being the most Staid Proper Duke she'd ever met, eye patch or not, and that meant that if she married him—which she very much would not—he would try to curtail her in some way, even if he promised that he wouldn't, and she'd be on display like all the other Society ladies who were too afraid to even approach the card tables.

"No."

She spoke quietly, but firmly. Not letting on that he had both raised her hopes and dashed them within minutes of each other.

"No?" His hand tightened where it held her to him.

"No," she repeated, pulling his fingers off her skin. "I won't marry you just because it seems like a good idea now that you've done—that, and I've done—this, and we've . . ."

"That's not the entire reason why. We both like art."

She shoved him so he did fall off the sofa then, landing on the rug with a soft thump. She would have laughed at how comical he looked if her heart wasn't busy breaking.

She scooted over to the edge and peered over at him. He looked slightly dazed and, she was loath to admit, remarkably dashing, even though he didn't have a shirt on and he was only in his smallclothes.

Perhaps because of that.

"We both like *art*?" she said in an outraged tone of voice. Because if she allowed herself to really feel she would end up crying, and there was no way she wanted him to see her like that. Not when he'd just made the most pathetic marriage proposal after the most amazing moment.

It just wasn't fair.

He sat up and ran his hands through his hair, looking confused. "Well, yes. And I could help you in aiding those women, and you could put my money to good use, and we would have plenty to discuss."

Never mind. The first part wasn't the worst marriage proposal ever. This further explanation of what their married life would be like was.

She leaned over to the floor to gather her chemise, putting it on with trembling hands. His expression was—perplexed. As though he wasn't quite sure what was happening.

That made both of them.

She stood, shaking the chemise down so it covered her, at least, even though she was still entirely, shockingly undressed for being alone with an unmarried gentleman.

But even if all of Society burst in on them, she would not marry him. How did he not know that already?

"Where is my gown?" she asked. "You took it off, and now I don't know where it is." She couldn't speak to him any longer about this marriage thing, not without losing her temper, not without crying, not without telling him she loved him, of all things.

Not without any of that, and so she just had to get dressed and get home without saying anything on her mind.

"So—you don't wish to get married?" His voice sounded strained.

Good. She hoped he was feeling just an iota of all the pain she was. It was a terrible thought, but there it was.

"No, I don't wish to." She found her gown and stepped into it, then twisted her arms in back of herself to try to do up the buttons.

An impossible task.

"Here, let me," he said, getting up and going behind her. Still mostly naked, still warm, and solid, and everything she found desirable, except for how he felt about her.

"Why would you say such a thing?" she asked, at last. Say, not ask; he hadn't asked her to marry him, he'd just said he supposed they should get married. Not the same thing at all.

She felt him shrug as he continued her buttons. "I—I don't know," he replied, and he sounded stiff, and distant, and everything she'd thought he was when she first met him.

"Oh."

Silence as he finished.

"There you are." He patted her shoulder, awkwardly, and she resisted the urge to—well, she didn't know if she wanted to hit him or—no, she just wanted to hit him.

She definitely did not want to marry him.

She gathered herself and then turned to face him. Damn it, he hadn't put on a shirt or anything, and he was so gloriously handsome and just what she wanted that she was tempted to just forget all her worries, and scruples, and trepidation and say, *Yes, yes, I will marry you, you terribly unromantic person who isn't at all in love with me.*

Only she didn't.

"I don't even know how you lost your eye." She blurted it out, surprised even to hear herself say it. She hadn't realized she'd been thinking it until she spoke.

"My eye?" He sounded alarmed.

"Yes." She drew her hand up to his face and he flinched. Flinched! She snatched it away, feeling the color rush to her face. If she couldn't even touch him there, couldn't ask him, what was the point?

Perhaps you shouldn't have let him touch you there, a voice whispered inside her head.

Now you tell me, she whispered back.

"I—it's not important," he replied, of course stiffly, then turned to his left so his eye patch was no longer in view.

"Really?" She planted her hands on her hips. "It's not important that of the two eyes you were born with you only have one remaining?" She felt the sting all the way through her body. Similar to how he'd made her feel just a few minutes ago, only this time it wasn't pleasure she was experiencing.

He grimaced, and she felt her heart sink.

"Please call your carriage. I wish to go home."

He nodded, frowned, and picked his clothing up from the floor, pulling the bell at the same time. Margaret heard feet scurrying just as he was doing up the buttons on his trousers.

At least he was a speedy dresser, even if he had disappointed her in every other way.

"Your Grace?" the butler opened the door and stepped inside, clearly not looking at Margaret.

Of course, because she was there, and it was shocking, and he was a perfect servant.

"Call the carriage."

"I will just go wait in the hallway," Margaret said, plucking her cloak up from the chair she'd tossed it onto. Back when she thought she was in love with him, back before she'd gotten undressed, achieved ecstasy, and then had her heart dashed onto the ground.

The butler nodded, then left the room, leaving them alone.

"Margaret," he began, speaking in a pleading voice. What could he possibly have to say? Unless it was to further grind her heart into pieces?

"Good evening, Your Grace," she said, walking to the door as quickly as she could. She could not stand to be there one more minute.

"Good evening, my lady."

She was shaking as she shut the door.

How had it gone so horribly wrong? Lasham reviewed the events of the past few days, from accompanying her to confront those ruffians, his admiration and concern for her warring with one another, the argument on the drive home, the visit to the gardens, the party, then when she arrived at his house, took tea, and then he'd—they'd—well, that part was wonderful.

And then he'd said what was on his mind, just spoke it aloud, and it was as though it were the worst possible thing he could have said, and it made him feel as awkward and lonely as he'd ever felt.

Was this it, then? Was he doomed to forever be alone, simply because his words weren't right?

He winced as he recalled what he'd said—*I suppose we ought to consider getting married*. Not even a proposal, just a tentative suggestion that didn't speak of anything but propriety.

He was an idiot. And, damn it, he wasn't even *her* idiot. He was his own now, forever on his own, able to say what was on his mind—*I suppose we ought to consider getting married*—but unable to say what he felt, which was . . . He paused as he considered it.

What did he feel?

She challenged him.

She intrigued him.

She made him happy.

So did that mean . . . ?

Yes, damn it. He was in love with her. He loved her. He wanted to be with her forever and always, and he'd just ruined all of that because of his inability to say what he felt.

Was there ever such a pathetic wretch?

But wallowing in self-flagellation wasn't going to solve his problems.

What was? He thought for a moment, nodded once, then strode out of the room and headed up the stairs to his bedroom.

Annie took one look at Margaret as she walked into the house and gathered Margaret in her arms, making clucking noises of comfort into her hair. "Let's go to your room, sweet, and you can tell me all about it."

Margaret let Annie guide her upstairs, relieved that at least one person whom she loved also loved her in return.

Which was inaccurate, of course, because her sister loved her as well, and her brother-in-law cared for her because of Isabella. So two and a half people loved her, which was likely more than other people had in their lives.

Annie brought her into Margaret's bedroom, then planted Margaret in the middle of the room and undressed her, not saying a word—thankfully—about how disarranged her clothing was, because it was obviously not up to Annie's own standards.

Annie finally spoke when Margaret was in her night rail, a cozy robe wrapped over her, and seated in her chair. "What is it?"

Margaret bit her lip, trying to figure out just what to say.

"You're in love with him. Which I'd told you already."

Thank goodness Annie was so intuitive.

"Yes. And he proposed."

Annie wasn't that able to predict things, apparently, because her mouth dropped open in surprise. "And you said no?"

Well, put that way, it did seem ridiculous. You loved someone, he asked you to spend the rest of your life with him, and you turned him down.

"He doesn't love me."

"Well, why did he ask you then?" Practical Annie.

Margaret shrugged, feeling embarrassed and foolish. "He is a gentleman, and he thought that since—" She stopped, not sure just how to say it, or what to say, which was a rarity for her, since she always knew what to say. Until him.

"Since you and he were adventuring?" Annie said with a significant tone to the final word.

Margaret felt her face suffuse with color. "Yes."

"But if you love him, and obviously he feels something for you, else he wouldn't be adventuring with you—why not say yes?"

Very practical Annie. She would have had no problem agreeing to what the duke proposed, except— "Well, he didn't precisely ask. He just said he 'supposed we should consider getting married.'" She lowered her voice as she spoke his words, feeling the return of all the emotions she'd had when he'd said them: disappointment, sadness, frustration. Not the way one wished to feel when accepting a proposal.

Annie's eyebrows rose, and she nodded. "Ah, no wonder you look as you do. That is not a proposal, not the kind you deserve. If you had wanted to just consider getting married, you could have had Lord Collingwood. But you didn't, and that caused enough trouble to make us stay away for two years. We won't have to leave again, will we?"

Margaret shook her head. "No, I don't believe so. It is not as though the duke truly wishes to marry me; he just thought that was something he should do. He suggested, I declined, and now we are just back to our normal lives. Besides," she said, drawing her robe tighter around herself, "I can't leave now, not now that I've seen what needs to be done to help those women. And what would Lord Gantrey do, without me to lose to?" She tried to imbue her voice with a lighter tone, but it didn't quite work.

Annie wasn't fooled, either. "I'm sorry, my lady."

There wasn't much more to say, was there?

But there was so much more to feel.

And none of it good.

Georgiana and the Dragon

By A Lady of Mystery

⁂

"How is it worse?" Bless her father for going straight to the heart of the problem. He and her sisters were all looking at her, waiting for an answer.

"He's not who he appears."

"What your daughter means, Georgiana's father, is that I am not a half-clothed man in your daughter's company."

"What are you then?"

"The other person you really are, does he have more clothing?" Her youngest sister, of course, who always spoke what was on her mind.

He laughed, and Georgiana jumped; she hadn't heard him laugh before, she'd just heard him groan and mutter and tell her she was an unattractive not-princess.

It was a good sound, one that seemed to flow through her whole body.

"He's a dragon," she blurted out. "Not a man."

Chapter 28

*H*e saw her at her usual spot at the table, Lord Gantrey beside her, and Lord Collingwood seated opposite, which made him bristle. Because now he and Lord Collingwood had one more thing in common, having been rejected by her.

She looked paler than usual, but no less beautiful. She was wearing another jewellike color, this time a burnt umber shade that made her dark hair and brown eyes seem to sparkle even more. As he watched, she frowned and tossed a card onto the pile in the middle of the table.

"Why aren't you with her instead of hiding out here in the corner of the room?" Leave it to Jamie to get to the heart of the matter.

Lasham shrugged, feeling his jaw clamp tight.

"Ah." As though Jamie knew precisely what he was thinking—which he likely did, even if Lasham himself did not. "You did something to muck it all up, didn't you?"

Well, it did seem as though Jamie knew, then.

"How are you going to make it right?" Jamie nodded in her direction. "You won't find another woman who so suits you."

"How would you know?" It wasn't as though Jamie had spent any time when the two of them were together.

"Because you have been nearly happy, Lash." Jamie's voice was serious, markedly different from his usual bantering tone. "You wall yourself away in your house and your responsibilities, and that is all well and good, but you need to look for happiness. Lord knows it is in short enough supply," he muttered. "And you have seemed nearly happy lately, and the only difference that I can see is her in your life."

"You're correct. Only you're also correct that I mucked it up, and I'm not sure I can make it right again." He'd thought and thought, and come up with only a few ideas.

"Have you told her how you feel?"

Oh. Well, no, he hadn't thought of that. Grand gestures, gifts, promises to let her stay the way she was, yes. But not how he felt.

Jamie rolled his eyes at the expression on Lasham's face. "You're an idiot, Lash."

That was something he had thought of. Many times.

"I suppose I should do just that, then."

Jamie clapped him on the shoulder. "I look forward to greeting the Duchess of Lasham, provided you don't mess this up."

Lasham swallowed, knowing it was entirely

possible he would, but also just as determined that he wouldn't.

"My hand again, I believe." Margaret scooped up the pile of coins on the table and drew them toward her.

"It's interesting how often the luck runs your way, my lady." Lord Collingwood spoke in an insinuating tone, but then again, he always spoke that way, so perhaps he was not implying she was a cheater.

"Nearly a miracle, one would say," he added.

So much for thinking he wasn't implying anything.

"Are you making an accusation, my lord?" she asked in a flat tone of voice. "Because if you are, please do come out and say it directly."

"Spoken like a writer, my lady. I do so enjoy your little scribblings," Lord Collingwood said, this time with a sneer in his voice.

He really was a repugnant person; she was beyond relieved neither she nor her sister had ended up married to him.

Especially since her "little scribblings" enabled her to say no to his proposal.

"Well?" This time she couldn't keep her voice from trembling, something she saw he noticed, judging by the triumphant expression on his face.

"Well, then, Lady Margaret, I have to say that I do believe your winning to be the result of more than luck."

Lord Gantrey, the lovely man, spluttered at her side. "That is a very serious accusation, my lord. The lady has remarkable luck, to be sure, but she is also a skilled player, one to whom I am proud to have lost more times than I care to admit."

The other players, as well as the onlookers, all chuckled, lightening the mood and dispersing the silence that Lord Collingwood's comments had created.

"You are too kind, my lord," he replied. "*Too* kind," he repeated, stressing the first word. "I stand by what I said—I believe Lady Margaret's luck is too fortuitous to be merely luck."

Margaret felt her entire body starting to heat, as though someone had planted her in front of a blazing fireplace. Or in front of a terrible man who was determined to accuse her of something she had not done just because he was piqued by her, or her skill at cards, or how her sister had escaped him.

She rose, placing her hands on the table to still their shaking. "If you will excuse me, I do not wish to remain here and be accused of cheating. Please continue your play without me. Perhaps your luck will improve."

Lord Gantrey rose as well, taking her hands in his. "My lady, I do not believe these accusations. But," he said in a low murmur, "perhaps it would be best for you to stay away from the tables for a bit. Until Lord Collingwood's temper has eased. He has had ill luck lately, and it is unfortunate that much of it has been at your and your family's hands."

Of course. Now she had to stay away from doing the one thing that would give her freedom from people such as Lord Collingwood, because of his accusations. That was an irony she wished she did not have to contemplate. But none of that was Lord Gantrey's fault.

"Thank you, my lord, I am most grateful for your advice." She nodded, then walked quickly from the room, not meeting anyone's gaze as she left.

All she had to do was get her cloak and get into her carriage. She could handle that without causing a scandal, couldn't she?

"Miss," a voice called as she walked out of the house, her cloak wrapped tightly around herself.

Margaret paused on the step, glancing around to see who might have spoken. It was not a cultured accent, and if it was one of the women she'd helped, that meant there was something wrong.

Because of course there was something wrong, because everything was wrong.

And wasn't she the dramatic one. Worse than even one of her own heroines.

"Miss, pardon me." It was Sally, the woman who'd led them to where the rabble-rousers were drinking.

It definitely meant there was something wrong.

"What is it, Sally?" Margaret spoke in a low tone, glancing around to make sure nobody was about. No, nobody, of course not, since the party had just begun and Society wouldn't be finished until well into the wee hours. "Come over here," she said, drawing the other woman into the shadow cast by somebody's carriage. Not his, she would have recognized it, and wasn't she relieved he wasn't here tonight to witness her latest disgrace?

If he had been, he probably would have leaped in and tried to salvage her reputation, which just would have worsened it, because everyone would think things—things that were true, to be sure, but things—and then she would be the woman who had been accused of cheating and who had done things with the duke whom she wouldn't be marrying.

"It's them men, miss. Some of them got drunk, and now they're demanding that a few of the girls, the ones who work there, and who was just there having a pint, keep them company. You know, that way," as though Margaret didn't already have a crystal-clear idea of what was happening.

Her throat tightened. Women who had nowhere to turn for help. Women who had no choice because of men's superior strength.

Women who couldn't say no if they wanted to.

"Let's go, then," she said, looking down the row of carriages for hers. Thankfully, it wasn't too far down the line, and she took Sally's arm and headed toward it, feeling her heart racing, as much at the thought of being able to help as at the danger the women were in.

He'd watched as Lord Collingwood had said something to her, something that made her turn even paler, then bright red as an angry flush stained her cheeks. His hands had clenched into fists, and he'd been about to stride toward them to demand what was going on, only he knew, just as he knew his name was Vortigern, that she would not appreciate that. Would likely resent it, actually.

So he watched as she spoke, then rose, her entire demeanor exhibiting fury and sadness and an almost tangible sense of desolation.

Had he done that? That last part, that terribly alone part?

In a selfish perhaps-she-does-care-for-me way, he hoped so. Maybe then he'd have a chance at happiness. With her.

He followed when she left, and while he didn't hear what the woman said who approached her, he knew it was nothing good, judging by their reactions. So when she went to her carriage, he went to his. And told his coachman to follow her at a discreet distance.

Sally shared what she knew about what was happening while Margaret and Annie listened. It didn't sound good, but then again, it didn't sound as though anything had happened yet.

"And then I thought that since we couldn't go to ask anyone for help, and most of the men around are too scairt of that gang to do anything, that we'd come and ask you. I didn't see that scary-looking fellow with you, though. It'd be better if he were here."

Margaret and Annie shared a glance. "It would be better, but he is not," Margaret said at last. "And I cannot get him at this late hour."

Or at any time, she thought for a brief, heart-rending moment before pushing the truth away.

"We'll have to do," Annie said firmly. "We can't leave those girls with them gents, not without trying to get them to stop."

"No, we can't." Margaret couldn't bear the idea that any woman was frightened simply because of her gender. It wasn't fair, not at all, and she wished she were a man, or at least had the strength and position of one, so she could walk in and scatter the crowd as easily as Vortig—that is, the duke could if he employed his looks, his attitude, and his resonant voice all at the same time.

They arrived at the pub about ten minutes later, Margaret having secured her embroidery needles, even though she knew they wouldn't actually be a deterrent to anybody who wished to harm her.

Sally got out first, her expression tightening as she heard the ruckus from inside the pub.

Annie and Margaret followed, all three of them walking quickly to the door. Margaret told John Coachman just to wait, to keep the horses ready, in case they needed to make a quick escape.

Margaret took a deep breath, preparing for whatever would be on the other side.

The sight that greeted them did not seem, at first, to be all that awful until Margaret saw the girls' strained expressions and how the men had positioned the chairs so the girls would have to get through several of them to leave the room.

And the feeling in the room was one of menace, made more so by the expression on a few of the men, who appeared to be getting drunk as well as angry. Not a good combination.

"Pardon me, gentlemen," Margaret said brightly. As though she hadn't just walked into a room filled with workingmen who were filled with gin and ire.

"Oh, it's the lady back again," the large ringleader said with a sneer. His sneer was better than Lord Collingwood's; she would have to tell that latter gentleman he might want to take lessons from this one.

"Yes, and I have a duty to these women," although to call them "women" when they were so clearly frightened girls felt wrong, but she didn't want to edit herself at this moment.

The man tilted back on his chair so it was on two legs. A clear demonstration of how little her presence was affecting him. "Go on home to your fancy life. We don't want none of what you're selling here. Do we, lads?"

Most of the men nodded in agreement, and one of them kept his stare on her as he drew a terrified-looking woman against him.

Margaret swallowed, feeling the embroidery needles tucked up against her forearm, knowing they were not going to help, not at all. Not against these men. Men who were likely desperate, and she couldn't fault them for their desperation, but she could fault them for taking out their fury at their own powerlessness on these girls.

"My lady, this doesn't seem good," Annie said, close in her ear.

Annie had never been more accurate in her life. And yet still Margaret had to do something, to try to break through their anger just enough to get these girls out of immediate danger.

"I don't have a choice, Annie," she replied in a quiet voice.

Annie tugged on her sleeve. "You do. You don't owe nobody here. We can walk out now, and we can find help, and send it in."

Margaret glanced to where the belligerent-looking leader was still canted back on his chair, holding a dram of whiskey to his mouth and drinking it as though it were water.

"We don't have the benefit of that kind of time."

Nobody was paying attention to them any longer, except the one who'd drawn the woman closer. He still stared at her, his lip curled in derision.

She couldn't blame him for his scorn; it wasn't as though she were anything more than a lady and her lady's maid, with a rail-thin coachman somewhere outside. Not to mention those embroidery needles.

Perhaps she could just stitch what she wanted to say.

"If I might, gentlemen," Margaret began again, trying to keep her voice from trembling. Because if they did decide she was more than a nuisance? Things could be very unpleasant for her as well as every other woman in the room.

The leader righted his chair again and stood, kicking his chair in back of him so it skittered against the wall.

"Look here, miss. We don't want trouble. But we also don't want to hear what you have to say, can you understand that?" He crossed his arms over his chest and planted his feet wide in a combative stance.

"I can," Margaret said. "I absolutely would not wish to listen to me speak, either, if it kept me from enjoying my evening. And if you just listen for a moment, you can return to your pints and your—your liquor." She was doing a terrible job, she and Annie were only moments away from being tossed out, and that was the best scenario. She took a deep breath and continued, "Only some of these women are needed urgently, at this very moment." She had no chance of persuading the men that they should allow the girls to leave, so she was going to have to make something up. She could do it, it was what she did for a living, wasn't it?

She wished she was able to plot this particular tale out as well as she did her serials. As it was, she was going to have to make something up on the spot.

The leader took a few more steps closer, a skeptical expression on his face. "Where are they needed so urgently, then?"

She put a bright smile on her face. "I am so glad you asked. The Quality Employment Agency has asked its workers to go to their office to—to take advantage of an emergency placement." They all looked confused. No wonder, she had no idea what she was saying, either. "That is, there is an emergency, and the—the—"

"The Duke of Lasham requires workers for jobs that begin tomorrow, and we are filling the positions now. And not only the women are wanted. There is work for the men among you as well, at least men who can take an honest day's wage for an honest day's work."

His voice resonated through the pub, seeming like it carried its own weight, as though she could reach up and touch it.

She turned, blinking as she drank in the sight of him. He stood in the open door, framed by the light from the streetlamps, looking large, and omnipotent, and powerful. As a duke should be.

There was a moment's silence, then a clamor as the pub's inhabitants all shouted their desire to work, to do whatever the duke wanted, accompanied by a scraping of chairs as people rose to get closer to the man who held their destiny—for the moment, at least—in his large, capable hands.

She lifted her chin and met his gaze, nodding in acknowledgment of what he'd done. Of what he'd said.

Thank you, she mouthed, and he nodded back, something in his expression making her squirm with—with something.

Of course, you ninny, you're still in love with him, a voice in her head said.

Well, true enough, the more pragmatic voice agreed.

And he might not care enough for her, but he'd done this. He'd followed her—again—and he'd rescued her—again—and this time, she could acknowledge, even without his prompting, that she'd needed rescuing.

Lasham exhaled as the people crowded around him, wishing he could just push through them to her, but knowing his effort would be for naught if he didn't see this thing through.

He gestured to his coachman and footman to join him, glad that both were fairly large men who would appear to be an impediment, should the crowd grow unruly again.

"Your Grace?" His coachman's gaze was on the duke, but kept darting around, as though looking for trouble. Good man.

"Yes, just take these people's names and tell them all to report to the house tomorrow at eight o'clock sharp." And in the meantime, he'd figure out what to do with all of them, now that he'd spoken. Meecham was bound to have some ideas, no doubt having something to do with equal work and rights and the like. He gave a mental shrug; it wasn't anything he wasn't in favor of already, and the process to get things implemented could be—no, always was—ridiculously slow, so if he could speed it along for a few people, out of the many who needed it? And save her in the process?

So much the better.

A part of him was furious with her for putting herself in danger again, but another part was proud of her for sticking to her resolution and facing the danger, even though it was, obviously, *dangerous*.

He'd known what she was up to as soon as he saw where her carriage was headed, and he'd been grateful he'd kept the pistols in the coach, and even more grateful he hadn't had to use them.

"My lord, that is, Your Grace, thank you so much for this chance." It was the woman who'd brought them here initially. "My girls, they are hard workers, they won't disappoint you."

"I'm certain they won't," Lasham replied. "Just go see my man over there," he said, gesturing to the coachman, now armed with a tablet and a pencil. He spread his hands to get their attention, then spoke again.

"If everyone could just go give your names, and receive further instruction, then you can all go home for the evening. You'll need to rest if you're to work hard tomorrow," he said, knowing that no matter what he and Meecham devised for them to do, that would be true.

They shuffled about, the palpable energy and antagonism from just a few moments ago dissipating as the people dispersed, and he was finally able to go to her.

"Margaret, I—"

Her tone was flat, nearly brittle. "Yes, thank you for the rescue." She lifted her chin. "I did require it, and it was very clever of you to follow me."

"That's not why I did it." He spoke in a low tone only she could hear.

And she obviously did hear it—he saw her swallow, and take a deep breath, as though—as

though she were bracing for something or relieved.

He had no idea which.

"Can you—that is, would you please come with
me?" He held his breath, hoping she would at
least give him this courtesy.

And then the rest would be up to him.

GEORGIANA AND THE DRAGON

By A Lady of Mystery

Her entire family looked at her for a long moment, then all three of them opened their respective mouths and howled. In laughter.

At her.

"A dragon?" Her father pointed one arm toward the man, holding the other over his stomach. "That man there?"

"At least tell us something we can believe for a moment, Georgie," Mary, her youngest sister, said.

Georgiana glanced over at the man——she would have to find out if he had a name besides man-who-was-a-dragon—and rolled her eyes.

He grimaced, opened his mouth, and flames shot out, scorching the sapling that her younger sister had planted a few years ago.

"Does that prove it?" he asked, as the smoke settled.

Chapter 29

Damn it, but why did he still look so handsome? She hadn't expected him to lose his height or his breadth or anything, but she'd hoped that some of what she had been feeling might be showing on his face as well.

Instead, he was still handsome.

"Please?" He gestured to her carriage and she paused, glancing back at Annie, whose expression was encouraging. She rolled her eyes at her extremely optimistic and misguided friend, but allowed him to help her into the carriage.

He sat beside her, as he had those other times, and her body reacted immediately. To his warmth, his closeness, his very maleness inhabiting the coach. To him.

"Well?" She had to break the silence, she was itching to ask him questions, even as she wanted to pretend to be as cool and collected as he was.

"I followed you."

"Yes, I gathered that," she said in a dry tone.

"Since you appeared at the same place I was." She paused. "Thank you. As I said."

"You're welcome." He shifted, and she felt his leg touch hers. Her body sparked at the contact, and she had to push down the sharp rush of desire that flooded her. But she couldn't think about that any longer, no matter what he might say now.

Actually, because of what he might say. Maybe this time he would mention that since they both drew breath they had things in common, and shouldn't they consider spending the rest of their lives together, just breathing?

Or he could tell her that since he'd told her the secret to his first name—a secret anyone could discover, by the way—he was forced to marry her so she wouldn't reveal it.

"I don't know what to say," he began, then stopped abruptly.

Now that opinion they actually did have in common.

And then she laughed as she thought about it. "But you do, don't you see?" She shook her head. "You just said the exact right thing to disperse that crowd." *And you said the exact wrong thing to get me to marry you, but perhaps that was the point.*

She felt him shake his head next to her. "Is that what I did? I thought I just wielded my power as a duke, as a man of means. It wasn't what I said."

She softened at hearing how—how bleak he sounded. Especially as he said the last few words.

Dear Lord, but she loved him. Even now, even after he'd taken her heart and made it feel all happy and warm and protected, and then trampled it so it broke into shards. Even now.

She was definitely never using herself as a heroine, she knew that, since she didn't want to write a woman who was still in love after being so treated.

"You said the right thing." She spoke in a soft voice, one that was meant to reassure, but seemed to have the opposite effect.

"That's even worse, then." His tone was bitter, nearly savage in its intensity.

Now she didn't know what to say. She didn't even know what he meant, much less how to respond.

"I was eighteen." His words sounded as though he were propelling them from his lungs. Forceful, quick, and urgent. "I was home from school, and feeling as though I were finally my own man. Finally feeling as though I could be a good duke after all." He uttered a derisive snort. "Which I was not. Not then."

He laid his hand, palm up, on his thigh, and she took it without thinking. The warmth of it easing into other places they weren't touching.

"And I spent all evening drinking, alone, and then I decided I needed more wine. I went to the wine cellar, and popped open a bottle of champagne, and then this," he said, raising their intertwined hands to gesture to his eye patch, "happened."

Margaret took a few moments to process what he'd said. "You—you weren't in a battle? Or a duel?"

He snorted again. "Nothing nearly as honorable as either of those things."

"You—you lost your eye to a champagne cork?"

"Yes," he bit out.

"But—" What could she possibly say to such a revelation? "But that is so odd."

"You could say that," he replied, and she couldn't tell if he was upset or sarcastic or anything. "Although that odd event did result in my losing an eye. Peripheral vision. Depth perception. Those things."

"And all this time you haven't told anyone? You've just let them wonder why?"

She felt him shrug. "It isn't important." As he'd said before, when she'd asked.

"But it is." She curled her fingers around his as she tried to explain. "It isn't just your title that makes you who you are. It's—it's how you carry yourself, and how you honor your position. It's how you walk into a room as though you are daring anyone to ask about your eye, or anything else, for that matter." And she hadn't quite realized it until she'd said it aloud just how—how impressive he was. Even though he wasn't able to say what he felt.

Was she just hoping he hadn't been able to say what he meant before? She couldn't succumb to that tempting thought, or she'd never find out what he would say because she'd be too busy kissing him, inarticulate boor that he was.

That part made her very angry. At herself.

"Why would anyone want to know anything

about me?" He sounded genuinely curious. "About me, that is, about Vortigern."

He didn't know. He had no clue, did he, about how people saw him, and more specifically, what she felt about him. "Why wouldn't they? They only wouldn't if you made it impossible for them to know you. All they see is who you present. And it's not Vortigern, the man who lost his eye through a careless—and you have to admit, almost humorous—youthful escapade. They see the duke, the man who holds his responsibilities with as much weight as he does his title."

"And you?" He spoke so softly, so hesitantly, she almost couldn't hear him.

"I don't know anymore," she replied, wishing it weren't true.

I don't know anymore. The words resonated through his whole being, making him feel as though he'd been shot. Wounded, at least.

If he didn't get this right this time he would be doomed to be alone forever. No pressure, though. He drew a deep breath and tried to get it right.

"I—" he began, only to stop as the coach slowed.

Damn it. Now they were at his house, and he hadn't said anything to let her know how he felt, what he felt, and he could see the rest of his life passing before him, alone, always missing her, and yet not able to—

"May I come in?" she asked, poking him on the arm. Apparently he'd spent too long panicking about how he couldn't speak to her that he couldn't speak to her.

An irony he did not appreciate.

"Yes, of course." He rapped on the roof to let his footman know to open the door, then waited as she descended, following her. Breathing her scent in quick, surreptitious sniffs that, if she caught him at it, would most definitely make her want to turn on her heel and march right back out again.

Thankfully, she didn't notice.

"In here," he said, escorting her into the room— their room—before turning to his butler—who hadn't batted an eyelash; he should tell Meecham to make sure the man got a raise in pay—before asking for—

For what? This wasn't a social call, it was far too late and too odd for that. So tea was out. Neither could he offer her spirits, because then it would seem he was wanting to get her loosened up or something, and he certainly did not want to have it appear that he was trying to do that. Even though he wished she would loosen up, but it wouldn't be because of him or his liquor, he knew that for certain.

"That will be all," he said at last, pulling the door shut behind them.

And now they were alone. Together.

As they had been just the night before, was it?

And he'd so horribly mucked it up.

"You were about to say?" she said as he turned back to her.

He drew a deep breath.

GEORGIANA AND THE DRAGON

By A Lady of Mystery

All three of her family members bore precisely the same expression: shock mixed with a smidge of awe.

"Does that prove it?" Georgiana asked. "And if it does, can we move on to how we can help him?"

"Help me how?" the dragon/man asked.

Georgiana looked at him, feeling her mouth drop open, too. "Don't you want to learn how to be a man?"

His face twisted into a distasteful expression. "No, not at all. From what I can see, humans run around hurting one another. Dragons just eat and breathe fire and fly around."

Georgiana blinked. "So you'd rather be a dragon?"

He nodded. "Yes, and so would you if you knew what it was like."

"Tell me, then," Georgiana replied.

Chapter 30

"Tell me," Margaret said, when he just stood there, gaping at her as though she'd sprouted an additional head.

No, I'm just foolishly in love with you, she thought sourly.

"Can we sit?" He didn't wait for her reply, just took her arm and guided her to the sofa—their sofa.

She blushed as she remembered it, then felt the burning sting of his casual suggestion all over again.

He waited for her to sit down, then placed himself at the opposite end of the sofa, a nearly precise repeat of the night they'd first met, back when she'd stumbled into that room looking for peace and found him.

Who'd done the exact opposite of bringing her peace. Not that he'd brought her war, actually, but he had brought her longing, and desire, and passion, and hope, and intrigue, and disappointment.

And here she was again.

"Well?" It was harder to get him to speak than it was one of her reluctant heroes. Perhaps she should write his words for him.

But then she would never know how he truly felt. If he truly felt at all, or just wanted her because she was convenient, even though she was anything but.

"I can't believe we were able to walk out of that pub without at least one person trying to punch me in the nose," he said at last.

"I might've myself, given enough time," she said. He swallowed, the movement of his throat making his cravat move.

She wished he'd take it off.

No, she didn't.

Yes, she absolutely did.

He laughed, that rare smile of his making her heart ache. "It is so much easier to say what you mean through your actions, isn't it?" he said in a rueful tone of voice.

She was about to voice her agreement when she thought of something.

"It is," she said, sliding over on the sofa to him. He watched her with a wary look in his eye. As though she might punch him. "Instead of asking you to tell me what you feel, how about I show you how I feel?" She smiled. "No words, I promise."

Because she knew him, didn't she? She knew he would find the right words, eventually, but that his actions the other evening said what he might not even know himself. That this was important, this thing between them, and that even as he was likely berating himself—as she was berating him also, honestly—what he did, how he behaved, said more about what he meant than what he said.

"No words?" His voice was rough, low, and sent a shiver through her.

"Not unless you want me to stop." She bit her lip, feeling as though she were on a precipice, about to fling herself off it, and having that moment of hesitation, only determined to still do it.

Do it. Yes, *that*.

"Then I won't speak," he replied, his words redolent with all sorts of meaning she understood perfectly.

She moved closer and brought her hands up to his cravat, beginning to undo the folds. It was a complicated knot, and she huffed out a breath in frustration as it didn't come undone right away, but swatted his hand away when he would have helped. "I am showing you, I do not want your help."

One eyebrow rose. "At least not until later, I assume," he said in a smoky tone of voice. Oh, if only he could just say things like that to her all the time, she might never leave this room. Their room.

She got the cravat undone, then drew it from around his neck and placed the fabric on the back of the sofa, leaning in to his neck as she did so.

She let her mouth hover over his neck, then pressed her lips against the column of his throat, feeling his body react. "You can do whatever you want," she murmured. "Just don't say anything."

He immediately placed his arms around her,

pulling her to him, his mouth finding hers and claiming it in a kiss that spoke volumes.

There were worse ways to communicate, she thought, as his tongue licked and sucked, his teeth nibbling on her lower lip, his hands holding her against his body so tightly, so strongly, it made her feel as though she were a cherished possession.

But he wasn't holding her as though she were precious, or breakable; he was holding her as though he knew she could get away, if she wanted to, but he really did not want her to. As though he wanted to do whatever he wished, and at the moment, she knew he could. Because it would be what she wished as well.

Her nipples tightened, and her breasts felt heavy, straining against the layers of fabric she wore. She needed to feel his skin on hers, and she couldn't tell him to take everything off—no talking—so she would have to take matters into her own hand.

So to speak.

She broke the kiss, both of them gasping, and she slid her hands under his coat, pushing it off his broad shoulders and helping tug it off his arms. When it was free of his body, she tossed it on the floor, figuring dukes would have legions of servants to deal with it later.

Then she went to work on the buttons of his shirt, feeling his gaze intent upon her face. She made the mistake of glancing up into his eye for a moment, and her breath caught.

If only he had been able to say some of what

she saw on his face now, they would already have done this, and plighted their respective troths to each other, and been on their way to figuring out how to live with each other without compromise.

She had to look away, return to focusing on his shirt, because she didn't want his staff to find them, hours later, still gazing into each other's eyes. Although that event—having stayed the entire evening with him alone in a room—would force their hands as well. That would be too scandalous even for such a discreet staff as the duke seemed to have. And Annie wouldn't be shy about making her opinion known, for that matter.

She tugged the shirt out from his trousers, then raised it from his lower abdomen up over his head. His stomach muscles were tightened, and she could see the individual definition of his abdomen, and that sight definitely made her feel way more squirmy than before. She wanted to lean down and lick each ridge, kiss the skin on his hard stomach, draw her tongue through the narrow line of hair that led down there.

She felt his breath hitch as she tossed the shirt to join its compatriot coat, then he nodded to her, not saying anything, but making his request absolutely clear as though he had spoken it aloud: *I want you to take your gown off.*

She smiled back and turned sideways so he could get at her buttons, which he did immediately. And what's more, he kissed the exposed area with each undoing of a button, so that by the time all of them were undone, she was a shivering mess of want and desire and sexual awareness.

Then she stood and pushed the gown off her shoulders to her waist, then shimmied a little so the gown went sliding down her hips to the ground.

She wore only her corset and chemise, standing in front of him, her hands laced behind her back, which had the advantage of making her breasts thrust out more prominently.

Which she only deemed an advantage when she saw how he was looking at her.

He rose swiftly from the sofa and approached her, his hands at the waistband to his trousers, his fingers beginning to undo his own buttons.

She reached forward and put her fingers on his wrist, then shook her head, a sly smile on her lips. She put her hands to the laces of her corset and undid it, then allowed it to fall to the ground.

Then, standing only in her chemise, she stepped forward to him, wrapping her arms around his neck and pulling him down for a kiss. He was so tall she could tell it was awkward for him to kiss her like this, but from the noises he was making in his throat he didn't seem to notice. She stood on tiptoe as they kissed, as she pressed her breasts into his warm, hard chest.

His hands were at her waist, holding her still so he could kiss her as he wished, and she pushed closer in still, now able to feel his erection against her stomach. It was a hard, throbbing reminder of what they were doing, and hopefully, how he felt.

His hands had slid away from her waist lower to cup the curves of her buttocks, helping to raise her up so they were more of a height. So they could kiss more comfortably.

Although none of this was comfortable. It was fiery, passionate, exciting, and so filled with meaning it would take an entire dictionary to define it, but it was not comfortable.

His hand slid between and lower, his fingers sliding along her slit where she was already wet.

She started at his touch, breaking the kiss, and she gazed at him in shock and nervousness at his having her felt all that, all the way she was feeling.

He didn't say anything, since he was following instructions, after all, but he kept his gaze on her and then his tongue licked his lip in a sensuous, evocative gesture that made her knees weak.

She heard her breath catch, and it seemed he did, too, since his gaze turned predatory. He stepped forward and grasped the lower edge of her chemise and drew it up, but didn't remove it entirely. Instead, he pulled it up over her head and let it hang there, making her momentarily blind.

And, likely, looking rather odd, but all thoughts of how she looked fled when his mouth found her breast, his hands were wrapped around her body, and he was sucking her nipple into his mouth, his fingers caressing her back, the curve of her backside, her hips. His erection pushing into her, his mouth moving now to the other breast, her entire body feeling as though it were sparked with wires that sizzled with each touch.

She could tell by his movement and the sound that he was getting onto his knees, and then she felt his fingers on her, there, and then his mouth, his tongue, sliding into the moist wet heat of her, and she gasped, feeling her knees tremble again as he kissed her.

Her hands were in his hair, clutching him to her, and she felt him chuckle, then reach up to unclasp her hands. She couldn't help but let out a noise of disappointment when he removed his mouth, but that noise turned into a gasp as she felt him pick her up as though she weighed nothing and walk her to the sofa, where he laid her gently down.

She lay there, still unseeing, but hearing the noises he was making—the shuck of trousers coming down those strong, long legs, the rustle of more fabric as he undid his smallclothes, and she bit her lip, wishing she could see him in all his naked glory.

And then she felt him get onto the sofa, one knee to the right of her thigh, the other nudging at her hip to make room for her. His penis touching her stomach, close to there, but not close enough, and then he reached up and removed the chemise so she could see him.

"Oh," she said in a mixture of surprise and excitement. His chest was right there, sprinkled with some dark hair, his nipples standing up from the flat planes of his chest.

He hadn't taken the eye patch off, but that was the only item of clothing that remained. His body was stupendous, a large, muscled work of art that truly eclipsed anything found in a gallery. Hard, smooth, and so profoundly masculine it made her hurt, but in a good way. A very good way.

She reached her hand up and put her fingers on the eye patch, keeping her gaze on his face. His expression tightened, but he nodded, and her fingers slipped to the back of his head where she undid the knot holding the patch in place.

It fell onto her chest and stayed there. She didn't move to brush it off or anything, just kept her eyes on his face.

It was disturbing. The skin was stretched tight over where the eye had been, raised scarring showing how repairs had been attempted. His eyebrow was unscathed, and looked out of place above the ravaged area of his eye.

She reached up to touch the corner of where his eye had been. He flinched, but allowed it, letting out a deep breath as she touched her fingertip to his skin.

Now he was as naked and exposed as he'd ever been. Now she could see the real Vortigern.

The question was, did the real Vortigern feel as strongly about her as she did about him? His actions—not his words—would tell her every-thing she needed to know.

GEORGIANA AND THE DRAGON

By A Lady of Mystery

"Instead of telling you, how about I show you?"

Georgiana wrinkled her brow, as did the other members of her family.

"How would you do that, then?" her father asked.

The dragon/man glanced at each of them in turn, settling his gaze at last on Georgiana. "By turning you into one."

"Oh," Georgiana gasped. She looked at her family, all of whose faces were expressing varying degrees of shock and excitement. "Father?"

Her father planted his fists on his hips and settled back on his heels. Only to say the exact opposite of what Georgiana expected.

"Why not?"

The dragon/man smiled as he spread his arms. "Why not indeed?"

And Georgiana nodded.

Chapter 31

*V*ortigern held his breath as she ran her fingers over the scarring. He made a point of not looking in the glass after he'd washed his face, and had gotten skilled at putting the patch on without having to look at himself.

"Well?" he said at last, knowing he wasn't supposed to be speaking, but unable to help himself.

"It is off-putting, and distinctive, and unusual." She met his gaze and smiled. "Like you."

And he let his breath out as her words washed over him. He bent his head and closed his eye, feeling the sting of tears. He hadn't cried in years, but now it felt right.

She gathered him into his arms and he let his weight fall onto her, resisting the urge to ask if he was too heavy. If he was, she would tell him. She would speak up and say what was on her mind. He knew that about her, just as he knew it was equally difficult for him to do so.

She ran her fingers over his back, into the hair at the nape of his neck, and wrapped one of her legs around him, pushing their lower bodies even closer together, a fact his throbbing cock very much appreciated.

He raised his head and met her gaze again, this time hoping that what he felt about her was in his expression.

She smiled, but didn't say anything. Just moved her hand so it was between them, on him, and then she nudged his leg up so she had room enough to run her hand up and down his shaft, gripping and squeezing.

He opened his mouth to say something, but she shook her head, leaning up to place her mouth on his as her movements below increased. He placed his hand on hers and moved the head of his cock toward her entrance, slowly, in case that wasn't what she wanted after all.

Judging by how she widened her legs and pushed him toward her as well, it was what she wanted, too.

And wasn't he delighted they agreed on something.

He rose up on one arm and glanced down, seeing the dark curls on her mound, his cock brushing those soft hairs. And nearly spent right then and there, only he'd be damned if he was going to come outside her. He wanted in, and so he pushed, stopping when she made a noise in her throat, but her hand on his arse, pushing him farther in, made him continue.

And then he was home. Inside her, her body a warm, wet, welcoming place, her kisses growing more frantic as her body accommodated his size.

Even if he were allowed to speak, he didn't think he could, not at this moment, not when his cock was throbbing and pulsing inside her, her fingers were splayed on his lower back, her tongue was inside his mouth, and he knew he wouldn't last too long. He hoped he lasted long enough to bring her some pleasure as well, but that was less important than that she knew, she understood, what he felt about her.

I love you, he said in his head as he began to move, withdrawing a bit so as to be able to push back home again.

And again, thrusting and pulling and withdrawing, building up a rhythm that she matched, her body answering each of his movements with one of her own that only served to heighten his pleasure.

Dear God, how had he gone so long without being inside her? Without knowing what home truly was?

She broke the kiss and flung her head back, and he dropped his head down to her neck, where he bit her tender skin, all the while still moving, the grip of her hands intensifying.

And then it happened, one final thrust and he climaxed, roaring as he did so, feeling the waves of pleasure wash over him as he shook.

And dropped down on her, their bodies slick with sweat, her hands still all over him, her hair tangled, her chest heaving, as his was.

They were silent for a few long minutes, he as comfortable as he'd ever been, knowing she was the same. Knowing it because he knew her, and she knew him, and hopefully by now she knew how he felt.

"I suppose," she began in a deliberately lowered voice, a clear imitation of that time before when he'd spoken so stupidly. *I suppose we ought to consider getting married.* Had anyone ever made a worse proposal?

"No talking, remember?" he murmured, his mouth tucked into her shoulder.

She nodded, shifting to make herself more comfortable under him, but not asking him to move.

He hoped she never would.

"Yes."

Her word was spoken so quietly, even though they were as close physically as two people could be, he nearly didn't hear her. And then that was all he heard, as what she'd said reverberated through his whole body.

That one word—"yes." "Yes" meaning *I suppose we ought to consider getting married*, yes to *Do you love me?*, yes to *Do you know I love you?* and on and on until the "yeses" crowded his brain, made it impossible for him to think of anything but her, and their future, and how much he loved her.

"Yes," he replied, then closed his eye and smiled.

Margaret took a deep breath before heading into the ballroom. She knew Vortigern would be there, but not until later, he'd said. She wanted to do this before their engagement was announced, since it was important that she remain who she was despite who she was going to be.

Or something like that.

Lord Collingwood hadn't stopped with just accusing her of cheating to her face—he'd also made the social rounds, planting seeds of suspicion in everyone's ears. Why he was so determined to blacken her reputation was beyond her, but there it was. Perhaps something to do with being scorned? Although he hadn't wanted her in the first place. No matter, but it did matter to her dealings with people.

"Lady Margaret Sawford," the butler announced. The room quieted, and she heard the rustle of fabric as people swiveled in her direction.

Wonderful. Lord Collingwood had done more damage than she'd realized. The bastard.

She descended the stairs into the ballroom, glancing at the gaming table where Lord Gantrey already sat, a reassuring warm smile on his face. At least one person remained in her corner. Although more of them would flock there once they knew she would be the Duchess of Lasham, which was why it was crucial to do this now, before they knew.

"My lady." It was her hostess, who glanced around nervously, as though someone would challenge her for having invited the cheater.

As though all the people in this ballroom already were absolutely pure of heart and had never done anything wrong themselves. Margaret nearly snorted, only that would be terribly rude. Much worse than treating her servants poorly, as more than a few people here had done, according to Annie. More than keeping their creditors waiting while they continued to buy more, as most of the people here did. Even more than making it clear that one loathed one's spouse, as a smattering of people here did.

And when did she become so judgmental? This wasn't about others, this was only about her. She spotted Lord Collingwood at another of the tables and made her way to his side, waiting for him to acknowledge her, since she knew damn well he was well aware that she was there.

"A word, my lord," she said at last, when it seemed he wasn't going to meet her gaze. Then he did turn his head, his eyebrows raised in an insufferably condescending way.

Or perhaps she was just reading him that way.

"Yes, my lady? Are you here to share how you've bilked these lovely people through your nefarious practices?"

So she was not just reading him. And she had to admit he had a lovely grasp on the English language—"nefarious practices," indeed.

"My lord, I do not know where you reached the conclusion that I have been cheating." She raised her head so she was addressing everyone in the vicinity, a good thing given they were all staring at her. "I am skilled at cards, that I will admit. If you would rather believe I cheated than that I could beat you at a game, well—" and she shrugged her shoulders as though to show what she thought about that.

"The thing is, I cannot prove I have not cheated just as you cannot prove I have." She narrowed her gaze at him. "Unless you do have proof? And neglected to provide it when you accused me?"

He glared at her, two red spots of color on his cheek. Still seated, the ultimate insult when a lady was addressing a gentleman in conversation.

"If I were my sister, I would have used my actions instead of my words," she said, spotting Vortigern in the distance and shooting him a conspiratorial wink, "as when Isabella punched you for saying things about me." Several members of the crowd gasped, and turned their scrutiny to Lord Collingwood, as she'd intended. "And yet it seems you have not learned your lesson not to talk about me, even though I have refused your suit and have made my own way in the world through my own skills since my parents have refused me because of you." Of course it still stung, but she would get over it, especially now that she had someone to love who also loved her.

"But it seems you like to bear a grudge, my lord, so I will tell you now, and forever, that I will not have you, no matter how much you might accuse me of cheating. Nor will I waste one more thought on you, since there are other people who deserve my attention." She caught Vortigern's gaze again and smiled, just for him. "So if you wish to accuse me of cheating, please go ahead, but keep in mind that proof will be required, and that your past actions regarding me are bound to be considered when people are hearing what you have to say." She glanced around the room, smiling at Lord Gantrey until finally resting her gaze on him. Her love. The man who was able to render her inarticulate through his actions, which he'd proven multiple times already.

If the gossips knew of that, she would definitely deserve her scandalous reputation. But since she was shortly to be his duchess, it wouldn't matter much anyway.

He stepped forward, her proud, layered, difficult, intelligent, sensual husband-to-be, and took her arm, leading her out of the ballroom without saying a word. As it should be.

Dear Lady Margaret,

Normally I do not intrude on your writing, since it has done so well in our little paper, but I and some of our readers are concerned about Georgiana's fate. We are worried she will be eaten by the dragon, or that she will want to stay a dragon. Wouldn't it be preferable to have the dragon save her from some dangerous situation, and then have them both spend the rest of their days as humans?
Signed,
Mr. Garrett, Editor in Chief

Dear Mr. Garrett:

No, it would not be preferable.
Signed,
Lady Margaret Sawford (aka A Lady of Mystery)

GEORGIANA AND THE DRAGON

By a Lady of Mystery

"This feels tremendous!" Georgiana shouted to him—his name was George, oddly enough—as they flew above the city, scouting for the best places to find water for Georgiana's family. As she'd been doing when she first met him.

Her father hadn't been delighted that she'd chosen to become a dragon, but then they'd pointed out the benefits—easily accessible fire, travel was easier (if not precisely comfortable), and nobody would dare not pay him for his work, given who his son-in-law was.

They did turn back into humans every so often, just to check that they truly did prefer dragondom, but inevitably got tired of walking on two legs after about a day and switched back.

It wasn't the ending many would have chosen, but then again, only one person was Georgiana, and that was Georgiana herself.

And she chose her dragon.

Epilogue

"It's not so bad. Not as good as the ices, but still, not so bad."

Vortigern considered his eel pie, which he'd eaten half of already, whereas Margaret had only gotten through a few bites.

He'd expended considerable energy that morning, waking her to take her in a quick, rough burst of lovemaking, then spent considerably more time and effort after that to bring her pleasure.

She could still feel the ripples of it through her body. She shivered in reaction.

"Are you cold?" he said in a concerned voice.

She shook her head, laughing. "No, just remembering."

"Oh," he replied in a knowing tone.

"Duke, Mrs. Duke." Two of Sally's girls, now employed at a factory Vortigern had investments in, approached them, matching smiles on their faces.

"Good morning, girls." Margaret returned their curtsey. "How are you today?"

The younger one gazed at Vortigern's half-eaten pie. "Hungry." Her elder sister elbowed her, her face turning bright pink.

"Let's do something about that, then," he said, gesturing to the eel pie shop.

They'd begun spending Saturday mornings here, and now the inhabitants of the neighborhood were nearly not frightened or intimidated at seeing him in their midst. It helped that Margaret "unduked" him, which meant removing his cravat, messing up his hair, and making sure he was in his oldest clothing—a fact his valet did not yet appreciate. And now she was pleased to see a few changes in the area; the women walked with their heads held higher, the men had more work, the children even seemed to play more loudly.

And whenever she would worry that he didn't have time to come here with her, he'd tell her she was showing him another adventure, and he wouldn't allow her to miss out on it.

So far their entire married life was an adventure, juggling how to be a nearly proper duchess with being a responsible woman and an author.

She hadn't had to give anything up, not that he would ask.

She waited on the street as he paid inside for the pies, appreciating the symmetry of the eels laid out just so in the window.

The girls tumbled out of the shop, both of them with delighted expressions on their faces, pies clutched in their hands. "Thank you, Duke," they both said.

The younger one paused in her devouring of the treat. "How did you lose your eye then, Duke?"

"Allow me to tell the story," Margaret said with a smile.

". . . And then the bear approached him, and to save his life, he held a piece of chicken in front of his face, which the bear swiped his paw at, but he also took his eye," she finished. Vortigern shot an amused glance her way as she spoke, but didn't say anything. "It was a terrible tragedy, but at least the duke—my husband—survived," she said.

Margaret thought the bear story was one of her more inventive—thus far, he'd lost his eye fighting pirates in the South Seas (which was far too clichéd for her liking), in a duel fighting over a lady's honor (raising the question which lady, which just made Margaret jealous, even though it was a mythical lady), in a horse-riding accident (too dull and messy), and as a result of a broken window (How did the window break? Was anyone punished, given that it was an aristocrat's eye that had been lost?).

And anytime Margaret offered up another story, her husband—her love—just smiled at her and didn't say a word, instead showing her just what he thought of his imaginative wife later, when they were alone.

She glanced at the one-eyed man in question. "I suppose we should be getting back now," she said. "We have to go meet with some ladies who have never had eel pie in their lives," she said to the girls.

Their eyes widened as though that were an impossibility.

She was due to speak at a fund-raising effort to

help more of the poorer London neighborhoods. The fact she was now a duchess meant that Society ladies were tumbling over themselves to attend, and give, so they could say they knew the Duchess of Lasham.

It wasn't as bad as she had thought it might be. It was much better, in fact, especially since she had him.

"I suppose so," he replied, holding out his arm.

Author's Note: About the Accident

All of us have heard, at one point or another, an admonition to be careful or you'll lose an eye (perhaps the most well-known one is in *A Christmas Story*, where Ralphie is warned about the dangers of the air rifle he wants for Christmas).

And every New Year's Eve, the media has stories about the dangers of losing an eye from a champagne cork, which is how Vortigern, the hero of *One-Eyed Dukes Are Wild*, lost his eye.

It might seem like an apocryphal story, but one of our modern-day inventions, the interval windshield wiper, came about because of such a real-life accident, which my husband, Scott, told me about, which then inspired Vortigern's injury.

Robert Kearns, an engineer, lost his eye to an errant champagne cork on his wedding night in 1953. He was then inspired to develop the wiper, which mimics an eye's blinking motion rather than the constant back-and-forth that was the standard.

AVON BOOKS

The Diamond Standard of Romance

Visit AVONROMANCE.COM

Come celebrate 75 years of Avon Books
as each month we look toward the future
and celebrate the past!

Join us online for more information about our
75th anniversary e-book promotions,
author events and reader activities.
A full year of new voices and classic stories.
All created by the very best writers of romantic fiction.

*Diamonds Always
Sparkle, Shimmer, and Shine!*